Those Ties That Bind

by

Kim Janine Ligon

Dedication

Thank you Jim once again for your unfailing support as I crafted a new story. And for another terrific title! With loving thanks!

Praise for Kim Janine Ligon...

Debut Novel *Polly's List*

"The perfect balance of suspense and romance, danger and mischief."

~ Terry Newman, Author of *Heartquake*

"*Polly's List* is really a cozy mystery and romantic suspense all rolled into one."

~ Anastasia Abboud,
Author of *Tremors Through Time*

Landing On Her Feet

"This is an inspiring story of love, faith, forgiveness, and redemption."

~ D.V. Stone's Around the Fire
book and author blog

"Exceptional Suspense. Well drawn characters. Lovers of romantic suspense, especially with a well drawn "bad guy" who operates on only one cylinder—himself and his needs—will dive into this book and not let go until the very end."

~ Kat Henry Doran, Wild Women Reviews

Acknowledgements

Special thanks to:

*Millie for your usual spot on first reader insights. You make this easier!

*Amy for providing the perfect Greek words!

*Chad and Mary for stocking my books and hosting my book signings. It's always a thrill to see my books on your shelves.

*My new book club friends: the Northriver Readers, the Illumen and Moundville friends, and the O'Fallon Bookworm Buddies. Thanks for your support and encouragement. You make this journey more fun!

*Lori, Lisa, and Luke for your invaluable medical knowledge and assistance. Nice to have such expertise in the family!

*Kevin for your helpful information on West Point.

*My blog followers. You were with me when publishing was only a dream and you continue to bless me with your encouraging words.

*My incomparable editor, Dianne Rich who coaxes the best from me. I can't do it without you!

*My publisher, The Wild Rose Press. I love growing in this garden you lovingly tend surrounded by my uber-supportive fellow Roses.

*The good Lord who plants stories on my heart so they can bloom on these book pages.

* There are not words adequate to say how you have blessed me. I am humbled and appreciative of your continuing support. As long as you keep reading my stories, I'll continue to write them. Thank you from the bottom of a heart overflowing with love and gratitude.

Chapter One

Dr. Chase Merrick entered Trauma Room 4 wearing a look of concerned weariness. He reread the chart in his hand. Seventeen years old. Major blood loss. Going in and out of consciousness. Fluctuating blood pressure. Premature labor gone woefully wrong. No baby was transported with her.

"Nurse, did anyone from The Center accompany her?" he asked.

"Not this time. No official transfer paperwork. The only things I know are her name is Rose Rich and her blood type is O positive. We started the IV as you requested and gave her the injection to contract the uterus and slow the blood loss. The blood bank is sending down three units for immediate transfusion. Oh, here they are."

The nurse met the blood bank technician at the door. She started the transfusion in the left arm since the IV fluids were running into the right arm. Then she hung another bag of IV fluids.

Dr. Merrick stepped to the young girl's bedside and gently grasped her hand. It was cold. "Rose, wake up. You're in the hospital emergency room. I'm Dr. Merrick. Can you hear me?" He kept gently rubbing her icy hands between his own large, warm ones. "Rose, can you hear me?"

The girl thrashed her legs from side to side and

tried to pull her arms out of the restraints necessary to hold the IVs in place. The doctor gently put pressure on her shoulder and quietly talked to her. She stopped moving and made mewling sounds. Her mouth moved. No words were audible. Dr. Merrick leaned closer. His ear hovered just above her lips.

"You're in the hospital, Rose. We're trying to help you. Don't be frightened. I know you are hurting. We gave you pain medication. You should begin to feel better soon."

In barely a whisper, Rose sobbed, "Doc, not me again, don't. Please, I can't, please don't." Her eyes opened wide, then snapped closed.

Moments later, her hand slipped out of Dr. Merrick's. No pulse. He immediately began CPR. No response. An injection was given. The nurse rolled the crash cart to the bedside. The doctor yelled, "All clear. All clear. All clear." Everyone stepped away from the bed. He applied the paddles to the patient's chest and delivered a shock. No pulse.

Again he yelled, "All clear. All clear. All clear." The body shuddered as electricity coursed through it. Only a single flat line on the monitor. Ventilation breaths were administered. No change.

One more time, the physician yelled, "All clear. All clear. All clear." The charge of electricity shot through the patient's body once more. No change to the monitor. No pulse. No respiration. Nothing.

Dr. Merrick pronounced the patient dead at 10:08 a.m.

****

"Miss Langford," Margie Wright stuck her head in the CEO's office doorway, "Dr. Merrick is here. He needs to see you urgently."

"Send him in."

Evelyn Langford rose from her desk, slipped her suit jacket on, and walked across the office to meet her visitor. "Doctor, do we have an issue in the Emergency Room? Please sit down." She motioned to the chairs at a small table in the corner of the office.

"We have more than just an issue. I'm so angry I don't know if I can sit." The physician took several steps away from the CEO.

"Please, we've been colleagues for over twelve years and friends almost as long. You and I have always been able to discuss a problem and find an agreeable solution. Tell me what happened."

"You're right, Evelyn. You are one of the good guys. It isn't your fault. Sorry. I'm so furious I'm losing sight of the solution." Dr. Merrick took a deep breath and sat down. "I lost a patient in the Emergency Room a few minutes ago. Seventeen years old, but looked twelve. She was transported by ambulance from The Center. She was severely dehydrated, traumatic blood loss, and I was told by the ambulance driver she had just delivered a stillborn baby."

"I can understand that losing such a young patient is more than a little difficult," she said.

"That's only half the problem. This was the third emergency transfer from The Center in the past three months. They continue to ignore established protocols for these transfers. If this practice continues, I'm going to recommend that the State pull their license. These girls—not adult women—have been in extended labor by the time they are transported. The medical staff there has to be aware the patients are rapidly deteriorating into a critical state. Both the other times we were also told their babies were stillborn. Something is wrong out there. And this patient wasn't transported to the Emergency Room today until it was too late for me to do anything to prevent her death. We only had time to start IVs and a blood transfusion before I had to use the paddles from the crash cart. She was only moments away from being DOA by the time she rolled off the ambulance." The doctor took another deep breath.

"Did anyone from The Center accompany them? Family or medical staff?"

"Not today. And basically no paperwork. We had a name and blood type and a child-mother on the doorstep of death. It looks like the patient goes critical and they pile them into an ambulance and hope we can pull a miracle out of thin air. Today I had no more miracles."

"You're correct. Something is not right at The Center. I'll get to the bottom of it. I promise."

"It's not only that the mothers are transported so long after they should have been. Why are their babies stillborn? The mothers are only children themselves. We saved the other two, but it required extraordinary efforts. The Center should be sending them as soon as they are in distress, not hours later after they've delivered a dead child that might have survived if they'd come to us earlier. Childbirth, properly monitored, should not result in death, even with a very young mother." Dr. Merrick clenched his hand into a fist and hit the table. The dull thud rang through the office.

"I'll talk to The Center immediately and request the stillborn's body. We need to get this patient's paperwork to find out whom to contact about the death and to get appropriate permissions. Are you requesting autopsies for both mother and baby?"

"Yes. Maybe further examination will help determine where the problem is. We need to find out what's happening and get this resolved before we lose any more mothers. Or babies."

"Thank you for letting me know about the situation." The CEO clasped the physician's hand in hers.

"Thank you for seeing me immediately. The patient's name was Rose Rich according to the ambulance driver."

****

After Dr. Merrick left, Evelyn asked Margie to get the medical director at The Center on the phone. She buzzed in fifteen minutes later.

"Sorry, Miss Langford. I'm getting a run-around, but I do have the administrative assistant on the line. She says the medical director is unavailable."

"Fine, I'll talk to her." Evelyn picked up the phone. "Mrs. Rafferty, I'm calling as the President and CEO of Garland Regional Medical Center. It's about the young woman, Rose Rich, who was transported to us by ambulance this morning. She has died. It is imperative that I speak with your medical director immediately."

Evelyn heard muffled sounds in the background. The assistant had not placed the call on hold, only put her hand over the receiver. As Evelyn suspected, the medical director must have been standing next to her, because moments later, he came on the line.

"Who are you to insist on speaking to me immediately?" he demanded.

"I am the CEO of the medical center where a young girl died shortly after being transferred from your facility to my emergency department. She was the third such transfer in as many months. What is the problem there?" Evelyn tried to keep a controlled and professional tone, despite the man's imperious tone and reluctance to speak with her.

"It isn't my problem if your emergency room physicians aren't adequately prepared to save lives," he tersely stated.

"You know good and well the problem is not with Regional's doctors. If you continue to flaunt all reasonable protocols regarding hospital transfers from The Center, you will lose your facility license. I'm certain that is not what you want. I need all the paperwork for Rose Rich, including her next of kin contact information, so we can release the body to them. The medical examiner wants to autopsy her stillborn. We plan to autopsy the patient as well, when we can get permission from her family." Her voice did not betray the anger she was feeling.

"Fine, I'll courier over the paperwork. The stillborn's body is not available. It has been incinerated at the mother's request."

"We were told the delivery was only an hour ago. You've already disposed of the body? Don't you think some investigation should be done about the infant's cause of death?" She clamped her jaw down and shook with anger.

"You have incorrect information, the delivery wasn't an hour ago, it was at one this morning."

"That's worse. You withheld emergency medical treatment for over eight hours after delivery. Why would you put the mother at risk? You knew something had gone wrong when the baby was stillborn. The patient might have had a chance if she'd been transferred to us sooner. Get me the paperwork within the hour." The CEO slammed the phone down and took a deep breath trying to keep bile from rising into her throat.

Within twenty minutes, Margie brought in the paperwork from The Center. Evelyn personally tried the phone numbers on Rose Rich's paperwork.

She dialed the first number under the Next of Kin section. "We're sorry. This number is not in service." Maybe she misdialed. Evelyn tried it again. Same result.

The second number was in the same area code. Another "not in service" message.

The third number was in a different area code. "Hello, this is Taco Insanity. Have you tried our new Veggie Maniac stuffed full of peppers, onions, mushrooms, kale, and squash? What are you going crazy for?" a cheerful voice answered on the second ring.

"I am Evelyn Langford calling from Garland Regional Medical Center in Lansdale, Wisconsin. I'm looking for Rose Rich."

"Wisconsin? Just a minute, lady. Let me get the boss." The handset clattered as it hit the counter.

A few moments later a voice said, "Hi. This is Mitzi. I'm the shift manager. Who were you looking for?"

"Rose Rich or any family member of hers."

"We don't have any employee by that name. I'll be happy to ask around. Could you leave me a number and

I'll text you back?"

"Thank you for being so helpful. Where would I go to thank you in person?" Evelyn left her cell number and hung up. The Taco Insanity was in a suburb north of Chicago. Had Rose been a regular customer there who ordered her taco fix by phone for take out? Or had she accidentally stumbled on a valid number when completing her admission paperwork at The Center?

The email she'd sent half an hour earlier to another Next of Kin entry bounced back. Not a "valid address." Every bit of this patient's contact information was bogus.

She buzzed her assistant. "Margie, would you please schedule a special meeting with Dr. Chase Merrick, Dr. Luke Wetzel, Courtland Gaines, and Dr. Lisa Miller for seven thirty tomorrow morning. The topic is emergency transfers from The Obstetrical Center. Thank you."

A little before five that afternoon a text message from Mitzi popped up on Evelyn's phone.

—*Sorry. No one here knows Rose Rich.*—

Another dead end.

She needed to get this investigation launched before she left tomorrow evening. She hated to let it linger for a week while she was out of town.

Chapter Two

Evelyn Langford walked through the door from the garage into the kitchen and parked her purse, attaché case, and a pile of mail on the nearest pale gray granite countertop. She bent over and unlatched the crate next to the round oak kitchen table. The door sprang open.

A wiggling ball of fawn colored fur bounced around her feet making happy snorts, then made a beeline for the door to the backyard. By the time the little pug returned to the kitchen, his bowls of dog food and fresh water were waiting on the mat next to the crate. He barked a quick "thank you" and began wolfing down the food as if he hadn't eaten in days. His full mouth made his snorting louder.

"Gonzo, I'm sorry you have to stay crated up all day, but I'm certain there would be too many things to tempt you if I let you have unsupervised solo run of the house. I know you're missing her too." She petted the dog's back and stretched out his corkscrew tail. "Tomorrow, you'll be off on a new adventure. While I'm on vacation, the Merrick kids have volunteered to petsit with you so you don't have to go to a kennel. You know them. They've been here lots of times. Now you'll get to see where they live. I expect you to be on your very best behavior or they won't want to invite you back." The little dog never raised his head. He focused on munching the bowl of kibble.

Evelyn spent the rest of the evening packing her bags for the trip to the Gulf and gathering all of Gonzo's essentials to take to the Merricks in the morning. It was easier to pack what she would need for fun in the sun than to anticipate everything the little furball might require on his first overnight outing away from home. She planned to drop the dog off before she went to work, in case there were problems. If something arose, she could execute plan B for boarding Gonzo at the kennel or, in the worst case scenario, cancel her much anticipated trip.

****

Evelyn set the alarm for an hour earlier than normal. She had a lot to do before the seven thirty special meeting. First, she took Gonzo downstairs and fed him so he'd be ready to leave when she was. A shower, breakfast, and a travel mug of coffee. She was ready. She loaded the car with her suitcases and Gonzo's bags. It looked like he was moving in with the Merricks, in fairness a large part was his crate so he could sleep in a familiar place.

Gonzo was a furry mass of non-stop wiggle. He must have sensed something exciting was about to happen. Evelyn could hardly get him fastened into his car seat. Yes, the little dog had his own perch in the back seat so he was high enough to see out the window. She never thought she'd be one of *those* people, the ones who treat their pets like children. It wasn't her fault. Mama fell in love with the little furball as soon as he came in the house four years ago. He made Mama smile and kept her company while Evelyn was at work. He deserved some pampering. He'd been a wonderful companion for her mom, especially in the final months.

The five-year-old twins, Mallory and Tracy Merrick, and their older brothers, Timmy and Trevor, seemed almost as excited as the little dog. They ran out to meet Gonzo and his mistress as soon as they pulled in the driveway. The unleashed dog and the children raced into the house together.

Katrina Merrick opened the back door and asked, "Do you have time for a cup of coffee, Evelyn?"

"I'd love one, but I've got an early meeting. Here's Gonzo's schedule. He's used to being in his crate for extended periods if you don't want to mess with him while the kids are in school. He's a pretty good little guy. I don't think you'll have any problems. If you do, you can take him out to Dr. Gengler's to board. I warned them it might happen," Evelyn explained.

"Don't waste a moment worrying about him. The kids are over the moon excited about having him spend the week. They've been begging to get a dog. Gonzo is their test run to see if they can handle it."

"I hope you don't get stuck with a lot of extra work because of your boarder. Looks like you've got plenty to handle."

Katrina laughed. "The bigger I get, the slower I am. The kids are great help and so excited about the baby. The only controversy right now is whether I'm having a boy or a girl. The kids are arguing about which gender will be in control. Chase laughs and says it doesn't matter what the new baby is, we're already outnumbered. I know they'll do their part with Gonzo."

"You're certainly going to have your hands full."

"I'm used to it. I like it that way. I'm sure Gonzo staying here will cause a stir in the kindergarten class this week. Mallory was talking to my father on the phone last night and told him they were taking care of a pig for a week. When Pop asked if she didn't mean a pug, she refused to be corrected. She said everyone knows pigs have curly tails and snort. So does Gonzo. She wants to take him for Show and Tell if it's okay with you."

"Gonzo loves being the center of attention. Tell Mallory she may show off her guest pig." Evelyn laughed. "Thanks a million for doing this. He'll be happy with the kids to play with and probably not even notice I'm gone. I think I'll escape while he's distracted. Don't forget he can go to the kennel if need be."

"Enjoy your vacation. We'll be fine." Katrina waved her out of the kitchen.

Chapter Three

Evelyn found a cup of coffee waiting at her desk. Margie took such good care of her. She grabbed it and the notebook she'd made notes about Rose Rich in and went into the administrative conference room adjoining her office.

She joined Dr. Lisa Miller, VP of Patient Care Services already at the table nursing a cup of chai tea. She nodded "good morning" as she took a sip. Shortly, Courtland Gaines, CFO, came in carrying a tray holding a custom-made omelet from the cafeteria and a grande espresso coffee. Dr. Luke Wetzel, the Medical Director for Women and Children's Services, came in with his usual large, black coffee. Last to join the party, Dr. Chase Merrick, Medical Director for Emergency Services, arrived empty-handed. Margie slipped into her spot at the table and put a large cup of black coffee in front of the physician. He mouthed "thank you" and took a big swig.

"I appreciate everyone taking time to join me this morning. Yesterday, Dr. Merrick brought to my attention that we are experiencing a wave of young mothers coming into the Emergency Room from The Obstetrical Center. By the time we get them, they are already in a critical state. I would like the five of us to create a plan to address this issue. I've asked Margie to take minutes so we capture all our ideas. Once we are in agreement about how to proceed, I would like to have a joint meeting between our Board and The Obstetrical Center's Board of Directors to present our concerns and find a mutually agreeable solution to this ongoing issue."

Courtland Gaines pushed his plate to the side and wiped his mouth with a napkin. "I'm telling you, The Obstetrical Center is a magnet for wayward girls. They think if they make it here they'll get paid handsomely for the fruit of their promiscuity."

"I disagree with that," Evelyn Langford stated. "There were pregnant runaways in Garland County long before The Center existed."

"We know there are a number of healthy babies being born at The Center every month. For the most part, they do not require our emergency services," Dr. Wetzel said. "We must understand what is different about the ones who do end up in the Emergency Room. Is it a matter of education of The Center's staff to be able to better identify problem pregnancies requiring earlier specialized medical interventions? I would be happy to teach some classes to help raise their level of competency and comfort so they can recognize the problems more quickly."

"Thank you. You may have identified one of the issues. I am also concerned patients are being transported to us with little or no paperwork. Rose Rich's paperwork was couriered to me almost immediately after I requested it yesterday. It was worthless. None of the next of kin or emergency contact information was valid. We have a body in the morgue that is basically a Jane Doe," the CEO reported.

"And the baby was not transferred with the mother.

We need to have autopsies on both the mother and the child to determine why they died," Dr. Merrick said.

"Unfortunately, the child was immediately incinerated at The Center. I was told it was done at the mother's request. I also learned this birth occurred much earlier than we were initially led to believe," Evelyn said.

Dr. Miller spoke up, "I think the first step is to find out who our Jane Doe really is. I'm happy to contact Chief Davis and get his help in checking the National Runaway database to see if this girl has been reported missing. Providing false information on admission would be more likely if the patient were hiding something, like being a runaway."

"Don't you think that's a long shot? A waste of everyone's time?" Courtland Gaines asked.

"No, I don't or I wouldn't have volunteered to do it," Lisa Miller bristled.

"I think talking with Chief Davis is an excellent place to start. We can share Rose's fingerprints and picture from the electronic patient chart system with the police if it will help," Evelyn said.

"Thanks. I'll get started on this immediately," Dr. Miller said.

"I'll have Margie get a joint board meeting scheduled for early next week. I'll cancel my vacation and get this addressed," the CEO said.

"No. You need the time off, Miss Langford. Let us monitor the situation and have the meeting as soon as you return. It's highly unlikely a joint meeting could be scheduled so quickly. One week isn't going to change what's been happening over the last several months, but a vacation could do wonders for your stress level," Dr.

Merrick advised. "As your personal physician, I might even say the break is medically necessary." He smiled.

Dr. Miller added, "Another week will give me time to get information back from Chief Davis so we'll have a more complete picture of the issue when the boards meet jointly."

"Remember, if anything changes, I'll be here to take care of things, like I always am when you're not available," Courtland Gaines announced. "Nothing to worry about. You're leaving Regional in my capable hands."

"Thank you, doctors. You're right. There's nothing like a walk on the beach and the roar of the surf for stress relief and it may take some time to check those national resources. Thank you, Courtland. I didn't mean to infer you couldn't handle things in my absence. My flight is early tomorrow morning. I leave for Chicago this evening. I'll have my cell phone. I see Margie making notes, and I'm certain she'll get the joint board meeting scheduled as soon as possible after my return," Evelyn agreed.

Everyone filed out of the conference room. As he passed her, Courtland Gaines leaned over and whispered to his boss, "Try not to miss me too much while you're gone." He patted her back and winked. Then left the room.

The man made Evelyn's skin crawl. After an encounter with him she felt like she needed an immediate shower. He was careful to only be inappropriate when they were alone. Never with a witness. Someday he'd slip up.

Something was wrong at The Center, but what? Evelyn didn't want to mediate a battle royal between

The Obstetrical Center and Courtland Gaines. It could be the issue he had been looking for to get her out of his way. Permanently. He still thought she stole this job, his rightful job. Dr. Merrick was right. She needed a vacation.

The charming, manipulative Courtland—just call me Court—Gaines had been at the Lansdale Hospital thirty-five years as CFO. He believed he was the heir apparent to be CEO. But, twenty years ago, they hired the younger Evelyn Langford as the President/CEO. She had been with a larger hospital in Ohio before the accident brought her home. Her father, Dr. Russell Langford, had been president of the hospital medical staff until his untimely death in the car crash that crippled her mother.

Evelyn stepped into the CEO role and guided the small community hospital into an alliance with a larger medical system allowing the facility to offer many services the smaller hospital couldn't afford to provide if they had remained independent. She had been very proud when they officially became Garland Regional Medical Center instead of Lansdale Memorial Hospital five years ago.

It was the perfect match. Small town girl returns home after making good in the world outside Lansdale to take the reins at her father's hospital.

Perfect for everyone.

Except Courtland Gaines.

Chapter Four

Miss Langford buzzed Margie. "Please get the medical director at The Obstetrical Center on the line for me."

"Hello."

"Miss Langford, what do you want?" the physician snarled.

"Rose Rich's paperwork doesn't have any valid contact information. Her real name is probably not Rose Rich. We are coordinating with Chief Davis to check the National Runaway database to see if she is listed there."

"Why are you going to all this trouble for someone you don't even know? All you're required to do is to send the body to the morgue and you're done." Did he snort?

"I can't just dispose of her like garbage. If she was my child or my sister, I'd want to know what happened to her. I'd want an autopsy done to see why she died."

"We already know why she died. Complications in childbirth. Why do you have to act as if this was a major crime or malfeasance? Women do still die in childbirth, despite all the advances in medical science. This isn't an issue for the police. Garland Regional isn't going to be blamed for her death." He got louder with each word.

"You needn't yell. I can hear you. The patient

mumbled something to Dr. Merrick right before she died. She said '*Doc, not me again, don't. Please, I can't. Please don't.*' Does that make any sense to you?"

The physician hesitated a moment. "Why ask me? How would I know why a dying girl, who lied about who she was, said anything? She was probably delirious. Why do you think it has something to do with me?"

"She said *not me again*. I thought since she was your patient you might have some insight into her situation. Had she given birth at your center before?"

"How would I know off the top of my head? Hundreds of mothers have been through here. I haven't memorized all their names, faces, and personal situations."

"Don't worry about it. I'm sure Chief Davis will get to the bottom of this."

"There is nothing to get to the bottom of. I've reinstituted stricter protocols to trigger hospital transfers sooner for distressed patients. No need to pull in the local police or national resources. Let it go, okay?"

"It's good to know that in the future mothers in danger will be transported to us sooner, but it's too late to put the brakes on checking with the police. The wheels are already in motion. We've started the investigation," the CEO said.

"I am putting this on the record. I won't tolerate harassment of any kind. If you force my hand, you'll regret it. I promise," the physician said authoritatively.

"We both have to do what our professional ethics require. This is not personal. It has nothing to do with our relationship. I'll let you know if anything else comes up. I expect you to do the same. Goodbye." Miss Langford hung up.

****

Margie Wright stuck her head through the CEO's doorway. "You'd better get things wrapped up or you'll be super late getting to your airport hotel. I promise not to let anything important slip through the cracks while you're away."

"Oh, Margie, I never worry about your behavior while I'm out of town." Evelyn Langford laughed. She checked her phone. "You're right though. I need to get going. I haven't heard anything about Gonzo today. No news must be good news."

She grabbed her attaché case off the table by the door. Margie stopped her. "Unless your airline tickets are in there, leave it here. You're supposed to be going on vacation. No sense in taking work along with you. Buy a good trashy novel in the airport to read on the plane instead."

Evelyn smiled. "How did I get so lucky to have you take care of me? You're absolutely right. Thank you. I'll see you a week from Monday."

****

Evelyn was getting away later than she'd hoped, but earlier than she'd feared. Knowing the CEO was going out of town seemed to be the catalyst that brought all the minor crises bubbling throughout her facility to a head. Everyone wanted to see her for "just a minute" before she escaped. Margie efficiently deflected some of the issues by scheduling meetings for after her return. One or two she sent on to Courtland Gaines to resolve. Evelyn trusted her assistant's judgment. She knew what needed the CEO's immediate attention and what was an abandonment-panic-induced issue.

By the time the "Welcome to Illinois" sign shone in the headlights, Evelyn had begun to relax. It would be good to get some much needed stress relief. Seeing her college housemates always brought peace to her soul. No matter her current personal situation. She desperately wanted to laugh and enjoy the people who loved her without reservations and leave her small-town medical center CEO life behind for a bit. Dr. Merrick was right. She needed the vacation.

Chapter Five

Evelyn Langford leaned closer to the mirror opening her sable brown eyes wider. So this was what fifty looked like. She hadn't expected to get there so quickly. She had been blessed with Grandmother Shipley's great skin. Only a few wrinkles around the eyes and mouth. Her mother said they were "happy wrinkles" from smiling and laughing. After the last ten years, she was surprised there weren't more "worry wrinkles." No puffy eyes in the reflection. No number eleven vertical wrinkles above her nose between her eyebrows. Her hair was more silver than brown, but that had been true since before she turned thirty.

She finished braiding her waist-length brown and silver hair, slathered on the sunscreen her mother had insisted she use long before it was the norm, grabbed a giant travel cup full of steaming, black coffee, and quietly crept out the door to witness sunrise on the beach while her housemates remained snug in their beds snoozing. The sugar-white sand gently warmed her bare toes and the lapping waves beckoned her closer.

The beach at the Gulf of Mexico had always been her peaceful place. Something in the smell of the ocean and the sound of the waves, observing the magnificence of creation, had always renewed her heart, her spirit. She was thankful it hadn't changed after all this time.

She needed to be reminded of the good and beauty in the world after the trials of the past year. She teetered on the edge of overwhelming stress. The year had been a personal and professional train wreck.

Evelyn thought about their first trip to the Alabama Gulf coast during Spring Break freshman year at a small liberal arts college. The Fantastic Four, as the housemates called themselves, fled the cold Wisconsin spring, where snow still blanketed the ground with temperatures routinely below comfortable, to play in the sun and sand on the Gulf of Mexico.

They had rented this same seashell pink house directly on the beach then and every odd numbered year since their first trip. Now they came a little later in the year, usually the first week of May. It was the ideal time, the sweet spot between the ever wilder Spring Breakers and the post-school family vacationers. They held a weeklong birthday celebration: Evelyn's was May 1st; Beverly's on May 3rd; Liz's on May 4th; and Pam's on May 6th. This year would be the Big 5 - 0 for all of them. Certainly an occasion worth celebrating.

She strolled to the water's edge. The chilly water lapped over her feet. The sky burst with flashes of orange, red, pink, and yellow as the sun rose above the undulating horizon. Her cell phone's chirp interrupted the soothing sound of waves gently rolling onto the beach. No rest for a weary CEO even hundreds of miles away. When she saw who was calling, she let it ring several more times before she answered.

"A little early in the day for a crisis, isn't it Court?…Of course, I'm awake…No, I'm certain he doesn't want to lose his privileges…Shouldn't this be an issue for you to discuss with Dr. Merrick and the

Medical Staff…Okay. I'll talk to him when I return, but please discuss the issue with his peers first…Anything else?…Goodbye."

She pushed the End Call button and breathed deeply. The phone chirped again. Immediately.

"Speak of the devil," she said out loud, then answered.

****

Rance Thompson jogged down the beach soaking in the early morning sunshine and breathing in the brisk salt air. The shifting sand under his feet provided a little more strenuous workout than his usual one on an indoor rubberized track. He wasn't a gym rat, who had to exercise at all costs, but he tried to keep the aging process in check and not let his enjoyment of good food show in his still trim waistline.

Rance slowed as he neared a woman walking at the water's edge. She was too pale to have been here long. Not even a first day's tender pink glow. A long braid of silver and brown hair fell down the middle of her back until it brushed a little below her waist. Her modest white trimmed navy-blue bathing suit clung to well-placed curves making a very pleasant view, especially with the glorious sunrise surrounding her.

As he got nearer, he saw she was holding a phone to her ear. The conversation must have been upsetting. He hadn't tried to listen, but he couldn't help but overhear her end of the call.

"I just got off the phone with Court…If you didn't call about that, why did you call…Frank, threatening me is not going to make this better for you…You know very well I'm on vacation… It will have to wait until I get home. I can't do anything about it from hundreds of miles away even if I wanted to…Don't curse at me. I'm hanging up, Frank. Don't call back. I'll deal with you when I return home."

The woman pulled the phone away from her ear as Rance approached her. She was sobbing. Her hand holding the phone was trembling at her side.

"I didn't mean to eavesdrop, but do you need help?" Rance spoke softly as he approached her side.

"I'm sorry, what?" the woman snapped and turned to glare at him.

"Is there anything I can do to help? You seem to be crying."

She scowled and wiped tears away with the back of her hand.

"No. I don't need your help. Continue your run. Go on. Leave me alone." The voice was harsh and raspy. She wheeled around and stomped off in the opposite direction.

"Goodbye. I'm sorry I offended you," Rance said softly, sure the woman wasn't listening, then, reluctantly, continued jogging down the beach.

He should know better than to offer to help a strange woman. Today, they were all too independent to admit they needed support from anyone. Even the strongest person—male or female—needed a little help from time to time. People didn't cry like she was for no reason. He could have listened. Sometimes people felt better just to be heard. He was a good listener.

Evie walked a few yards. She stopped and looked behind her. The stranger continued retreating toward the sunrise.

Why couldn't she come for a walk on the beach without being hit on?

She stopped at the water's edge letting the gentle waves pull the sand out from under her feet. When she looked again, she no longer saw the runner.

Maybe she was being too sensitive. She had been crying. He seemed genuinely concerned. She shouldn't have sounded so harsh. No wonder they called her the Snow Queen behind her back.

Frank made her completely crazy. Why did she let him push all her buttons so easily? After a lifetime of practice, you'd think she would have developed automatic defenses against him. Well, she wasn't going to let him ruin the rest of this glorious vacation. Everyone else should be awake and stirring by now.

****

Halfway back to the house Evie spotted Beverly up to her knees in the surf taking pictures of the sunrise and the morning birds wading along the shore and soaring overhead. Her mass of strawberry blonde curls was even wilder than usual as the soft breeze rearranged them.

"Stop. That's a perfect pose with the sun rising barely above your shoulder," Beverly hollered then snapped several pictures. She waded out of the water and met Evie onshore. "I'm hoping to entice Mel into coming here. How will he be able to resist after seeing all these pictures?"

"You mean he's never been here?"

"Nope. You know Pam's family hasn't either. Some day we should come on an off year and invite everyone's significant others," Beverly thought out loud.

Evie laughed. "Make sure and give me plenty of notice so I can dredge up a main squeeze. It's been so long since I've had one I'm not sure I even know where I'd look."

"You're not the only one. We'd have to get the timing perfect to catch Liz when she's married again or at least in one of her committed relationships," Beverly added. "I'm becoming an almost competent photographer. Think this could be my next career after I'm done teaching kindergarten?"

"It would fit well with your plans to travel more when you're both retired," Evie agreed.

"Stranger things have happened."

The aroma of frying bacon and fresh brewed coffee greeted them at the patio door. Pam was a blonde blur scurrying around the kitchen scrambling eggs, plating flaky croissants from the bakery down the road, and pulling the pan of bacon out of the oven.

"You're just in time," Pam called. "Breakfast is almost ready." She handed a bowl of cut up fresh fruit to Beverly. "Let's eat on the patio. It's a magnificent morning."

Evie opened the door and picked up the plates and silverware, then followed Beverly to the table. Pam was behind her juggling a tray full of food.

"Good thing I waited tables in college. Some things you never forget how to do." Pam laughed, her green eyes twinkling.

"I never eat this much for breakfast," Evie protested. "Everyone doesn't live on a cattle ranch and chase four kids around! Sitting behind a desk doesn't burn nearly the same number of calories as you do."

The refreshing sea breeze provided the perfect counterpoint to the bright sunshine. The friends talked as if they had been together only last week instead of two years ago.

Breakfast was long finished. Pam was showing them pictures of her third child's high school graduation. You really noticed the passage of time when you saw how much her kids changed visit over visit. Since she was the only mother in the Fantastic Four, the rest of her friends happily played the role of Auntie spoiling her children with gifts for all occasions. This year Pam would have three kids in college. Could grandkids be far behind?

The patio door opened. Liz plopped down in the empty chair nearest the door. "Coffee. Where is the coffee?" Her cropped silver hair spiked wildly at the top of her head. "My word it's bright out here." She pulled a pair of sunglasses out of the pocket of her scarlet silk pajamas. She looked like an incognito movie star gracing them with her presence. Pam deposited an oversized, steaming mug of black coffee in front of Liz.

"Bless you. No wonder you've kept your original husband happy all these years." Liz moaned when the brew reached her lips.

"You sound like you never see the morning sun. Doesn't it shine on those New York City skyscrapers?" Evie teased.

"What about some breakfast?" Pam asked.

"I have it. Just keep the coffee coming." Liz slid deeper into the overstuffed cushions.

After the dishes were done, everyone got ready for the beach. They moved the entire entourage closer to the water dragging chairs, umbrellas, towels, and a cooler of bottled water and snacks. This first day they'd be back inside by noon. Years of experience had taught them nothing ruined their holiday more quickly than a first day sunburn. The afternoon would be spent playing cards and board games from the house's closet treasure trove.

It was the beginning of a week-long slumber party complete with eating the wrong things, drinking more than normal, whispered secrets, late nights, group activities, time alone, reading, laughing, crying, sun, and surf. It was invigorating and exhausting. In a word—perfect.

Saturday night was the official night for celebration and their traditional birthday bash. This was a big one. Fifty. Four college girls celebrating thirty years together. Friends through it all. Who would have imagined they'd still be sisters-of-the-heart?

Chapter Six

No birthday celebration at the Gulf would be complete without dinner at Constantine's. The restaurant with walls of floor-to-ceiling windows seemed suspended above the deep azure of the peaceful waters of the bay. It was the perfect place to enjoy the colorful sunset, indulge in incredible seafood and Greek specialties, and cap off the evening listening and dancing to live after-dinner music out on the veranda. Tonight, almost as if it were especially for them, an oldies cover band was playing music from the era when this Fantastic Four first visited Constantine's thirty years ago.

Old Constantine, now in his eighties, was still there and fondly remembered his sweet "dolls." His son, Theo, ran the restaurant now, but the meal ended the same way it always had with wonderful frothy cappuccinos and creamy tiramisu, on the house, in honor of their birthdays.

Constantine always joined them for dessert. He was very protective of the Fantastic Four, discouraging any male attention to his *kouklas mous* (dolls); a hold over from the days when he worried about them being too young and naïve to be on their own so far from home. It was an evening of strolls down memory lane, rollicking laughter, and a delightful celebration of their cherished friendships.

They finished the tiramisus and lingered over the luscious cappuccinos. A tall, muscularly built man with curly brown hair approached their table and bowed to Evie saying, "Excuse me for interrupting this fun, but I had to stop. It's good to see you smiling. You look radiant. I see it's a celebration dinner. Happy birthday."

He would probably get in trouble for stopping and more for the comment, but he couldn't resist her smile. So much more beautiful than the tears he'd witnessed streaming down her cheeks earlier in the week. He joined his three male dinner companions on the veranda where the band was beginning to play.

"*Koukla mou*," Constantine said, "Who is this man who likes to see you smile?"

"I was about to ask the same question," Beverly said.

"I don't know his name." Evie smiled. "I had a brief encounter with him on the beach at sunrise the first morning after we got here."

"Well, I think I'd find out his name, tout suite," Liz said. "You know, we're not getting any younger!"

"Back off, Liz, you've had your turn, four times as I recall. Give Evie some room to operate. We don't want her to be an old maid. Looking radiant to someone so handsome should be acted on!" Pam chimed in good naturedly.

"I think the Old Maid ship sailed a long time ago. Mama has been telling me I was one since I turned thirty, when as she was fond of saying, I let Greg get away," Evie said. The smile never left her face. "Mama never knew I didn't let him go. I shoved him away with all my might until the door hit him in the butt on his way out—and then I locked it!"

Evie's friends laughed remembering Greg not too fondly, the man who swept Evie off her feet despite repeated warnings from all of them. She finally listened to their advice. She didn't have to accept Greg's marriage proposal, with his baggage of two exes and four children, simply because of her age. There are worse things than being single after thirty. Being married to a player, like Greg, would have been at the top of the list.

"*Koukla mou.*" Constantine patted Evie's hand. "Be patient for the true love, like I had with my Rosa, God rest her soul. When it comes, you'll be glad you waited for your heart's desire. There is no age limit for passion to find you for the first time. Constantine knows about these things. Do not worry. It will happen for my sweet Evie."

"I don't worry about finding my soul mate. I hope I will, but at fifty, I'm not sure I would recognize my one and only love, even if he presented a certificate of authenticity from the Maker himself." Evie pushed her chair back from the table. "I think it's time to go out on the veranda and see how many of those old songs we can remember the words to."

The Fantastic Four strolled outside to enjoy a beautiful sunset, a gentle breeze, and music that reminded them of their much younger days. When they all had drinks in hand, Liz proposed a toast, "To friends who never fail you."

Pam added, "To the sisters of my heart."

"To friends who keep you laughing, especially when you feel like crying," Beverly said.

Evie finished the round of toasts, "To the Fantastic Four, friends who are even more fantastic at fifty!"

"Quiet down," Liz protested. "I just caught the eye of a thirty-something at the far table. He doesn't need to know I'm old enough to be his mother's eldest sister." The table erupted in laughter. Suddenly, everyone stopped laughing, and stared at Evie. Beverly pointed over her shoulder.

Evie turned to see what Beverly was signaling. There was Mr. Concerned with his three friends. "Good evening ladies. My name is Rance, and these fine gentlemen are Kyle, Peter, and John. If you would like to continue your celebration on the dance floor, we'd be honored to be your partners. I promise we won't step on your toes."

Liz introduced the Fantastic Four, first names only, and everyone paired off. Rance didn't waste any time claiming a reluctant Evie as his partner.

"You can't be the only one not dancing," Rance said, smiling as he took her hand. "You look like someone who knows her way around a dance floor."

"I do like to dance, although I don't get to very often. First, I think I owe you an apology. I was upset the other morning and now I realize you were only being kind when you stopped to check on me. I wasn't in a mood to accept any kindness at the time. I'm sorry I snapped at you."

"Consider the matter forgotten. Let's dance."

Evie stepped into his arms on the dance floor. And stayed there for the entire evening. Boy, could that man dance. They waltzed and cha chaed, two-stepped, and tangoed; at one point they even did a pretty mean samba. And no toes were stepped on even once. She couldn't remember the last time she'd had so much fun. With a man.

Four hours later, after lots of dancing, singing along to well-known oldies, and peals of laughter, the band went on another break. The Fantastic Four decided it was time to end their celebration. As Liz put it, "It's past time for old broads with early flights to call it a night."

"What happened to not telling our age?" Beverly laughed.

"They know we're old—we could sing every word to all of the songs the band played tonight!" Liz replied laughing.

The ladies hugged their impromptu dance partners. Rance held Evie a little longer than the others.

"You're a great dancer. I'm glad we ran into one another again, this time in happier circumstances. I hope you keep exercising your beautiful smile. Have a good flight home."

He bent down and kissed Evie on the cheek. She returned the kiss and fled before he noticed she was blushing. She was fifty years old. Why should she blush about a hug and a peck on the cheek? Must be hormonal.

Rance watched their dance partners leave the veranda. It was too bad they hadn't met again earlier in the week. Evie was a doll and fun, once you got past the barriers she put up. He could have sat and stared into her big brown eyes for hours. He loved the way they crinkled into little slits when she laughed. Maybe they'd meet again.

"C'mon, Dad." Kyle pulled Rance's arm. "This was fun, but remember, we have an early flight too."

"Thanks for not calling me Dad while the ladies were here! I didn't want them thinking I was too old for them." Rance laughed.

Rance's best friend, Peter, and his son, John, were in the car patiently waiting for them. "We didn't catch much out in the Gulf this trip, but we made up for it by reeling in some nice ones tonight!" Peter said.

The Fantastic Four lingered on the patio at the house before saying good night and goodbye. The week had flown by like the best of times frequently do. Tomorrow they'd return to their separate realities for another two years apart.

****

Evie settled into her first-class window seat prepared to enjoy the romance novel she'd never had time to read at the beach. One perk of her high stress job was it made first class seats possible. The trip had been everything she needed and wanted. Positively wonderful. Stress-relieving. Fun. Magnificent.

In years past, she'd look forward to giving Mama the update on the girls, their families, and love lives when she got home, but for the first time in twenty years, Mama wouldn't be there. Instead she'd have Frank to deal with—without Mama as the all important buffer—and the usual number of "crises" waiting for her after being away for a week. Margie's abilities only stretched so far. And Courtland Gaines couldn't magically solve every problem in her absence. No reason to worry about what was waiting at home. It would all be there tomorrow. She was still on vacation…a little longer.

Evie awoke to laughter from the row behind her. The flight attendant brought her a large cup of coffee and a breakfast snack of yogurt, apple slices, and a packet of wonderfully crunchy cinnamon cookies. She was surprisingly hungry. She'd gotten accustomed to Pam's ranch hand breakfasts this past week. Not a positive development. She was certain she wouldn't like the numbers her scales showed in the morning.

A few minutes after her tray was cleared, someone slid into the empty aisle seat. "Good morning, sleepy head. I'm sorry we disturbed your dreams." Rance sat next to her, looking as handsome as he had last night.

"Good morning. The dancing took more out of me than I thought. If I had to leave my dreams, it was nice to do it to laughter instead of the beeping alarm clock that will do the honors tomorrow morning." Evie smiled at her unexpected guest. His eyes were amazing. They beckoned you into their deep blue pools. She needed to pay attention. He was talking to her.

"We all had fun last night, but morning came too quickly. Early flights home are the worst part about vacation." Rance returned her smile. "I didn't realize you were from Chicago too. We never got around to personal details last night."

"I'm not. I live in Wisconsin, in a really small town you've probably never heard of about four hours from O'Hare. I usually fly in and out of Chicago."

"You've got me there. I don't know much about Wisconsin. The only place I've been in the dairy state is Madison. I went to a conference there. Where are your friends?"

"All headed home. Pam lives in Montana. Liz is in New York City. Beverly is in North Carolina. We all attended the same small college in Wisconsin, and we've been friends ever since. The trip to the Gulf for our birthdays is a long-standing tradition."

"Your group is more cosmopolitan than mine.

We're all from the Chicago area. Lived all my life in suburban Chicago. Went to school there." She had the brightest eyes. He hadn't lied about her smile; it lit her whole face.

"Was this your first trip to the Gulf coast?"

"Yep. It was our annual fishing trip. We'd done the Atlantic coast and the Keys, so we were ready for something different. We didn't have much luck fishing, but I'm glad I got to meet you...and your friends."

"I hope you enjoyed the Gulf. I think those sugar-white sand beaches are the most beautiful anywhere in the world," Evie said.

"They are lovely. And we had Chamber of Commerce weather—blue skies and gentle breezes every day. Is it always like this?"

"Over the years we've had a few clinker weeks where we stayed in and did jigsaw puzzles and complained about the weather, but for the most part this was typical. It's good to visit before hurricane season," Evie explained.

They talked as if they were old friends instead of new acquaintances. They even softly sang one of the romantic ballads from last night.

"It's a good thing no one else is in first class to hear our harmony." Rance laughed. "You have a voice almost as beautiful as the mouth it comes out of." He needed to think of something to say that didn't sound so cheesy.

"And you, sir, are a flatterer. But, don't stop. It will get you far with this small-town girl." Evie's laughter bubbled out. He was so easy to talk to.

All too soon, their conversation ended. The flight attendant tapped Rance on the shoulder and told him to return to his seat as they prepared for the approach to O'Hare.

"I hope to see you again, Evie. Here's my business card. Next time you're going to be in Chicago, give me a call. We can have dinner and go dancing or something." Rance handed her a card, lifted her hand, gently kissed it, and returned to his seat.

The card said:

Rance A. Thompson

Special Agent

Federal Bureau of Investigation

Chicago Field Office

Criminal Investigation Division

Wow, an FBI agent. He certainly was a kind man and so much fun. She'd hang on to the card. You never know when she'd be in Chicago, especially since she had such a pleasant reason to go. Evie leaned back in her seat smiling as the wheels touched down.

The landing was extremely smooth. Evie repacked her carry-on bag to deplane. Rance's friends, Peter and John, scooted out ahead of her.

Kyle stood in the aisle next to Evie's row and turned to Rance saying, "Dad, don't forget the bag under the seat in front of you."

"Got it. Thanks for reminding me. Don't want to leave it again," Rance replied grabbing the bag, blew a kiss to Evie, and followed Kyle onto the jet way.

Evie walked off the plane behind them. Dad? He wasn't wearing a wedding ring...of course, even married guys don't always wear one. Kyle's dad? They looked more like brothers. Was he divorced or widowed? Or still married and stepping out on the guys' holiday? Was she a vacation fling? She had his card, if she ever wanted to find out.

Wait, he didn't know her last name. Wouldn't you ask for someone's whole name, if you were seriously interested in them? He had given her his business card. He wasn't being secretive about who he was or how to find him.

She suspected he was way too young for her. He couldn't be forty yet. He was charming while it lasted and so easy on the eyes. Back to reality. After the last four hours of vacation—the drive home.

Chapter Seven

After a quick trip through the supermarket, the next stop was the Merrick house to retrieve their guest. "Does he have to leave now?" Tracy asked.

"We'd be happy to keep him all the time," Mallory added.

"Girls, Miss Langford needs to take Gonzo home. I'm sure since you did a good job, she'll let him come back and stay with us again," Chase Merrick said.

"I absolutely will," Evelyn agreed. "I didn't worry about him for a minute because I knew he was having lots of fun with all of you."

"They all played hard this week," Katrina said. "He wasn't a moment's problem. And he was definitely the hit of Show and Tell on Wednesday."

Tracy and Mallory hugged Gonzo with tears in their eyes. Even the boys said they'd be happy to petsit for Gonzo any time. They were delighted when Evelyn paid all four of them for their services despite their mother's protest.

Evelyn had trouble getting the wiggly furball into his car seat. He kept licking her hand and barking happy little yips. When they got home, she unhooked Gonzo and lifted him out of the seat. He squirmed out of her arms and raced to the door. She ran the garage door down and walked into the kitchen. She set the grocery bags on the granite counter just inside the door and reached for the light switch.

Wait.

A noise.

Something moved by the table.

Gonzo let loose a low growl followed by a sharp bark and backed out of the kitchen bumping into her feet.

"Who's there?" She reached into her purse and pulled out the pepper spray. "I know I'm not alone. Speak up. Now! Who are you?"

No answer. She quickly flipped on the lights and sprayed in the direction of the shadow near the kitchen table.

A male voice howled, "What in the blazes is wrong with you? It's me. Get out of the way. My arms are on fire. Lucky you missed my eyes." The man pushed past her to reach the kitchen sink. He grabbed the sprayer and shot water down one arm and then the other. He pulled paper towels off the roll and blotted his arms.

"Frank? It's your fault I sprayed you. Why didn't you answer me? Why would you let yourself in my house and sit waiting in the dark? You scared me out of my wits. Gonzo didn't even know who you were. Don't ever do that again."

"That dog hates me. He knew it was me. You made him vicious. He should have been put down as soon as his mistress was gone," Frank snarled.

"What an ugly sentiment. Animals can sense who likes them and who doesn't. Maybe Gonzo is reflecting the way you treat him."

"Boo hoo. Poor little dog. I don't have to justify coming into this house. I'm entitled to be here. This was my house too, remember? I was concerned about you. Check your cell phone. Your calls are going straight to voice mail. Where have you been? Your flight was on time and landed more than five hours ago."

She turned on her phone. Twenty missed calls in five hours. Frank was out of control.

"If it is any of your business, I stopped at the grocery store for a few things so I wouldn't have to go back out before morning. Then I stopped and retrieved Gonzo from the Merricks. It took a few minutes to settle my business there. What's so urgent? Can't it wait until morning?"

"When are we meeting with the executor on the estate? It's been sixty days."

"You're kidding. That's your emergency? You can't wait to get your hands on Mama's money? I thought it would be something important like your privileges at Garland Regional were suspended and you needed me to intercede again."

"That Gaines cretin has been trying to bump me out, but Merrick said no."

"I hope they got your attention this time."

"I'm not here to discuss your precious Garland Regional. You scheduled your vacation now because you knew I was anxious to get the estate resolved as quickly as possible. Your little holiday was timed specifically to annoy me." Frank's voice got louder.

"No, my dear brother, much as I love to irk you, this vacation has been scheduled for this week for more than two years. I know you didn't remember, but it was my birthday, my fiftieth birthday, and I was celebrating with my friends at the Gulf, like I have for the past thirty years.

"You know the executor couldn't make any disbursements until after all the public notices had been filed. I think our appointment at Lindstrom and Roggan is this Friday afternoon." Evie checked the calendar hanging above the phone on the kitchen wall. "Yes, it's at four o'clock on Friday. We're meeting with Hal Lindstrom in his office."

"It will be too late. I need my money now. Today," he choked out the words. The vein on his neck throbbed. His face flushed bright red. Was he having a panic attack? Or worse?

"You can't wait five more days? Surely, you have enough money to make it until Friday."

"You have to give me ten thousand dollars. I need it first thing tomorrow morning. I'll pay you back on Friday after we get our inheritance. I know you have it to spare. You always have extra money," Frank demanded.

"You should have money too. What about Dad's trust disbursement every month and your thriving practice? Why do you need ten thousand dollars in cash? What kind of trouble are you in?"

"You don't need to know why I need the money. You just have to give it to me. If you won't help me, I'll have to do something else. I'd rather not resort to them."

"What are you talking about? Them who? Is this related to all your trips into Chicago?"

"I can't tell you. Won't you give me the money without the third degree?"

"Frank, you know I care about you and would help if I could, but I don't have ten thousand in cash lying around the house," Evie explained.

"I know, it wasn't in the safe."

"You opened my safe? How dare you. If the money had been there would you have just taken it?"

"I lived here too. I know the combination. It's that urgent. Aren't you listening? Don't you understand anything I've been saying?"

"I'll see what I can do tomorrow. I can't give you anything now."

"Whatever happens next remember, I asked you first. If I have to do something extreme, it is all on you. It's your fault. You wouldn't help your only sibling, your living flesh and blood. Don't family ties mean anything to you? You are such a selfish witch."

"What kind of mess are you in? You told me The Langford Obstetrical Center was making money hand over fist. Where did it all go? Dad left you a thriving medical practice. What happened to all your patients?"

"You think it's helpful to point out my past financial failures instead of lending me what I need to get through this crisis?"

"Frank, I don't have ten thousand dollars in cash— *if* I wanted to help—you'd have to wait for the bank to open in the morning. Why don't we talk about this over lunch tomorrow?"

"It will be too damned late. Thanks for absolutely nothing."

He stormed out of the room. The front door slammed. He strode down the street beyond the hedges where he'd parked, got in the car, slammed the door, revved up the engine, and squealed his tires as he pulled away from the curb.

Gonzo rubbed against Evie's legs. She bent down, gathered him in her arms, and scratched between his ears. His contented snorting sounded almost like purring.

"So what trouble do you think my brother has fallen into now?" Evie asked the little dog.

Evie sat at the kitchen table having a bowl of vegetable soup for supper. She pulled her work e-mail up on the laptop computer. She might as well do this now. Tomorrow morning would be a zoo after being away for a week. Reading her e-mail would give her an inkling of what awaited tomorrow and in the week beyond.

Her cell phone rang.

Not Frank.

"Hello, Court. Is everything okay?"

"Can't a guy check on his favorite CEO without something being wrong?"

The voice was oily…too smooth…too creepy. Evie shivered.

"It's late. Did you need something specific?"

"Wanted you to know everything has been handled. Dr. Miller and I talked with Chief Davis," Court announced authoritatively. "The investigation is officially started about the Rich girl."

"That's what I expected. Was there anything else?"

"We got another mystery mother. She's still breathing though. Her baby is in the high-risk intensive care nursery."

Why did he sound almost gleeful?

"Another emergency transfer from The Center?"

"No, but another young woman who was brought by ambulance to the E.R. in labor. She refuses to tell us who she is or where she's from. She's in a bad way. They're putting her prints through the National

Runaway database. Chief Davis said it's standard protocol in a case like this." Why was he so excited about another young woman's distress?

"Thanks for letting me know."

"Wait, don't you want all the details?"

"Not tonight. I'm exhausted. Tomorrow is soon enough. Good night."

"But, Evie, you didn't tell me anything about your vacation."

"This isn't a social call, Courtland. Right now, I feel like the past week never happened. Good night."

Evie finished processing her e-mail and reviewing her calendar for the coming day. No surprises there. Court would undoubtedly make a beeline into administration first thing in the morning to give her all the grisly details about the new arrivals. What made that man tick?

She worried about Frank. He could be a pain in the butt, but he was family. Why couldn't he meet his expenses? Had he gotten involved in gambling or drugs? He was so secretive about all of the trips to Chicago. He didn't have a lot of restraint when he got interested in something; he would jump in with both feet. For being a trained medical professional, he was amazingly naïve about lots of life.

Evelyn seemed to have gotten all the common sense in the family. She'd make a point to talk to him tomorrow. Maybe there was something she could do that didn't involve giving him ten thousand dollars for an unknown reason.

She shut down the laptop and put it with her purse on the counter by the door. Then she double checked the locks on all the doors, turned out lights, scooped up the pug, and walked upstairs to her bedroom.

"I almost forgot to tell you, Gonzo, I met a man on this trip. He's an FBI agent from Chicago. A kind, good-looking guy who is a terrific dancer. I chatted with him on the plane most of the flight home. Even though he gave me his business card, I suspect I was only a vacation dalliance. He has a grown son. He's probably married. All the good ones are." She set her pet down on the bed.

Gonzo barked twice, then curled up on the right side of Evie's bed where he had his own pillow and blanket. She should make him sleep in his bed on the floor, but she liked the company of the little pug. It was kind of comforting to hear him snoring like a little motorboat all night. He had been so lost after Mama died. They needed each other. She'd missed him this past week.

Chapter Eight

Evelyn Langford was thankful for a relatively calm and normal first day back after a week off. Margie Wright, her long-time personal assistant, knew how Miss Langford liked things run and had no problem stepping in to make some decisions in the CEO's absence. Margie's conscientious approach to her job made everything easier. Lots of little nagging issues had already been resolved by the efficient Mrs. Wright by the time the CEO returned. More importantly, Courtland Gaines was kept out of pot stirring so normal operations could continue to run smoothly.

Margie reviewed the list of calls to return and appointments for the day with her boss. She was about to leave the CEO's office when she stopped. "And I guess Mr. Gaines already told you that Mrs. Kapper accompanied another young girl in labor into the Emergency Room last night."

"He did. He was eager to be the first one to deliver the sad news. Are they both on three?" the CEO asked.

"They are. I figured you'd want to go and check on them in person. You don't have anything scheduled for the next thirty minutes," the assistant said with a smile.

****

Evelyn Langford peered in the window to the High Risk Intensive Care Nursery. She sighed out loud. No matter how many babies she saw in the isolettes, they were each a minor miracle in their own right. Every tiny bed and incubator was occupied today. She stepped to the phone on the wall on the right side of the window and lifted the receiver.

"Good morning. I came to see our newest arrival. Would you please point him out?...Third row in the middle? He's so tiny, but look at that shock of red hair. Thank you." She hung up.

"All of two pounds and two ounces." Dr. Wetzel stepped to the window beside her. "It's going to be touch and go."

"I understand we have a meeting later this morning to discuss updates from our earlier called meeting and additional concerns—in general—not just about this little fellow. I wanted to see him for myself before we talked," the CEO explained.

"Then I'll save my speech for later in a more private spot. Dr. Merrick and I have some ideas."

"Good, although I don't relish the idea of being ganged up on by a team of docs." Miss Langford smiled broadly. "I'll see you at ten."

****

Evelyn checked in at the Obstetrical desk before going to see the red-headed baby's mother.

"Good morning, Miss Langford," Lori Bryers, the head nurse, said as the CEO approached the unit nursing station. "I thought we would be seeing you this morning."

"You make my visit sound ominous."

Lori laughed. "Sorry, it was unintended. Only I wish you would drop by for no reason at all except to shoot the breeze with an old friend. Not for this."

"I'd like nothing better. We old timers have to stick

together. I haven't forgotten we were in the same new employee orientation," the CEO said. "How is our patient doing?"

"She's been through hell but seems to be coming around. We know her name now. It's Lila. No last name yet but it's a start. And she's AB Negative. I just sent out an email to employees calling for donors for an impromptu blood drive."

"I'm AB Negative. I'll have Margie schedule me a donation time."

"Done. She put it on your schedule as soon as the request went out."

"Great. Has anyone called to check on Lila or come to visit?"

"Only Mrs. Kapper. She's in the waiting room crocheting a blanket for the little guy. I hate to be pessimistic, but I hope it doesn't become his shroud."

"Mama always said, 'from your mouth to God's ear.' I heard Mrs. Kapper found Lila and got her to the E.R."

"Yes—the other two also. Apparently, she has a knack for finding about to be mothers in distress," Nurse Bryers confirmed.

"Fortunate for them. Please let me know if anyone asks about Lila or her son."

Miss Langford found Mrs. Kapper sitting on a bench crocheting in the nearly empty waiting room. These days with the dads, grandparents, and siblings in the delivery rooms, there was a lot less need for the waiting area.

"Good morning, Mrs. Kapper. I hear you've been our Good Samaritan once again."

"Miss Langford, so nice to see you, my dear. Do

you have time to sit with me a minute?" The petite, white-haired woman patted the black Naugahyde-covered bench next to her.

"I do. I'm hoping you can tell me how you met Lila." Evelyn sat down and breathed in the lavender-scented haze surrounding Mrs. Kapper.

"Well, technically we've never met. Lila was sitting on the apple tree bench, same as the other girls. You remember my special seat, right?"

"The one in your orchard up on the hill? The seat Mr. Kapper built for you when you were pregnant with your first child so you'd have a place to rest on your daily walk?"

"You do remember. You're such a sweet girl. I've rested there in mid-constitutional every day since. I credit it with keeping me going strong at eighty. There is something about my orchard that attracts weary, frightened, pregnant girls." Mrs. Kapper chuckled. "I was out for my morning stroll. There she was, lying on the bench. She didn't want to go to the hospital, but I could see she was in labor—after six kids you know what it looks like. Her water broke and there was blood everywhere. I called an ambulance from my alert necklace; so glad the kids got me this." She patted the monitor hanging around her powdered, wrinkled neck next to a string of pearls. "We didn't get to talk much. Did you see Lila? She's a blonde-haired baby doll. So young. And her little red-headed boy. This blanket's for him." She held up the nearly complete lacy pale blue and white coverlet.

"You do beautiful work. You'll have to give me lessons someday. This sounds like it was a repeat of the previous two episodes."

"Exactly. I'm glad I didn't decide to be lazy and skip my walk today. Some greater power knew I was needed up the hill this morning and made me walk despite my achy knees."

"Miss Lila and her little guy are lucky you're a creature of habit. Thank you for getting her here so quickly." Miss Langford patted the woman's back. "I'll be checking in periodically. If you need anything, you know where my office is. If I'm not there, Mrs. Wright will be happy to help you."

The CEO noticed the new mother's room door was open. She knocked and stepped into the room. The young woman, really a girl, in the bed was asleep. IVs were inserted in both arms. One was delivering fluids and the other blood. A nurse was bent over the patient checking her vital signs. When she finished, she met Miss Langford at the door.

"Is she any better?"

. "She's not been conscious for any extended period of time. I couldn't really say. Dr. Wetzel has been keeping a close eye on her. He may have more information," the nurse responded.

"Thank you. I'll see him shortly."

****

"We contacted the admissions office at The Center as soon as the patient arrived by ambulance even though she had come from Mrs. Kapper's house. They deny she's one of theirs now or ever has been," Dr. Merrick said.

"They always say that when the girl isn't going to make it," Courtland Gaines said with a snort.

"No one said she isn't going to make it," Dr. Wetzel corrected him. "She's lost a lot of blood but is being transfused. Her son is tiny but holding his own. He's a fighter and doing remarkably well for one so small. We are seeing younger and younger girls come into the Emergency Room who look like they've had less than ideal prenatal care. It's not a good recipe for healthy babies or their young moms."

"Do The Center board members know what's going on out there?" Dr. Miller asked.

"They've already said this girl is not one of their mothers. We have no reason to tell them about Lila. In fact, it would be a breach of confidentiality to tell them. However, I do believe these cases and the emergency C-sections we've had to do on The Center's patients, need further discussion. Not only with their board, but their medical staff as well. This needs to be on the agenda for the joint meeting," Dr. Merrick said.

"I thought we had all agreed to the joint meeting before I left last week. Let me check with Margie on the status of the meeting." Evelyn picked up the phone to talk to her assistant. She hung up and said, "We're still trying to find a date that works for the majority of both boards. Fortunately, three of our board members are also on The Center's board. It is not final but we hope to have it scheduled soon. I hear your concerns. We will get to the bottom of this," she assured the physicians.

"Like Dr. Wetzel, I'll be happy to provide any education needed for The Center's medical staff. The more training they have, the less likely it is that we will have to see one of their mothers," Dr. Merrick added.

"I'm sure they would appreciate having physicians with your experience available to help them," Miss Langford noted.

****

At lunch time, Courtland Gaines breezed past the assistant's desk saying, "Official business." He entered the office and closed Evelyn's door before Margie could get out of her chair.

He plopped a brown grease-stained sack on the small conference table in the corner of the CEO's office. "C'mon. You need to eat something. I've got Mac's cheeseburgers—just the way I know you like them."

"You're being thoughtful. I didn't realize how late it was. Thank you." Sometimes Court could be kind. But at what cost?

"I always have your best interest at heart. Don't you understand that by now?"

"You're here. Tell me about Lila," Evelyn said.

"We have plenty of time later for depressing discussions. Instead, why don't you tell me about your vacation?"

"Court, I need to know if you have any new information about the young lady who came in the other night."

"But your time off…"

"Please, Court."

"Right. Unfortunately, we didn't learn anything more about the girl. When she was alert, she refused to give us additional information. Chief Davis hasn't gotten information back yet on her fingerprints. Dr. Wetzel estimated she was fourteen or fifteen."

"A baby herself. Yes, the doctor told me."

"The chief's hopeful we'll get a hit in the National Runaway database. It's probably the only way we'll find out who she is and why she almost gave birth in Mrs. Kapper's apple orchard. The baby may provide clues too if we can get permission to do DNA testing."

"Thank you. I appreciate the way you handled the issue in my absence."

"Speaking of absences, how was the vacation?"

A knock. The office door opened. "Your one o'clock is here, Miss Langford."

"Thank you, Margie. Please show him in. Mr. Gaines and I are finished."

Reluctantly, Courtland Gaines cleared off the conference table and left his boss's office.

****

After her one o'clock meeting, Evelyn Langford made a quick trip to the impromptu donation center set up in Conference Room B and donated her valuable serum for Lila and her little son.

****

It was after seven o'clock in the evening before Evie had a chance to check on her brother. Frank's phone rang without being answered. No answering service responded. Nothing. Maybe he was on the other line and hadn't activated the service yet. She turned off her computer and left the office.

****

Gonzo bolted out of his crate as soon as Evie opened its door. He wiggled in and out of her legs on the way to the back door. After a quick stop in the yard, he rushed back into the kitchen. Evie squatted to pick up the small dog.

"Gonzo, it isn't fair to you to stay crated all day after years of having the run of the house with Mama and her nurses to love on you all day long. I should look for a new home for you, but I'd miss you too much. Having you here is like having part of Mama still here. You understand, don't you, boy?" Evie snuggled the little furball close to her cheek and was rewarded with a tongue across her nose. Laughing, she wiped her face. "I'll take that as a yes. Let's get you some dinner, then I'll be ready for some."

Evie continued to talk to Gonzo while she made her microwave dinner. He stopped munching his kibble periodically to cock his head and stare with those bug-eyes as if he understood every word.

"We have a new young mother and her darling red-headed boy who are both fighting for their lives. I hope we don't lose them. It's so hard when they arrive in the ambulance in such bad shape. Courtland Gaines keeps trying to be 'friends' with me, and Frank is being imperious. I know. Same old. Same old. It makes me wish I was back on vacation."

After dinner, Evie started a load of laundry and sat at the kitchen table reviewing the pile of correspondence she'd brought home with her.

At ten p.m., she finally got through to her brother. "I've been worried about you. I've been trying to contact you all evening. You don't have your service activated."

"Oh, now you're worried about me? How touching," Frank snapped. "My service just called to let me know they've had a glitch with their system. Fortunately, the only missed calls I'm showing are yours. No patients have called."

"At least your patients are okay."

"My patients are always fine. Why wouldn't they be? Why were you looking for me?"

"I wanted to see if there is anything I can do to help. You sounded so desperate and stressed last night.

You're right, we are flesh and blood relatives. I want to be better support for you."

"It's too late," Frank said flatly. "I told you very specifically, I needed the money by this morning."

"What do you mean? Yesterday, you needed ten thousand dollars and today you don't? How can that be true?"

"I took care of the situation. I hope permanently, but if not, it will be on your head, not mine," Frank said with a snort.

"How did you get the cash today? You didn't have it yesterday."

"I didn't say I found the money. I said I took care of the situation. Look, I have an early induction in the morning. Did you need anything else?" The irritation in Frank's voice was clear.

"No. Sorry I bothered you. I'll see you Friday afternoon in Hal Lindstrom's office."

How did he resolve a ten-thousand-dollar problem overnight? Maybe one of his buddies was good for the money, but he didn't say he'd found a lender. Frank would never give Evie any credit for being concerned since she failed to do exactly what he wanted, when he wanted. She wouldn't worry about Frank. She couldn't be her brother's keeper. It was more than a full-time job.

The laundry was washed, dried, and put away. She was ready for bed. She let Gonzo out one more time and she climbed the stairs with the spoiled pet in her arms. She deposited Gonzo on the bed and his motorboat engine fired right up. She was asleep almost before her head hit the pillow. She needed another vacation already.

Chapter Nine

Lab coat clad Dr. Frank Langford stormed into Lindstrom and Roggan's reception area slamming the heavy door after he entered.

"It's four fifteen. Why haven't we started yet?" he bellowed at the receptionist.

Evelyn Langford intervened to shield the wide-eyed young woman from her brother's inappropriate behavior. "We haven't started because you weren't here. You're late. Sit down. Mr. Lindstrom will be right with us." She led her red-faced brother to a nearby chair.

Could two siblings be more different? She had Mama's go-with-the-flow temperament and Dad's think-before-you-speak-in-anger approach to conflict. Where did Frank get his ugly attitude from? Neither their father nor mother ever showed a temper to them as children.

A legal assistant led them into the attorney's office where Hal Lindstrom was waiting on the other side of a massive, highly polished, walnut desk. The silver-haired senior partner was the executor for both their parents' estates and oversaw the disbursements from the trust fund they received after their father's death.

"A pleasure to see you both." Hal Lindstrom came around the desk to meet them. He gave Evelyn a brief hug and extended his hand to Frank. "Hard to believe both of your parents are gone. Your mother was an elegant and classy lady right to the end, always smiling, no matter the situation. I knew her before either of you were born, when your father had first started his practice."

"We know who our mother was. Cut to the chase. We're here for the disbursements from the estate," Frank interrupted.

"Frank, please, contain yourself. Mr. Lindstrom, my brother, apparently, has other obligations today and doesn't want to be here any longer than is necessary," Evelyn apologized.

Hal Lindstrom shook his head and began, "This meeting will not take long as there are no disbursements to make from your mother's estate."

"You're lying!" Frank jumped to his feet, the vein on the side of his neck throbbing. "I saw the will. We each get fifty percent of her estate. Equal shares. There is no one else to inherit. Where is all the money?"

Evelyn pulled Frank back down into the burgundy leather chair beside her. "I'm sure Mr. Lindstrom will explain, if you will give him a chance."

"Thank you, Evelyn, I will," Mr. Lindstrom continued. "Your father has been gone for twenty years. He left your mother half of his estate, plus your family home. She consumed every penny of his bequest, and then some. Remember, she spent six months in the Rehab Center with a broken back and pelvis. She hadn't been out of a wheelchair since the accident. Your mother had extraordinary medical bills throughout the entire time since your father's death.

"Evelyn relocating from Ohio to live with her did forestall the need for outside paid help. But, as you know, her condition continued to decline to the point she needed an attendant twenty-four hours a day these past five years. Her bequest from your father's estate was completely exhausted."

"How had Mama been paying her bills if her inheritance was gone?" Evelyn asked.

"She got a reverse mortgage on the house about four years ago and was receiving monthly payments from that. They were adequate to meet her expenses up to the time of her death. I was concerned that we would have to take principal from your trust once she exhausted those funds," Mr. Lindstrom replied.

Frank leapt to his feet again and spoke loudly, "She can't have used it all. No one human being could run through all the money my father left her. And all the equity from the house. I don't believe it."

He spun around and pointed at his sister. "You took it, didn't you? You were right there, cozying up to her, being the dutiful daughter. You convinced her to give you all the money! You kept sneaking it away, a little at a time. No wonder you have cash to burn on exotic weeklong vacations."

Evelyn pushed up out of her chair and stood toe-to-toe with Frank. "You know I did not take anything from Mama. I moved back to Lansdale and lived with her because she asked me to. I purchased all the groceries to feed both of us and her nurses. I paid Mama rent every month like I would any landlord. It helped cover our utilities. You can look at her bank statements and you'll see my monthly deposits. We had to have additional staff because I couldn't stay with her all day, every day. She needed more care than I was equipped to provide while working full time. I am not the medical person in the family, Dr. Langford!"

"You better believe I'll be checking all the records. How could you let her get a reverse mortgage and dissolve our inheritance?" Frank grabbed Evelyn's arm.

"Mama did that without my knowledge. She was never mentally compromised. She still wrote out checks for all her own bills each month and worked with Mr. Schmidt at the bank if she needed any financial advice or assistance. You and I were both signatories on her checking account in case of emergencies. Perhaps I should look at the records to see if you were writing yourself checks out of Mama's account." Evelyn jerked her arm out of Frank's grasp and shoved him away.

"How dare you accuse me! I would not steal from my mother when all I had to do was wait for my share."

"But you think I would." Evelyn shook her head and slid back into her chair.

"There's nothing. No, it's worse than nothing," Frank grumbled. "We need to get the house on the market so we can pay off the mortgage lender. If it is worth more than was lent maybe something good will come from this after all."

"Frank, you aren't solely in charge. I am not putting the house on the market. I have no intention of moving. I'm not ready to leave the last place where we made so many happy memories with our parents…with each other. Are you so heartless and greedy that the money is the only thing you care about? You're the one who said we are the only flesh and blood the other still has. Have you forgotten?" Evelyn sobbed.

"There are other ways to address this issue," Mr. Lindstrom interjected. "Your father set up the trust to be in effect until you had both reached age forty and for the life of your mother. The terms of your trust have all been met with her death. The assets may be distributed now, half to each of you."

"Finally, some good news. I want everything I have coming to me, and I want it immediately," Frank insisted.

"Wonderful. I'll be able to pay off the mortgage company and stay in the house," Evelyn said.

"My sister has a brilliant idea. Lindstrom, get an appraisal done so we can get this resolved. Evie, get out your checkbook, I want exactly half of the value above the amount due to the mortgage company." Frank smirked. "How long will it take to wrap up the trust and divide the spoils?"

"Since you both agree, I will begin the process immediately. I'll be back in touch in two weeks and let you know when things will be done," the attorney responded.

"Make it as quickly as you can. I've waited long enough to get what's coming to me!"

"Frank Langford, if I weren't related to you, I'd never speak to you ever again. I am so ashamed of you." She laid her head down on her folded arms on the edge of the desk and softly sobbed. Frank left the room, slamming the door.

"Evelyn, I'm sorry you had to deal with your brother in high dudgeon. Your father was concerned about Frank's lack of compassion and inability to handle money. Your brother is the reason your inheritance was put in the trust, instead of directly split between you when your father died." Hal Lindstrom walked around the desk and patted her back. "He hoped that by the time the assets were divided Frank might be more mature and responsible. The mortgage company has already contacted me asking about the house. I'm sure the bank could loan you the money to pay it off on the basis of the trust being settled."

"Frank's right. I'm the one who has always been good with money. I'll either take it from savings or get a mortgage. Could I please have the information to get in touch with the lender? I'll try and get things in motion on Monday. Why is Frank so desperate to get his hands on more money? What on earth has he been doing with the income from the trust and his practice? Do you have any idea what he's involved in?"

"Frank has always been tightly wired. I've heard some rumors about The Center causing him to be overextended. They say when he maxed out his ability to raise money here in Lansdale he borrowed money in Chicago from some questionable sources. I don't know any specifics. Mostly, only rumors. I think the sooner you separate your financial future from his, the better. I'll get the appraisal together. After I let you know the amount, you can proceed with purchasing your home. If you need anything else, please don't hesitate to let me know." The attorney reached across the desk and closed the file.

"Thank you. I see why Dad thought you were the best person to administer their estates." She stood and gave him a hug, then left the office.

Sitting in her car, Evelyn laid her head on the steering wheel. Tears streamed down her cheeks and onto her lap. First, she lost her father, then Mama, and now Frank was dead to her. She was all alone. Fifty years old and for the first time in her life, she was truly alone except for one snoring, bug-eyed little dog.

****

Mother's Day and for the first time in twenty years, there was no one to make the special salmon quiche for—Mama wasn't waiting for breakfast in her bed. Evie sat at the kitchen table staring into the backyard. The lilac bushes were beginning to bloom.

"I remember the year Frank and I saved our allowances and bought those flowering shrubs for Mother's Day. I think Dad helped by doing a little pre-negotiating with the nursery man. I'm not sure if she was more excited when they were delivered or we were. We blindfolded her and led her into the yard. She squealed with delight when she saw her favorite blooming bushes planted outside the kitchen window. Oh, Mama, will I ever stop missing you?" Evie sighed out loud. "You would be so disappointed in your son's behavior."

When Gonzo heard "Mama," he jumped out of his bed in the corner of the kitchen and raced into the first-floor bedroom. He barked three times. Evie rose and walked into Mama's room.

"What's wrong, boy? You miss her as much as I do, don't you?" The little dog rubbed against her legs and plopped down across her slippers. "I know. It's not getting easier for either of us. We had to know this day would come. She was eighty-five and the doctors said it was miraculous that she'd survived more than twenty years after the accident. The time has gone so quickly. I never imagined what my life would be like without her. At least we won't be kicked out of our home. I'll make sure of it." She stooped over and gathered the whimpering furball in her arms. "We've got each other. I guess it will have to be enough for now."

****

Evelyn Langford's phone chimed indicating an incoming text about ten thirty p.m. Sweet Lila with no last name was gone. Her little boy was holding his own, but they seemed no closer to finding whose daughter she was or where she came from before appearing in Mrs. Kapper's orchard.

Chapter Ten

It took longer than Evelyn Langford had hoped to schedule the joint board meeting between Garland Regional Medical Center and The Langford Obstetrical Center. The three members in common were Mr. Schmidt, the banker; the minister, Reverend Cox; and Muriel Whistler, co-owner of Whistler's Diner on the Square. The room was nearly full when Dr. Frank Langford, clad in a lab coat with a stethoscope looped over his shoulders, rushed through the conference room door.

"Sorry to be running late. Babies have a wonderful way of appearing on their own timeline, regardless of what is booked on my schedule." He laughed and sat next to Dr. Chase Merrick. He spoke to everyone in the room except his sister who was sitting directly across the table from him.

The Chairman of the Langford Obstetrical Center board, Reverend Cox, was also Vice Chair of the Garland Regional Medical Center board so he was asked to lead the joint meeting. The other Regional board members were Dr. Gengler, the veterinarian; Angie Westby, elementary school teacher; and William Ritterskamp, dairy farmer. The Langford Obstetrical Center remaining board members were Mikal Reynolds, volunteer coordinator; Elsie Dennis, business owner of Knitting Pretty; and Hank Shuster, hog farmer.

Dr. Wetzel spoke first. "The medical staff responsible for the women and children's department here at Garland Regional are concerned about the number of extremely young mothers we are seeing come from The Center and that some of them do not seem to have had appropriate prenatal care. I know they are already pregnant when you get them, but I'd recommend that you take a more aggressive approach with these young women in making certain they have the right nutrition and supplements. I would be happy to provide some literature outlining these recommendations and I will be glad to teach staff in-services to help raise everyone's competence level in dealing with these special mothers."

Mikal Reynolds was interested in seeing the literature to use in her volunteer work not only with The Center, but with the unwed mothers she counseled.

Dr. Merrick addressed the issues the Emergency Room staff were seeing, "The delays in transporting distressed women and girls in labor to Garland is dramatically impacting our ability to successfully take life-saving measures with them. The rapid incineration of stillborn bodies without allowing time for autopsies means the reason for the infant deaths remains a mystery. We need more post-mortem access to the mothers and children to identify the reasons for their demises. I will add my offer to Dr. Wetzel's to in-service the staff on more expansive emergency situation recognition and treatment."

Dr. Frank Langford said, "The Center would welcome the Garland Regional Medical Center's physicians. We can always use additional training.

Healthy mothers having healthy babies to go to happy homes is the ultimate goal of The Langford Obstetrical Center. Please contact my assistant, Mrs. Fran Rafferty, to arrange a time for these valuable classes when it will best work for you. I'll make certain my staff can attend."

Miss Langford said, "I'm encouraged by the spirit of cooperation in this room. I believe that by working together we can ensure Dr. Langford's ultimate stated goal is met. My concerns are related to the lack of proper paperwork accompanying these emergency transfers. We get little or no medical records information and the next of kin information is frequently missing or completely bogus. It makes death notifications, getting permissions, and general communication with the patients' families practically impossible."

"I believe I can address that particular issue, Miss Langford. For those of you who may not know me, I am Tom Peterman, local attorney and a partner in the Langford Obstetrical Center. I am pleased with this opportunity to have a discussion in a professional manner so it is not reduced to a public family squabble." It took all of Evelyn Langford's poise and self control to stay silent. He continued, "Mothers-to-be come to The Center for a variety of reasons. They are not all runaways or unwed. Some are more mature women in difficult situations who feel the best long-term option for their child is to be adopted. We collect adequate information to address the legalities of arranging for their care and for the adoption of their babies. We try not to pry into circumstances in these sensitive situations beyond what is essential to the safe delivery of the child and its subsequent adoption."

Chief Davis interrupted the attorney, "How does The Center vet the pregnant teenagers who appear on their doorstep? Clearly, they should have more scrutiny than your usual patients since they are not of legal age."

"We go through the same vetting process with all our mothers-to-be regardless of their age, race, or socioeconomic status," Dr. Langford responded. "Our focus is getting them excellent prenatal care as quickly as possible, then matching them with the perfect prospective adoptive parents for their child."

"So the answer is, you chose to look the other way rather than ask uncomfortable, unprofitable questions?" the chief asked.

"I think this discussion is taking a turn that no one wants to pursue," Reverend Cox said ignoring raised hands of members wanting to speak. "All in favor of tabling this discussion until a meeting following the additional training at The Center say aye...opposed? Motion carries. The next order of business is continued ongoing joint meetings."

The board members of both institutions unanimously agreed regular meetings between them should happen more frequently. A routine quarterly meeting was set. It was the only substantive action taken. Both boards asked to be kept in the loop on the queries related to the recent young mother deaths. They didn't rule out meeting sooner than three months from now, if the situation warranted joint action.

On the way out of the room, Dr. Frank Langford leaned over to his sister and snarled, "See the can of worms you've opened. I hope you're proud of yourself."

****

"It's about time this was resolved." Frank Langford plopped down in the wing back chair across the huge walnut desk from Hal Lindstrom. "It's been a month since I requested all I'm owed. You certainly took your sweet time about it."

"It's not Mr. Lindstrom's fault. It took some time for him to cash out the investments in the trust and for me to arrange financing for the house so I could pay you and the mortgage company off in full, as you demanded." Evelyn did not look up from her checkbook.

"Yeah, you're so busy managing a runaway search service, you don't have time for the important business of meeting your personal financial obligations." Frank glared as if focusing a laser at his sister's head.

"I need both your signatures to indicate you have been paid your portion of the trust assets and this business will be completed." Hal Lindstrom pushed the papers across the desk to Frank. "Please sign on the bottom line and initial in each spot where there is an X. Take your time and read it carefully. This is a final legal document."

"Just give me the checks and I'll sign. I don't need to read it. I have what I want." Frank scribbled his signature and initials throughout the document, then shoved it across the desktop to his sister. He took the check from her. "Not as much as I'd hoped for, but it will have to do." Then he got the one from the attorney. "This is more like it."

Turning to his sister, Frank said, "I haven't heard any more about the issue at the hospital, so I guess it's resolved as well?"

"I'm waiting to hear from Chief Davis. We don't know any more than we did three weeks ago. I don't believe anything has changed with any of your patients," Evelyn responded.

She walked around the desk and hugged Hal Lindstrom. "Thank you for getting this resolved so quickly and professionally. I greatly appreciate your help." She left the office without a backward glance.

"Well, aren't we Miss High and Mighty? Can you believe she left without even saying goodbye to me? Talk about sore losers."

Hal Lindstrom did not look up from his paperwork. The assistant came to the door and showed Frank out of the office.

****

Evie walked into the kitchen, set the grocery bags on the counter, and released the dog from his crate. "Well, Gonzo, it's officially all ours!"

Gonzo cocked his head then yipped three times putting his seal of approval on the news.

She put the groceries away and fed Gonzo, then walked around the first floor gently touching the well-used pieces of furniture, remembering the happy family who once lived there. How had they gotten to this stressful situation? Growing up, Frank had gladly played the role of big brother—protecting little Evie from rogue dogs, bullies, and snakes. He seemed to take great pride in making sure she was safe and contented. Now, they weren't even on speaking terms. She couldn't remember the last time they'd had a friendly conversation with one another or shared a meal together. They maintained an icy professional relationship. Nothing more.

Evie sat down on the sofa and looked around the room. Tears welled up in her eyes threatening to overflow to her cheeks at any moment. Gonzo sat at her feet whimpering until she pulled him onto her lap. His tongue curled out of his mouth and swiped across her cheek licking up the tears as they fell. "Thanks, Gonzo. I needed the reminder I'm not alone."

Chapter Eleven

Margie stood at the office door. "I'm sorry to bother you, Miss Langford, but Chief Davis is here with another gentleman and asked if you could spare him a few minutes. Your calendar is clear for the next half hour."

"Please show them in. I hope they have news about our patients." She straightened the papers on her desk, tucked a stray hair behind her ear, and stood to greet her guests.

"Miss Langford, thank you for seeing us without an appointment." Chief Davis extended his hand. "There's been a break in the case. I wanted you to hear about it right from the horse's mouth. Evelyn Langford, meet Special Agent Rance Thompson from the FBI's Chicago office. Rance Thompson, this is Evelyn Langford, Garland Regional Medical Center's CEO. She's the one who had her staff alert me about the young patients who died here."

The name was the same, no mistaking those curls, or those blue eyes. It was indeed Rance from the beach. He looked very professional in his navy suit with white shirt and a red striped tie. He stepped forward with his hand extended. "Miss Langford, it is a great pleasure to meet you."

She grasped his hand. "The pleasure is all mine, Mr. Thompson." She scanned his face. No glimmer of recognition. No extra squeeze. No lingering handshake. No nothing.

They sat down at the small conference table in the corner of the office.

"Miss Langford, your and Dr. Miller's instincts were spot on. The young woman you knew as Rose Rich was in the National Runaway database. Her real name was Rosalie Richardson, and she was from the northern suburbs of Chicago," Chief Davis said.

"Rosalie was almost fifteen when she went missing two and a half years ago. Her parents never believed she ran away. She was a happy kid, got good grades, and had lots of friends. Prior to her disappearance, her family said they'd never had a moment's problem with her. Rosalie was on her way home from high school one evening after volleyball practice. She was walking with two of her teammates, Sarah Kelley and Sonia Gables. All three girls did not come home that night and have not been seen since. Their parents are affluent. Originally it was thought to be a kidnapping, but no ransom demands were made for any of them. The local authorities decided the three friends must have run away together.

"Your call about Rosalie is the first indication anyone has had regarding their whereabouts in all this time. Understandably, all three sets of parents were relieved to get word about Rosalie even if the initial news was bad. The Kelley and Gables parents gave us permission to look at any records on their girls that may help find them. Fortunately, they'd had them fingerprinted as small children, so we have that additional information to use in confirming their identities," Agent Thompson reported.

Chief Davis said, "I also wanted to let you know that we have identified the girl who was admitted while you were gone. Mr. Gaines sent me her fingerprints. Her name is Lila Masterson. She's been missing ten months. Ran away from her grandmother's home in a small town in Illinois outside of Chicago. We're trying to contact the grandmother now."

"We lost Lila a couple of days ago. Her little boy is growing. He should be able to move out of the High Risk nursery soon. I hope you are able to get in touch with her relatives." She turned to the FBI agent. "Do you believe they are all runaways? If all this is the tragic result of a juvenile stunt gone horribly wrong, I don't understand why the FBI is involved," Evelyn said.

"Rosalie Richardson was a minor, her death was under mysterious circumstances, and it happened across the state line from where she went missing. Combine that with a similar story about the Masterson girl and they became FBI cases. We are coordinating with Chief Davis and treating these as possible human trafficking cases. We plan to go out to the facility where the Richardson girl gave birth later today. We're hoping The Obstetrical Center staff might recognize Sarah and Sonia as Rosalie's friends. Maybe they were all together. My greatest wish is to find the other girls alive here in Lansdale."

"Interesting the first three are from the northern Chicago suburbs. The only valid phone number on the patient's paperwork was for a fast-food Mexican restaurant, Taco Insanity, in the same area. They didn't know a Rose Rich. It might be productive to see if they knew Rosalie Richardson," Miss Langford said.

"If they do, why would a runaway trying to disappear give out a valid number? Maybe they haven't been missing by choice," the agent said. "That makes my investigation even more appropriate." He handed some pictures to Evelyn.

She stared at the photographs of the three smiling teenagers. She took a deep breath. "I pray you're right they're still alive. They're all so young."

"Miss Langford, please tell the Medical Examiner the Richardsons have given permission for Rosalie's autopsy. They would have for the baby too, if the body had not immediately been incinerated," Chief Davis said. "They have also signed all the appropriate releases for any hospital records and Langford Obstetrical Center records that will help solve this case.

"I'll let Dr. Balder know immediately. Are you leaving for The Center now?"

"Yes. That is the other reason we stopped to see you first. I have a favor to ask. Would you come with us? I'm hoping you will have some influence and can ensure Dr. Langford's full cooperation with this investigation," the chief requested.

She laughed. "I'm not sure anyone can guarantee Dr. Langford's complete cooperation, least of all me."

"Frank Langford? Same last name? Is he your husband?" Agent Thompson asked.

"Thankfully, no. He is, however, my very stubborn, opinionated, older brother. The Langford Obstetrical Center is his." She smiled. "I have a committee meeting scheduled in just a few minutes. I could have Margie rearrange some things to go with you after it finishes. Why don't you grab a bite of early lunch. Our cafeteria has good food. Then we can go out there about twelve thirty. Will that work for you both?"

"Great." Rance smiled and shook her hand again. "I'm looking forward to working with you, Miss Langford. We'll be back at twelve thirty."

"Margie, would you please show these gentlemen to the cafeteria and call Dr. Langford's office to schedule a one o'clock appointment. Tell Mrs. Rafferty it is with Chief Davis and it is not optional. She needs to fit us in. Then, please clear my afternoon, thanks."

Rance Thompson followed Margie Wright and Chief Davis to the hospital cafeteria.

Evelyn had trouble concentrating on the issues in the Personnel Committee. She may not be able to get her brother out of this mess. What had he done? If the Feds were involved this wouldn't be easily swept under the rug. And why was Rance Thompson acting like they have never met? Maybe he didn't remember her. Not a very happy thought.

****

Fran Rafferty looked up from her computer screen. "Good afternoon, Miss Langford, Chief Davis. Dr. Langford should be here in a few minutes. He's finishing morning rounds. I don't believe I know this gentleman." The willowy, coal-black-haired woman stood and extended her hand.

The agent reached across her cluttered desk. "Good afternoon, I'm FBI Special Agent Rance Thompson. Nice to meet you, Mrs. Rafferty." He shook her hand and gave her his business card.

The woman smiled like a cat lapping up cream. "The pleasure is all mine, Special Agent Thompson. Please, have a seat on the sofa. There is some literature about The Center on the coffee table, if you are interested," she almost purred. She pointed to the small, low table in front of the three beige Naugahyde-covered chairs they sat down in.

The full color multi-page brochure showed The Langford Obstetrical Center's well manicured, landscaped grounds with a three-story dormitory and several administrative buildings and dotted with whitewashed guest cottages for adoptive parents, as well as pictures of smiling mothers and babies with beaming fathers. There was an explanation of their service matching babies with parents in a private adoption. The mothers and prospective parents would meet before the birth and could live on the grounds near one another in the last two months of the pregnancy. This allowed them to fully discuss the legal terms of the adoption and get to know one another better. The legal fees, room and board, and medical costs for mother and baby were all included in one fee to The Center.

"Are the photographs of actual patients or are they professional models?" the agent asked.

"Oh, those are all happy patients. We had a little contest last year to see who would be in the new brochures. Lots of people vied to appear in it. Those family portraits are of the adoptive parents with their new baby. Understandably, most of the birth mothers did not want to be part of the brochure. Please, take it with you. We're very proud of the work we do here. The bulletin board to your right is full of babies who were born here and found new parents before leaving. We have five or six adoptions every month."

Rance Thompson walked over to examine the pictures of smiling, healthy babies—a majority of them Caucasian—in the arms of their new parents. The board showed the families by the month the babies were born, a whole year's worth of adoptions.

"Lots of beautiful children. I had no idea Wisconsin was the redhead capital of the United States."

"We draw mothers from across the nation, not just Wisconsin," Dr. Langford said as he strode into the reception area. "The Langford Obstetrical Center has a well-deserved, excellent, national reputation." He did not stop to introduce himself.

"He's back," Mrs. Rafferty said nodding toward the doctor's office door. "Please go in."

"Dr. Langford, thank you for taking the time to see us on short notice," Chief Davis said.

"According to Mrs. Rafferty, I wasn't given the option to refuse," the physician said tersely.

"Mrs. Rafferty was correct. I gave those instructions. We needed to see you today. It's about the patient you called Rose Rich," Evelyn said.

"It's important, Dr. Langford. We need your help with this investigation." The agent stepped forward with his hand extended. "I'm Special Agent Rance Thompson from the FBI's Chicago division office."

Frank glared at his sister and ignored the agent's extended hand. "Really? The FBI? It wasn't enough for you to involve the local police? What in the blue blazes have you done?"

"Miss Langford has not done anything wrong. In fact, the call regarding the patient who died at Garland Regional recently is the first lead we've had in a case that had gone cold for more than two and a half years," Agent Thompson said.

"Since when is death in childbirth a matter for an

FBI investigation? Don't you have enough terrorists and bank robbers to track down?" the doctor sniped.

"More than enough, Dr. Langford. The girl you called Rose Rich is actually a seventeen-year-old named Rosalie Richardson who has been missing, classified as a runaway, for the past two and a half years. Her pregnancy, the circumstances of her death, and the fact she was found in a state where she did not reside led us to reopen this investigation as a possible human trafficking case," the agent responded.

"It seems like a gigantic leap of logic that being found in Wisconsin and dying in childbirth means there is a human trafficking ring at work here. But I'm only a country physician, not an FBI special agent," Dr. Langford said sarcastically.

"Unfortunately, this case has all the elements of a typical human trafficking case, and we are finding them all across the country in urban and rural areas. I don't want to waste your time, doctor. We are here because Rosalie Richardson disappeared at the same time as two other girls. We were hoping they were together here in Lansdale. I would like to show you and your staff pictures of Sonia Gables and Sarah Kelley to see if they might have visited their friend while she was a patient here. Would you please look at the pictures?" He pushed the two freshman class pictures across the desk. One of a smiling freckle-faced strawberry blonde and one of a girl with a ring of ebony curls framing her face.

"I'm sure I won't recognize them. I don't have time to monitor who is visiting our patients. I'm a very busy physician." Dr. Langford never looked down.

"Please. It may be a matter of life and death. Frank,

have a heart," Evelyn said.

Frank picked up the pictures. He visibly paled. His eyes twitched. He quickly dropped the photographs back on the desk. "Never seen them. Now I have work to do. Miss Langford knows the way out."

"One more minute, please. I also have questions about a Lila Masterson." The agent pulled another picture from the file and put it on the desk in front of Dr. Langford.

"I was very clear with the Garland Regional staff. This Lila girl was never one of our patients. I said that from the beginning. It is still true."

"May we show the pictures of all four girls to your staff?" Chief Davis asked.

"No. They're busy caring for patients. Leave the pictures with me and I'll share them in the staff meeting tomorrow morning. I can't have everyone's work disrupted because of the antics of four wayward teenagers." Frank quickly put the pictures in his lab coat pocket. "Is there anything else?"

"Yes, there is," Evelyn said. "Did Rosalie have prospective adoptive parents here at the time of the birth? They might remember meeting Sarah and Sonia."

"She did have, but they didn't stay after the baby died. They went home empty-handed before the girl was transferred to Garland. I'm afraid I can't release their names without a warrant due to privacy issues." Frank pushed away from his desk and rose out of his chair.

"We do have a release from Miss Richardson's parents to have access to her medical records. I'm officially requesting them now," Chief Davis said.

"I will have copies of them prepared and sent to

your office. The release from her parents does not entitle you to know the identity of the potential adoptive parents. Is there anything else?" the doctor said testily.

"No, thank you, Dr. Langford. Please, contact me if anyone recognizes any of the young women," Chief Davis said. "If knowing the planned adoptive parents' identity becomes necessary in this case, I'll be back with a warrant."

As they passed Mrs. Rafferty's desk, she said, "Chief, I've requested the medical records you wanted. You should have them in the morning by courier. Special Agent Thompson, please don't hesitate to let me know if you need anything else. Goodbye, Miss Langford. Have a lovely rest of your day."

The visitors left the building. Fran went into Frank's office. "Well, well, well, what kind of trouble have you gotten us into now? It isn't every day we get to entertain the FBI."

Frank quickly finished shredding the documents in his hand. "Eavesdropping again, Mrs. Rafferty?"

"Since I have a financial interest in your continued success, Dr. Langford, I don't want you to screw up this lucrative business." Fran hiked up her slim black skirt, sat down on the corner of his desk, crossed her legs, and put her hand on Frank's shoulder. "Do you want me to pass the pictures around, as the FBI requested?"

"What pictures?" Frank picked up the phone and stopped. He turned to his assistant and said, "What about having dinner with me tonight? You can make reservations at Shangri-La for dinner at seven, if you're interested."

"Why, Dr. Langford, I'd be delighted." Fran stood

to leave. "I thought the Campbells took a red-headed, healthy baby boy home. What's this nonsense about Rose's baby being stillborn?"

"Don't you have a lot of work to finish before we leave for dinner?"

"I do for a fact, Dr. Langford. I must have been mistaken about the Campbells." Fran left the office smiling.

****

Back at the hospital, Evelyn asked if Chief Davis and Special Agent Thompson would like to look at Rosalie's hospital medical record since her parents had signed a release. Chief Davis had to leave, but the agent eagerly took her up on the offer. She made arrangements for him to get a limited access password for the computerized patient records system and set him up with a computer in the administrative conference room.

"I'll check in later. It'll be interesting to see if you uncover anything new." She returned to her office to finish up some paperwork.

****

Margie stuck her head in the office. "Hey, boss, it's almost six and I'm leaving. Everything is locked except your office and the conference room. I'll see you in the morning."

"Thanks, Margie. Time got away from me. I'll go check on Mr. Thompson. Have a good evening."

"Oh, the FBI agent isn't here. He left about an hour ago. He had a six o'clock conference call and wanted to get checked in at the motel before it started."

Miss Langford turned out the lights and locked the door to the conference room and her office.

****

"Can you believe it? He didn't indicate in any way that he remembered who I am," Evie told Gonzo as she filled his dish. "Talk about ego crushing. I know it was simply an evening of dancing and a plane ride and it was over a month ago, but a girl would like to think the guy would acknowledge he'd met her before. I must not have made much of an impression on FBI Special Agent Rance Thompson. I guess I'm definitely over the hill. Or he does remember me and he's embarrassed about running into me again because he is married and doesn't want me to know. Either way, it's a confidence killer."

Gonzo never stopped eating. "You wouldn't pay attention to me either except you want to eat!" She reached down and scratched the dog's back. He yipped in response.

Chapter Twelve

"Good morning, Miss Langford," Margie said. "Chief Davis and Agent Thompson are already in the administrative conference room. They've asked that you join them at ten o'clock for an update call. I've rearranged your schedule so you can. Would you like me to get it on your calendar for the rest of the week? They said it would be a daily call and they would like your participation."

"Yes. Thanks, Margie."

A few minutes before ten, Evelyn Langford tapped lightly on the door to the conference room adjoining her office and cracked it open. Agent Thompson was on the phone but waved her in.

"Yes, all three of us are here now. I'm going to put you on speaker," the agent said.

Chief Davis reported that Rosalie Richardson's medical records from The Center were delivered to his office first thing this morning. He brought them to the meeting and was reviewing them with the agent. Unfortunately, all the information about the prospective adoptive parents had been redacted from the record. There was no mention of the birth, alive or stillborn.

Rance Thompson reported that the electronic patient record system at the hospital may be able to be searched for information on the missing girls. He asked Evelyn Langford if she would provide some IT assistance today to make that happen. She agreed and messaged the appropriate people.

The Chicago FBI office staff reported on other actions they were taking to reconstruct the disappearance of Rosalie and her two friends. The trail was very cold, but they were making progress.

After the call, Special Agent Thompson and Chief Davis had some questions about what they'd found in Rosalie's hospital records.

"Margie thought you found something on the computer. How can I help?"

"I noticed Rosalie's electronic chart included a color picture and her fingerprints. Why are they part of the chart?"

"The color pictures were introduced about two years ago to help reduce insurance fraud. When an insurance card is presented, we compare the picture of the person we have on file to the person in front of us. You'd be surprised how many people give their insurance card to their uninsured cousin or sister or even their next-door neighbor," the CEO explained.

"Is the fingerprint another part of the fraud prevention effort?"

"Although it could be another form of identification for that purpose, we implemented it primarily to assist in trauma situations. Unlike the pictures, which we take of everyone, the fingerprints are voluntary. Everyone doesn't want to be fingerprinted, for obvious reasons. The theory on fingerprint identification is, if you are in our database and you come into the emergency department unconscious, we would be able to begin treatment and notify your next of kin more quickly since we would know positively who you are, whether you could speak or not. We would know what you are allergic to and your blood type—all things needed to expedite your safe emergency treatment. We belong to a nationwide trauma system so it would be helpful if you travel outside of Lansdale.

"For all other times, fingerprints are a means to quickly complete your registration by verifying key information on file, rather than having to repeat it every time you use one of our services," Miss Langford explained. "And lots of parents volunteered to have their children in the database, in case of an emergency when they weren't home or in the event of a kidnapping. We work with Chief Davis and his department to share the juvenile prints and pictures, if the parents want us to."

"We make a sweep about once a year and offer fingerprinting as a service to the community," Chief Davis explained. "At the time of the initial fingerprinting, the parents can also opt for adding the prints to the trauma database Miss Langford told you about. We've had lots of takers. It has helped relieve a lot of worry for parents. For adults, I can personally testify to it making registrations for routine outpatient work much quicker. Thankfully I haven't had to test the emergency use of them."

"If we search the pictures and fingerprints in your database we could compare them to the pictures I have with me and electronically match them with the FBI facial recognition and fingerprint databases. If Rosalie Richardson was using a false name, there's a good chance that Sonia Kelley and Sarah Gables could have registered at your facility under aliases as well," the agent said.

"I thought you left the pictures with Dr. Langford," the CEO said.

"I'd never leave my only copy with anyone. We can get them electronically downloaded from the Bureau when we're ready to do the matching. Do you have someone here I can work with to create an electronic file?"

"Yes, I contacted our IT department earlier thinking they might be able to help. I'm sure they can get our information in a useable format for you. If the girls were in the area when Rosalie's baby was born, it's possible they used some of our services. This is very exciting."

"I'm cautiously optimistic about finding the missing girls. Thanks, I'd like to meet your IT team now, if they're available."

There was a knock at the door and Alan Wells entered the room. "Margie said you needed some IT help this morning, Miss Langford."

"You're right on cue. Special Agent Rance Thompson, please meet Alan Wells, our Director of Information Technology. Alan, this is Rance Thompson. He's the FBI Special Agent assigned to a case involving some of our patients. He needs some data from the computerized patient care records including fingerprints and photographs for a specific group of patients. We need to deliver the data with the patient number identifiers, no names, for this pass. Mr. Thompson, I'll leave you in Alan's capable hands. I'm certain he can get you what you need. Please let me know if you require anything else."

Courtland Gaines charged into the conference

room. "Don't run off so fast. I discovered moments ago that we have the FBI in my hospital investigating the mystery I shared with them and no one has even bothered to talk to me."

"I'm sorry, Court. You weren't available yesterday," Evelyn said tersely.

"I am now." He strode across the room, hand extended. "Courtland Gaines. I'm sure you recognize my name from the initial report when the last young woman was admitted. Glad you Federal boys are taking this seriously. You are?"

"Special Agent Rance Thompson. And I haven't seen the report from you yet."

"I'll remedy that immediately. I happen to have a copy right here." Court pulled a sheaf of papers from his coat pocket. "Let me know if you have any questions at all. My office extension and personal cell number are on the top of page one. Call any time. Day or night."

"Thank you for your assistance." Mr. Wells opened the conference room door and the agent turned to him. "Alan, ready to get started?"

"Follow me." They left together. Courtland Gaines stood in the middle of the office glaring.

"Explain to me why the IT guy has access to the FBI and I don't. I'm one of those who started this ball rolling. This is my case," Court demanded.

"The IT guy is working on a major project to give the FBI a way to review thousands of files electronically. The last time I looked, your area of expertise was finance, not computer systems. Is there anything else you need, Court?"

The CFO shook his head and left the conference

room.

****

At the end of the day, Margie buzzed the CEO. "Miss Langford, it's time to go to the Board Room. Mr. Thompson is in the conference room. I blocked the room for him for the rest of the week. I hope it was okay."

"Thanks, Margie. You have great instincts. I appreciate you taking care of our guest. You're right. It's almost Board meeting time."

Chapter Thirteen

Dr. Frank Langford stormed into the CEO's office despite her assistant's best efforts to stop him. "Have you totally lost your mind? Are you trying to destroy my business? Since when is it your responsibility to round up runaways at the expense of your own flesh and blood's success?"

Frank flung the front page of the *Lansdale Gazette* with pictures of Rosalie, Sonia, Sarah, and Lila under the full-page banner headline of "MISSING" on the CEO's desk.

"I'm mad enough to kill you. Don't you have a brain? This is unforgivable. You've gone too far. How did you even get those pictures to give to the paper? I shredded them!" Frank screamed. The vein on his neck throbbed with every word.

"I gave them to the editor and asked for the front-page story," Chief Davis said from the conference table.

Frank's face flamed beet red, redder than Evelyn had ever seen him before. "Why didn't you speak up? I was having a private family conversation with my sister!"

"I'm quite certain Mrs. Wright tried to tell you I was in a meeting when you bulled your way in here. Special Agent Thompson and Chief Davis are continuing their investigation looking for the other girls who are still missing. We are strategizing about next steps. Would you like to join us? I'm sure you would have valuable insights to share," Evelyn calmly said.

"I am much too busy to waste any of my time looking for badly behaved teenagers." Frank wheeled around to leave. He stopped short of the door. "Miss Langford, I will talk to you privately at a later date. You should keep in mind that there are slander and libel laws in this state. You are skating on thin ice. Both you and your precious medical center." He left the room and slammed the door.

Mrs. Wright tapped on the door and stepped in. "Sorry, I tried to stop him, but he charged past me."

"I know. It's not your fault my brother behaved like a braying jackass. It's okay. Thank you." Margie retreated to the outer office. Evelyn scanned the newspaper Frank had thrown on her desk. "Chief, this is a great story, and the pictures are very clear. The accompanying descriptions are excellent."

Agent Thompson said, "Hopefully, someone will recall seeing the girls together. This was an inspired idea. Especially, since Dr. Langford, by his own admission, did not share the pictures with his staff."

"In a small town, the weekly newspaper reaches more people than just about any other means of communication," Chief Davis said. "I hope someone recognizes them. That's why I wanted all four pictures lined up together on the front page. The missing girls might even see it and come to us, especially after the story tells about Rosalie and Lila's deaths. They may be frightened and in hiding. Maybe this will assure them we want to safely return them home. What are the next steps?"

The agent said, "I see from the newspaper story

there is a local hotline for anonymous tips about the girls. Thank you for setting it up. We'll get some bogus information, but we might also get some solid leads. It will take some time to filter through everything. If you need any help with follow up, let me know and I'll request additional Federal resources to assist."

"Some of our local schoolteachers and counselors volunteered to help man the phones and provide any guidance, if the girls happen to call in. Mrs. Christopher rounded up teams to answer calls. I thought it was a terrific idea," Chief Davis said. "I think we're covered with adequate resources for the immediate future. We'll make sure and pass along any actionable information. I better get back to the office and see if our article is generating any calls yet." The officer picked up his hat and left the room.

Rance Thompson asked, "Are you safe with Dr. Langford in the state he's in?"

"Frank's bark has always been worse than his bite, although I confess, I don't believe I've ever seen him this angry. The vein on his neck was throbbing and his face was so red. I wasn't worried for my safety, but I was afraid he might have a stroke. Don't worry about me. You have enough other things to think about. We need to find out how those girls got from the Chicago area to Lansdale and if they're still alive."

"You know your brother better than I do, but he seems like someone who could rapidly spiral out of control, especially if he was cornered. You shouldn't be alone with him until all this settles down. Just to be on the safe side."

"That's an easy promise to make and one I will be more than happy to keep. I'll be fine," she assured him.

"Thanks. I would like to talk to Mr. Wells again so we can start the file comparisons this morning."

Evelyn said, "I believe he is on his way to the conference room to meet with you."

Mr. Wells walked in moments later and Agent Thompson went to work with the IT staff.

****

At the end of the day, Evelyn knocked on the conference room door and cracked it open. The FBI agent was on the phone but waved her in.

"We'll keep running down the hotline calls, they've had over fifty since the article hit the paper this morning…Yes, the hospital has gone above and beyond to help us. Their IT staff really knows their stuff…Yes, Miss Langford has been especially helpful. I'll pass along the department's thanks…I agree…I don't know what the problem is yet, but I have a gut feeling Dr. Langford knows more than he's saying…No, not married, brother and sister…No, that isn't impeding our progress…Okay, I'll be on the ten o'clock status call in the morning. Chief Davis and Miss Langford will join me. Thanks. Good night."

He ended his call. "Good evening, Miss Langford. It has been one long, but very productive day. Mr. Wells had the data files for me before ten this morning. I'll write an official FBI Thank You memo for his personnel file. I interviewed Dr. Chase Merrick this afternoon on the specifics about Rosalie Richardson's emergency transport here and subsequent death. I also spoke with Dr. Luke Wetzel about Lila Masterson's delivery and baby boy. You have really cooperative and competent people on staff."

"Thanks. The memos for their files will be

especially appreciated at evaluation time. I have been blessed with great people who know their jobs. What were you saying about Dr. Langford?"

The conference room door swung open. Courtland Gaines strode in. "Why is she in this update and I was not invited?" he demanded.

"This was not an official update. Miss Langford came in as I finished my internal status call with the Chicago office. We were discussing the Garland Regional staff who have been helping me. We have a once daily status call at ten o'clock again tomorrow morning that involves all parties," Agent Thompson explained.

"I'm definitely a party to this investigation and I wasn't on the call today," Court bellowed.

"You are welcome to come tomorrow morning. You know we put the pictures in the paper and set up the hotline. There wasn't much else discussed on today's call. Now, if you'll excuse me, I'm leaving for the day," Thompson said.

"I have a terrific idea," Court said. "Why don't we three have dinner together and we can strategize about next steps? My treat at the Country Club. We can use one of the small private dining rooms."

"I'm sorry, I'm not available," the CEO quickly begged off.

"Then I guess it's guys' night out," Court slapped Rance Thompson on the back. "Shall we?"

****

As she pulled into her driveway, Evie's cell phone rang. Frank. If she didn't take it now he'd keep bugging her all night until she did.

"Hello, Frank. What can I do for you?"

"I need to see you now. We aren't finished with this morning's discussion. Not by a long shot. How dare you embarrass me in front of the police chief and that blasted Special Agent?"

"You heard Chief Davis. I had nothing to do with the article in the paper. What more could we possibly have to talk about?"

"Why are you cooperating with them? I heard the Medical Center released data files to them so they can search for those patients quickly and electronically. Why don't you just say no?"

"You must be kidding. These requests are coming from the Federal government. You don't say no to the FBI, you cooperate. Why are you so worried they might find those girls? Did you have something to do with their disappearances? Have you seen them?"

"Oh, great. First, you call in the law over a perfectly natural thing and now you're accusing me of crimes worthy of the FBI's attention? What did I ever do to you?" She held the phone away from her ear as his voice grew louder and angrier sounding.

"Frank, I don't enjoy being yelled at. I'm hanging up. You're not being rational about this whole situation. You're giving me a headache."

"There will be hell to pay…" She pressed the End Call button.

****

After a light supper and some reading for work, Evie carried the little dog to her bedroom and deposited him on his pillow. "The FBI agent is worried about my safety around Frank. I'm worried about Courtland Gaines sticking his nose into this. I'm not sure either of them is particularly stable. I know Frank is in a mess over his head. I don't think there's going to be an easy way out. I don't know why I'm so concerned about it. My fretting won't change a thing except make me lose sleep. A problem you never seem to have." The pug snored loudly from his special spot.

Chapter Fourteen

"We had fifty calls before six o'clock to the hotline yesterday. Chief Davis was right about the paper being the best way to reach a large number of people," Rance began.

Courtland Gaines raced into the room. "I thought it was a ten o'clock update. Did you start early?"

"You haven't missed a thing, Court," Evelyn assured him.

Chief Davis continued the report. "There were ten phone calls from phone numbers inside The Langford Obstetrical Center. None of those people would identify themselves, but they all said they had seen three of the girls. Sonia was going by Sophie and Sarah was using Sally, but no one ever heard their last names. They were seen with Rosalie more than once. No one has seen them since Rosalie's death. If ten people saw them in The Center, doesn't it seem likely Dr. Langford saw them at least once?"

"Wow, ten staff members called. You said there were fifty calls. Were the others credible callers?" Evelyn asked.

"About fifty-fifty. There were some who clearly hadn't seen the girls but were more than willing to give their names and phone numbers. Some swore they saw them all three together after Rosalie was dead. You always get a few lonely souls who just want to talk with someone so they imagine encounters with the missing people," Rance said.

"I guess they don't realize what valuable resources they're wasting," Courtland chimed in.

"Some do, some don't. We had twelve anonymous callers spread throughout the day that came from Unknown Caller cell phones. They all reported having seen Sonia and Sarah hitchhiking on the county highway going south out of town day before yesterday in the early morning. Each caller had the same description of what they were wearing. Half the callers were male and half were female."

"Isn't that a good thing? To have so much detail? Chief Davis, did you send anyone to check the highways? Did you alert the Iowa and Illinois State Patrols to be looking for them?" the CEO asked excitedly.

"Actually, it's not a good thing. If you asked twelve random people who had been shopping in a grocery store the day before yesterday at the time it was robbed to describe the robbers, they would probably not agree on how many bandits they saw or their sex. They wouldn't agree on what they were wearing, hair color, body type, or height. When you get so much detail that is an exact match, it's usually because it has been rehearsed. It's false information. Someone is trying their best to make us believe the girls aren't in Wisconsin any longer, so the FBI will leave Lansdale. When you weigh those twelve reports against the ten people who saw them at The Center and with Rosalie's death here, my gut says they're still around town," Chief Davis explained.

"Do you believe Dr. Langford is intentionally

being obstructive? Do you think he was responsible for some of the hitchhiker calls?" she asked.

"Possibly, but half of them were a female voice," the agent said.

"Fran Rafferty. If the male voice was Frank's, I'd bet the female voice was Fran's. They are close. It's disappointing to think my brother is hiding the truth. What happens next?" Evelyn asked.

"I'm not sure. We need to continue working the hotline tips. I keep hoping the missing girls will turn themselves in. That they are able to get free and escape," Rance said.

"What if they can't? I can't imagine what their parents are going through. I keep praying we find the last two alive. And soon. What about Lila Masterson? Any reports on her?"

"People have reported seeing her. The reports seem to be credible. They came from inside The Center. So I'm almost positive she was a patient there, even though Dr. Langford denies it. Our problem is that the calls from The Center have all been anonymous so we have nothing to force them to give us her records. Even if her grandmother agrees to request them," Chief Davis said.

"There has to be someone who will help. Someone brave enough to give us their name. I wish I knew what to do," Evelyn said.

"Maybe I could reason with Dr. Langford man to man," Court suggested. "That would take the family and law overtones out of the inquiry. He might respond to me more favorably than any of you."

"You understand, you wouldn't be asking in any official capacity," Rance clarified.

"And you're not authorized to make any offers of

any deals on law enforcement's behalf," Chief Davis added.

"Oh, sure, I understand what you're saying. Just thought I could help," Court said.

"As long as you understand the parameters, I don't think it could hurt. Who knows, you might get through to him," Rance agreed.

"Did you find anything from the electronic records review?" Evelyn asked.

"Sonia and Sarah were both seen in the outpatient area for blood tests. I matched their fingerprints to the ones on file so now we know the names they were under at The Center. I've requested the outpatient and The Center medical records since we have the parents' releases," Rance reported.

"What exciting news. If we get their records from The Center, will we be able to track their babies' adoptive parents?" Evelyn asked.

"Perhaps, or it may be like Rosalie's and we'll still be looking for them," the agent said.

"Would it help to know who the two patients were who had emergency room visits after childbirth at The Center before Rosalie? The two who lived? I could ask Dr. Merrick who they were and possibly find more fingerprints and pictures to match," the CEO volunteered.

"Excellent idea," Rance said. "I think that wraps up our current update. Thanks for all your help. I'm looking forward to getting tomorrow's reports."

****

Evelyn Langford tracked down Dr. Merrick over the lunch hour and explained what she needed. He said she would have it before the ten o'clock call tomorrow morning. Her day was packed with meetings bleeding into the evening when she had the Finance Committee meeting over dinner.

****

"Courtland Gaines, what are you doing here?" Fran Rafferty asked. "I thought we had agreed not to be seen together."

"I need to see Frank."

"He's not in. What's this all about?"

"You need to rein him in. The FBI believes he is intentionally obstructing their investigation. This is serious."

"How could you possibly know what the FBI believes?"

"I've managed to become friends with the lead agent, Rance Thompson. We're like this." Court held up his hand with two fingers mashed together.

"Don't get too comfortable. I can only deal with delusions of grandeur from one man at a time. I'll talk to Frank. He takes every incursion so personally. You've delivered your message. Now, leave before someone sees us together."

Chapter Fifteen

"Good morning, Miss Langford. Dr. Merrick dropped this off for you early this morning. He said you needed it first thing." Margie handed her boss a large manila envelope.

"Thanks." Evelyn took the envelope into her office and pulled the door shut.

Dr. Merrick found both the patients who had transferred from The Center before Rosalie and had copies of their Patient Information and E.R. Record sheets in the envelope. Sybil Russell and Carley Addams were the names on the charts. Both files had pictures, but no fingerprints.

She pressed the intercom button. "Margie, I'll be tied up for a while on some phone calls. Please don't disturb me unless it is Chief Davis or Special Agent Thompson."

She poured herself a cup of coffee and sat down to contact the people on Sybil and Carley's next of kin lists. She started with Sybil Russell's patient admission form. She dialed the first contact number under next of kin. "We're sorry. This number is not in service." The next number listed didn't give an out of service message—it made a blaring noise with static, then disconnected.

The third number began ringing. "Good morning, this is Dave at Taco Insanity. Have you tried our new

Insanity Under the Sea packed with shrimp, crab, and lobster bites? What are you crazy for?"

Evelyn hesitated a moment. "May I speak with Mitzi, the shift manager?"

"Sorry ma'am, she manages store number 27. This is store number 22."

"Oh, I didn't realize Taco Insanity was a chain."

"Yep. We're giving those other guys a run for their money. At least in Chicagoland."

"Could you help me? Do a Sybil Russell or Carley Addams work there?"

"No, they don't. Maybe they work at another store."

"Are they regular customers there?"

The voice hesitated. "I'm not sure. Why? Are they in some kind of trouble?"

"Not with me, but they could need help. Do you know them?"

"I might. I've been here five years. I see a lot of people coming through. I know some Sybils and Carleys but I don't usually learn last names. What do they look like?"

"Before I answer that, what is your position at Taco Insanity?"

"I'm a shift manager, Dave. That's how I know Mitzi. I've only been the manager the last two years."

"The pictures I have are of teenagers. One is a long haired, blue-eyed blonde who is Sybil Russell and Carley Addams has chin length hair that looks mostly brown but has some kind of highlights in it. Brown eyes too. Not too much to go on I'm afraid. It may have been several years since they were in your area, if they ever were."

"Are they usually together? Does the Sybil girl have a pretty smile?"

"They probably were together a lot. I don't have a smiling picture so I don't know."

"It's a long shot, but there were two girls who used to come in almost every day after school. I think they were Sybil and Carley. That Carley was real bubbly and kind of crazy acting. She dyed her hair bright green for St. Patrick's Day one year. She was always coming in with different colors streaked in her hair. She ordered a Porkarito Taco every single day. Sometimes two."

"What is a Porkarito Taco?"

"Three slices of bacon, ham, sausage, pulled pork, and cheese smothered in BBQ salsa."

"Goodness. You've given me some good information that will help confirm if Carley and Sybil are from your area. Thank you for your help."

"Sure thing. Have an insanely great day!"

****

She started to send an email to the address listed on the admission form. "Wait a minute," she said out loud. "I recognize one of those emails." She started scrolling back through the emails she tried right after Rosalie's death. "I knew it. It's the same fake email address Rosalie used. Is this a coincidence or were they connected?"

The phone numbers on Carley Addams' admission paperwork matched Sybil Russell's exactly, including the number for Taco Insanity store number 22. The bogus email was also on the second set of paperwork.

Evelyn paced around her office. Dead ends all the way around? Or another link to North Chicago suburbs?

She pressed the intercom button. "Margie, do you

know if Special Agent Thompson is still in the building?"

"He is, but I think he's on the law enforcement conference call. Chief Davis went into the conference room about thirty minutes ago. Do you want me to let them know you need to see them?"

"No, I'll go to the conference room. Thanks." Evelyn quietly slipped into the adjoining room holding the files from Dr. Merrick. She frowned when she saw Courtland Gaines taking notes.

When the conference call ended, she stepped forward. "Sorry I missed the call. I got so busy with this new information that I lost track of the time. I think you'll want to see this." She laid the files on the table. "These are the mothers who were emergency transfers from The Center in the two months before Rosalie Richardson came in. We got the same story on them. No baby because they were supposedly stillborns and the bodies were immediately incinerated. These girls survived only due to heroic efforts by the emergency room physicians and staff.

"They arrived with paperwork, unlike the Richardson girl. I've been through all the contact information and it is bogus, just like hers was, even down to the same fake email address on one of the contacts. However, there was one curious coincidence." Evelyn explained the Taco Insanity connection to them. "I'm willing to bet if we run Sybil and Carley through the runaway database they will show as missing too and from the northern suburbs of Chicago," Evelyn said.

"I'll be happy to do it." Chief Davis took the extra records copies she had. "Your instincts have been spot on so far, Miss Langford. Let's hope there is a link here that will take us closer to the Kelley and Gables girls."

"No fingerprints on these two, only pictures?" Rance asked. "I'll need their patient numbers so I can match the electronic pictures to the facial recognition database from the file we have. I also need the dates of their admissions."

"The information is in these files. I'll write it down for you," Evelyn offered. She made quick notes and handed them to the FBI agent.

"We had thirty-five more hot line calls. Five were the 'hitchhiking south' ones. Ten were from extensions in The Center. Two of them said all three of the girls had been pregnant, not just Rosalie. One of them was certain Rosalie had delivered a baby a year ago and this was her second pregnancy. One reported that Lila was also pregnant and had been in The Center, but disappeared under mysterious circumstances," Chief Davis reported.

"That makes sense. Lila was found in the morning at Mrs. Kapper's. I don't think we'll make much progress with her case until we can get a warrant to see The Center's medical records on Lila Masterson," Evelyn commented.

"I need something solid. Like a named source to give us a credible lead. If just one of those hotline callers from The Center would tell us who they are, it would be the break we need. Right now we have nothing to link the Masterson girl to The Center to force a warrant," Rance reported.

"Mr. Gaines, what did you learn from Dr. Langford? You didn't report on it earlier," Chief Davis asked.

Court hesitated, then said, "I wasn't able to talk

with the doctor directly, but I did talk with his administrative assistant and stressed the importance of better cooperation with the FBI. I think she got the message loud and clear." He sat back in the chair with a smug look on his face.

"Thank you. Mr. Thompson, will you be going back to Chicago this weekend?" Chief Davis asked.

"No, I won't. I have some things to follow up on that are more easily done from here. Our next regular update will be Monday morning. I hope to have some good news from further file comparisons. Hope you all have a lovely weekend," the agent said.

****

The Garland Regional Medical Center Annual Service Awards Dinner Friday evening at the Events Center on the fairgrounds was a huge success. Lots of hugs and celebrating. It was one of Evelyn Langford's favorite activities of the year. The Chairman of the Board, Charles Jungers, personally put the CEO's twenty-year pin on her lapel. Then Miss Langford turned to her right and placed a twenty-year pin on Nurse Lori Bryers's jacket and on five other staff members who had been in the same new employee orientation with the CEO. Time had flown by.

****

Saturday morning, Rance ventured into Whistler's Café for breakfast. He was surprised to hear someone calling his name. Dr. Chase Merrick and his wife, Katrina, and their four children were eating in a front booth. "Pull up a chair, Agent Thompson. There's plenty of room," Dr. Merrick invited.

"Thanks. It's nice to not have to eat alone. Please call me Rance."

Chase Merrick introduced his family to the agent. Timmy and Trevor recommended the chocolate chip pancakes with extra whipping cream. The twins, Mallory and Tracy, said the best thing was the cinnamon French toast. Rance opted for the daily special, bacon and eggs with hash browns and toast. It was refreshing to enjoy a meal with the outgoing Merrick children.

"If you don't mind me asking, when is the baby due?"

"We're getting a new brother in July!" Timmy and Trevor announced together.

"No. We're getting a new sister in July!" the twins insisted.

"As you heard, it's July. We just don't know yet what we're getting." Chase Merrick laughed.

"You're going to have your hands full, Mrs. Merrick," Rance said.

"The more the merrier. If this one is as good as the other four, I'll have no complaints," she said.

****

Rance struggled out of the uncomfortable chair at the motel room desk. He had cricks in his neck and back. No wonder. He'd been sitting there staring at the computer screen since he got back from breakfast four hours ago. His cell phone chimed.

"Special Agent Thompson…Kyle? Is everything okay?…Where are you?…I'm staying at the Pine Grove Motel. I have a room with two beds. Want to come on in tonight and stay here?… Okay. We can meet for brunch in the morning. Whistler's had a good breakfast today, but they're closed on Sunday. The Shangri-La is supposed to have a good brunch buffet…I'll make a reservation for ten thirty tomorrow morning for two. You're sure everything is all right?…Love you too…See you tomorrow." He pushed End Call.

It would be good to see his son. What mysterious thing was compelling Kyle to drive to Lansdale this weekend?

****

Kyle got out of his car at the same time as Rance pulled into the parking lot. He parked beside his son's vehicle. Rance laughed when they stood next to one another by Kyle's car. They both had on black slacks, red shirts open at the neck, and a black tweed sport coat.

"Great minds think alike," Kyle said. They hugged one another and walked into the Shangri-La together.

The brunch buffet was loaded with all kinds of breakfast and lunch dishes: ham, bacon, sausage, fried potatoes, oatmeal, an omelet station, fried chicken, prime rib, lasagna, four different vegetables, rice, potatoes, a salad bar, and a table full of desserts. There was no excuse for leaving hungry. They started with breakfast items.

"It's good to see you. Must be something really important for you to come all this way to talk to me in person." Kyle had grown into a fine, young man. Someone a dad could be proud of.

Kyle's cheeks flushed. "It is. Probably the most important thing in my life—after finding you."

"Okay. That sounds serious. Do you want me to guess or are you going to reveal the secret?"

His son took a deep breath. Then another. "Dad, I'm planning to ask Jamie to marry me."

"When?"

"Tomorrow night. It's the two year anniversary of our first date. I have the ring." He pulled a small, black velvet box out of his sport coat pocket. "I wasn't sure when you'd be home, so I decided to come to see you. I didn't want to miss proposing on our special day."

"Jamie is a very lucky girl to have such a thoughtful husband-to-be."

"No, I'm the lucky one. She is amazing. What do you think?" He opened the box. A small solitaire diamond surrounded by sapphires glistened inside.

"It's lovely. The gems match her eyes," Rance approved.

"That's why I picked this one." Kyle looked pleased with himself as he snapped the box shut and tucked it carefully away in his pocket.

"Did you want to see me in person so I could talk you out of it?" Rance smiled.

"Yes and no. Your opinion is important to me, but I am determined to follow through with my plan," Kyle said seriously.

"You are your mother's son. She always had a plan too. I think you're probably ready for this big leap. And you and Jamie are good together. You're a lot more mature than I was at twenty. I appreciate being asked my opinion. How soon do you want to say the vows?"

"Jamie and I need to talk about when—assuming she says yes. It means so much to have your blessing. I'm not sure what I would have done if you hadn't thought it was a good idea. I'm having lunch tomorrow with Mr. Colby at his club, to ask his permission before I ask her tomorrow night. I know it's old fashioned, but I want to start us off on the right foot. She's an only child too. They're pretty protective of her."

"Sounds like you have all the bases covered. Wish I could give you sage marital advice, but, as you know, I can't. I couldn't be prouder of you. I know your mom is too." He patted his son on the back. "I think the prime rib is calling my name. Let's go for round two."

"You go ahead. I need to make a pit stop. I'll be right back."

Rance strolled to the buffet table and Kyle walked to the lobby hostess stand, not to the restroom. He found their waiter. He gave him a credit card. For once Kyle would beat his dad to the check. The waiter said he'd return it and the receipt after they were through eating.

A group of six women who looked to be fresh from church services all in their Sunday best came in the front door. Kyle stopped to let them cross in front of him. Wait. He knew that woman.

He tapped the tall woman in an emerald-green brocade dress on the shoulder. She turned smiling. "Yes?"

"It is you, isn't it, Evie? From the beach?"

The woman's smile broadened. "Kyle! What a surprise, it's so good to see you. What are you doing in Wisconsin?"

"Visiting with Dad. He's here on business. I needed to see him. Come with me. He'll want to know you're here."

"Not now. I think I know where he's working. Don't say anything. I'll surprise him tomorrow," she said laughing. "Enjoy the rest of your visit."

The maître d' took Evelyn's party to a table on the far side of the room away from Kyle and Rance's table.

She sat down with her back to the room. Kyle loaded one more plate of food from the buffet and joined his dad.

They finished eating almost simultaneously. After Rance signaled for the check, the waiter came to the table with a receipt and credit card which he handed to Kyle.

Rance chuckled. "I guess you are grown up enough to get married. Thanks for brunch."

****

Evie sat at her dressing table brushing her hair. "I can't wait to see Rance Thompson's face in the morning when I tell him the jig is up. I'm positive he's married. He had to remember me; even his son knew who I was. A wife at home is the only explanation for refusing to recognize me publicly. Although, he was never secretive about who he was. He gave me his business card. Maybe he's only being professional and doesn't want Frank to know we'd met before. I'm not sure of anything, but running into Kyle here gives me a good reason to ask now. Don't you think so, Gonzo?"

The pug stared at her with his bug-eyes, cocked his head, and barked twice.

"Me too!" she said and crawled into bed.

Chapter Sixteen

Evelyn Langford strode into the conference room at nine fifty-five a.m. Monday morning wearing the scarlet red ensemble her Mama called her "take no prisoners" suit. Rance Thompson was in the room alone. She sat down across the table from him.

"Everyone else is running a little slow today," Rance said.

"Maybe they didn't have as nice a Sunday as we did and they're still tired," Evelyn said.

"Okay." Rance looked confused.

"Did you enjoy your brunch at Shangri-La yesterday morning?"

Rance made a point to take a breath. "Yes, were you there?"

"Did Kyle enjoy his?" Evelyn smiled wickedly. Rance blanched.

Courtland Gaines came into the room trailed by Chief Davis.

"Time for the call," Rance said softly.

Chief Davis reported, "Sybil Russell and Carley Addams both got hits on the National Runaway database. They've been missing about a year and a half. Same scenario except those are their actual names. Teenage girls coming home from a sporting event. They were both cheerleaders. They rode the bus to the game and back, then Sybil drove them to a post-game party. On the way home from the party around midnight, they had car trouble. Their vehicle was found the next morning, but no sign of the girls. And they are from the north suburbs of Chicago. We're trying to contact their families now."

"I was able to pull their hospital records out of the electronic files. I think it's time to take the pictures of these girls out to The Center and see what Dr. Langford has to say about them," Rance said.

"Is that really necessary?" Court asked. "Shouldn't we wait until we confirm they really are who you think they are? Why not wait until we talk to the parents?"

"Because time is critical and I think they are with Sonia and Sarah and I'm praying they are all still alive," Rance said tersely.

"I'm happy to deliver the pictures to Dr. Langford," Court volunteered.

"No. This is official business. Law enforcement business. I'll go myself," Rance said.

"If they're from the area the Taco Insanity is in, should we send their pictures to Dave, the shift manager to see if Carley is the Porkarito girl?" Evelyn asked.

"Let's wait until we hear from their families," Chief Davis said.

"After that we can consider sending the pictures if it is necessary," the agent agreed. "I believe that's all our business for this morning. I'm going to The Center now. I'll let everyone know if I discover anything significant."

****

Fran Rafferty was on the telephone when Rance Thompson walked into the waiting area. She waved him over and mouthed "Sorry." She finished the call and asked, "What brings Special Agent Thompson to The Langford Obstetrical Center today?"

"I'd like to speak with Dr. Langford if he is available."

"May I tell him what it's in reference to?"

"The FBI's ongoing investigation."

"One moment, please." Fran Rafferty scooted her chair away from the desk and gently knocked on Dr. Langford's office door, then opened it, and walked in closing the door behind her.

Rance took the opportunity to look at the "Baby" bulletin board while she was gone. He noted there was rarely more than one baby posted in a day. He looked at the dates on his card. There were adopted babies—a girl and a boy on the two dates in question. There was a baby boy on the date Rosalie died. Those smiling parents looked familiar, where had he seen them before? The baby's name was Joshua Campbell. He was certain he'd seen those people somewhere recently.

"I'm sorry. Dr. Langford is on his way out of the building for an appointment expected to take the rest of the day. Is there anything I can help you with?" Fran asked as she stepped back to her desk.

A door slammed. Dr. Langford must have a back door out of his office. How convenient.

"No. Thank you for checking. I needed to speak with him personally," Rance said.

"If you change your mind, you know where to find me. I know a lot more about the inner workings of The Center than you may realize. Let me give you my card." Fran reached into the top desk drawer and pulled out a business card. She flipped it over and wrote a number on the back. "This is my personal cell number. The number on the front is my direct line here at The Center. Feel free to use either one. Any time."

Rance quickly pocketed the card. "Thank you again. I'll be in touch."

****

Evelyn knocked on the conference room door and cracked it open. Rance waved her in. He was on the phone. "Things are progressing wonderfully. Really starting to come together. I should have additional data in the morning...terrific. It will all be detailed in my daily report. I'll get it off to you later this evening. Thanks. Good night." Agent Thompson ended the call.

"Sounds like Alan was able to get what you needed," Evelyn said.

"I don't have it all yet but we're on the right track. I continue to be optimistic."

"That's wonderful."

"I have a lot of updates from my work today. What about getting a preview of tomorrow's update over dinner tonight, unless you don't want to hear it until Mr. Gaines does?" Agent Thompson asked.

"I'd love to get the latest information. Mr. Gaines can wait his turn. We have some other issues to discuss. Personal things. I don't think it's a good idea to eat in a public place where we could be overheard. This is a small town and rumors spread quickly. How do you feel about pizza?" Evelyn asked.

"Love it! I need to go to my motel and file my daily report while everything is fresh in my mind. I saw there's a Ray's Pizza Place right across the street from the motel. Is it any good?"

"Best in town."

"Honestly, I'd probably be eating pizza at home

tonight too. What's your favorite?"

"I pretty much like it all. I trust your judgment. Get what you like. All I have is caffeine free diet pop, so if you want anything else, you'll have to get that too."

"Pop? Like soda pop?" the agent questioned.

"Yep, I forgot for a moment, you're not a native." She laughed. "It's almost six thirty. Want to do seven thirty? Will that give you enough time to complete your report? Ray's can turn around just about anything in thirty minutes." She wrote her address and cell phone number on the back of her card. "You'll need these."

"Second time today a woman gave me her personal cell phone number."

"Who was the first one?" Evelyn asked with a raised eyebrow.

"I'll tell you all about it as part of the update tonight. It won't take me long to get what I need for my report." He stuffed a large file folder into his briefcase, left a stack of others on the table, and shut down his laptop. "I'll see you in an hour at your house with dinner in hand."

****

Evie got home, freed Gonzo, and peeled out of her business suit. She put on a pair of black knit slacks and a three-quarter sleeve cotton sweater with a geometric pattern in black and white with a splash of red across the front. She unwound the bun on her head and brushed out her long hair leaving it flowing down her back with a red ribbon for a headband.

At seven thirty, on the dot, the doorbell chimed. Gonzo raced to the front of the house barking all the way. She opened the door. Rance Thompson was there. He'd changed into a bright blue polo shirt and khakis.

Just smelling the Ray's pizza he held in his hands made her hungry. Minutes earlier she thought she was too tired to eat.

Gonzo sniffed Rance's shoes and circled him twice making a low growl.

"Gonzo, Rance is our friend. He's the one I told you about. Stop growling at him," Evelyn scolded.

The little dog's corkscrew tail unfurled as he looked down with his head bent and little jowls brushing the floor. Rance handed the pizza to Evie and reached down to pet the furball. In a moment, Gonzo was wiggling all over with his tail screwed back tightly and making happy snorts.

"What exactly did you tell this little fellow to give him such a bad impression of me?" he asked laughing.

"None of your business!" A blush raced across her cheeks as she led the way to the kitchen.

"Do you have paper plates?" Rance asked as she deposited the pizza on the kitchen table. "Then we wouldn't have much to clean up when we're through eating."

"I like the way you think, Special Agent Thompson. Diet caffeine-free cola?"

"Please, with lots of ice. Want to eat here in the kitchen?"

"Works for me." She poured drinks and put them on the table with the silverware, parmesan cheese, and paper plates. For a few minutes, they concentrated on savoring the pizza while it was hot and gooey. The Ray's Deluxe was packed with meat and veggies of all kinds: green peppers, savory onions, pepperoni, sausage, ham, mushrooms, and three kinds of cheese. It melted together creating a flavor that left your mouth delighted.

"You were right about this pizza. It's outstanding."

"Glad you like it. Ray's is the only true specialty pizza place in town. You can get it other places, but along with a variety of other things."

There was an awkward silence. Rance looked around the cheery kitchen with its bright yellow patterned wallpaper and oak cabinets. It was built for creating feasts, with lots of countertop space and double ovens. The stove was an industrial sized six-burner gas monster. There was a counter extension where four stools waited for people to stop for a snack.

"Penny for your thoughts," Rance said.

"When you first got here, I wondered if you remembered meeting me." She could feel heat spreading across her cheeks. How foolish. She was a more than grown woman. She sounded like a thirteen-year-old girl mooning after the unattainable dashing captain of the basketball team.

"Let's see. It was the first week of May in the early morning. The ocean was on my left. The sun was rising in front of you. The sugar-white sand was warm beneath my feet," Rance began.

"Okay. You didn't forget meeting me," Evelyn said. "Running into Kyle at Shangri-La yesterday convinced me that for some reason you didn't want to get reacquainted. What's the story?"

"Kyle saw you yesterday? The stinker didn't let me know."

"I asked him to let me surprise you."

"You certainly did."

"So why did you ignore me for a week if you remembered who I was?"

"Of course I'd remember meeting a beautiful woman on the beach…it hasn't been that long since I held you in my arms dancing under the stars. You look more like the woman I remember with your hair down and dressed casually. I can't believe the prim and proper Garland Regional Medical Center CEO, Miss Evelyn Langford, is my Evie." He winked.

"Your Evie? When you deplaned in Chicago, you hadn't even asked my last name. How were you ever going to find *your* Evie again?"

"I have an unwavering belief in Divine intervention. When people are meant to be together, a path is made clear. And I thought if you were interested, you'd contact me. Women don't have to wait to be called these days. I did give you my card. Maybe that was a signal I'd answer your call." Rance laughed.

"Why did you act like we'd never met once you got here? And avoided being alone with me anywhere?"

"Evie, I have a job to do and until we made some progress, I couldn't afford any distractions. An agent has to get the lay of the land on a case. Who wants to help? Who doesn't? Who has something to hide? I love your radiant smile and you're a great dancer, but your brother is a person of interest in this case. I had to be certain where you stood, how you were involved. I probably should have waited longer but you running into Kyle blew my cover. We've discovered so much information on these cold cases. I'm encouraged by our progress, and I trust you. I thought I could afford to take the time to address some unfinished personal business now."

She shook her head. "You are right. Finding the girls is much more important than anything between us.

I confess, I'm relieved you were putting business first. I appreciate your approach. Usually I'm the one who's all business all the time. I'm not sure I would have confronted you if I hadn't seen Kyle and he clearly remembered me."

"Do you want to know what we discovered today?" he asked.

"Did you learn anything more about Frank's involvement? I remember Rosalie saying '*Doc, not me again*' right before she died. Two babies before age eighteen? I wonder if there is any way to confirm the information."

"I went out to The Center today to try and have a surprise visit with your brother. While I was waiting for Mrs. Rafferty to check his availability, I took the opportunity to look at the board in Administration. There were babies adopted on the days Sybil Russell and Carley Addams gave birth and one when Rosalie Richardson did. I recognized the couple holding a little red-headed boy born the day Rosalie died. I couldn't place them until later this afternoon when I was looking at the brochure I had picked up the first day when we visited The Center. A couple was on page four holding a little red-headed girl born eighteen months ago. I'm sure it's the same couple in the picture with a red-headed boy when Rosalie died. The brochure identified them as David and Millie Campbell of Arlington, Texas," Rance explained.

"They adopted a baby eighteen months ago from The Center and came back for a second one this month?" She picked up the brochure to look at the Campbells. "Two little redheads would fit perfectly in their family. Both of the parents have red hair. And didn't one of the hotline calls say that Rosalie was having a second baby there? So what happens next?"

"I contacted the Dallas office for assistance in finding the Campbells. If they did adopt two children from The Center, they should know if the same girl was the mother of both children. This could be a major breakthrough and the first concrete evidence that Rosalie's child was not stillborn. The more information we have, the more likely it is that we'll be able to tie everything together. This probably isn't the way to win you over, but your brother is high on my list of involved parties. I'm sure he has seen Sonia Gables and Sarah Kelley. He denied knowing Lila Masterson when she was in the hospital, but I'd bet my life that he's lying. No doubt since Sybil Russell and Carley Addams were emergency transfers from The Center, he'd recognize them too."

"How can you be so certain?"

"It's a gut reaction based on years of experience."

"I wish I could allay your fears but I'm afraid my brother has stepped into a bigger tangle than he will ever be able to find his way out of." Evie shook her head. "Oh, you said you'd gotten two personal cell phone numbers from women today. Who was the first one?"

"Fran Rafferty when I went to see Dr. Langford."

"And why would you need her personal cell phone number?"

"Whoa. I didn't ask for it. She thought I should have it without any prompting from me. Are you jealous?"

"No. Should I be? Are you in relationships with other women that I know nothing about?" Evie asked trying to sound light and unconcerned, but there was no smile on her face.

"Oh? The way you asked the question implies you and I are in a relationship," he teased.

She hesitated a moment. "It did sound that way, but I didn't mean to imply we have a relationship. So what did Kyle come to town for?"

"Okay, you want to change the subject. Am I getting a little too close to the truth?" He smiled. "Kyle's planning to pop the question to his girlfriend of two years and wanted to talk it over. I like Jamie and they're good together. I couldn't be happier."

"That is good news. How nice that he wanted to talk it over with his parent."

"Yeah. I'm lucky. Kyle has always been a thoughtful kid and now he's a compassionate young man." He glanced at his watch. "I hate to eat and run but I need to be ready for the ten o'clock conference call, so I should probably call it a night. I'll see you in the morning. Have sweet dreams and keep those prayers coming. We're going to need all the help we can get to get to the bottom of this bevy of missing girl cases."

Evie and Gonzo walked him to the front door. He kissed her on the cheek and scratched Gonzo behind the ears.

"Thanks for bringing dinner. See you in the morning."

Rance waved and got in the car. "Good night." He backed out of the driveway.

Evie turned to go back in the house. She picked up Gonzo. "I never asked the burning question point blank and Rance wasn't biting on the hints I dropped about

Kyle's parents." She nuzzled the dog against her cheek. "Maybe I don't really want to know if there is a clueless Mrs. Thompson waiting at home. What do you think?" Gonzo replied with a low growl.

Wait.

A black foreign car was parked down the street, idling at the curb. She walked down the sidewalk toward the vehicle still holding the pug. The car quickly pulled away and moved out of sight.

It had to be Court.

Not a good sign.

Chapter Seventeen

After the ten a.m. conference call, Rance shared a flyer which was printed on neon yellow paper. It said:

Pregnant? Need help?
For Confidential Assistance
Call 1-800-899-9999
Adoption Placements &
Financial Compensation
Up To $5K Per Healthy Baby
Contact Attorney Tom Peterman

"Do you think this is how they're attracting pregnant runaways? Paying them for their babies? Where did you find this?" Evelyn asked.

"It was posted on a tree along the state route. I'm sure five thousand dollars looks like a fortune to a pregnant teenage girl. Especially if she's a homeless runaway. There's a huge market for healthy Caucasian babies. Lots of people are on long waiting lists for adoptions. The private adoption attorneys are cashing in on that. If someone can afford the deluxe experience of The Langford Obstetrical Center, it makes sense they would use their money to go to the head of the line. Plus they get to know the baby's mother and the girl gets comfortable that her newborn is going to a good family. It's a win-win, especially for Tom Peterman and Dr. Langford," the special agent replied.

"I had no idea they were recruiting pregnant girls

willing to put their children up for adoption. I never thought about how the mothers-to-be knew to contact The Center. What do they do with them after they give birth? Pay them off and kick them out? What about the mothers whose babies don't make it? Do they get paid anything?" Chief Davis wondered out loud.

"I don't know," Rance said. "I need to talk with Tom Peterman about how the adoption process is working from his side. I called and have an appointment on Thursday morning to see him."

"Tom's a reasonable guy. I can't believe he'd be involved in anything that wasn't one hundred percent legal. He and his wife adopted three kids themselves. He began concentrating on the private adoption business when he realized they weren't the only frustrated wanna-be-parents. The red tape for an adoption can be overwhelming, especially for people with no legal background," Evelyn said.

"Sounds like he has nothing to hide," Court observed.

"I called the Dallas office to request their assistance in finding the couple we have reason to believe adopted the Richardson baby. They were understandably reluctant to answer questions about the adoptions from a random caller claiming to be the FBI. However, they did agree to meet in person with an agent tomorrow morning in the Dallas office at ten. Mark Richards, the Dallas Field Office Supervisor, will be there. I'll be on the laptop on the video call with all three of them to conduct the interview." Rance was clearly pleased about the break in the case.

"That's so exciting. If they confirm Rosalie Richardson was the mother of both their children, we'll know the stillborn story is a lie. Will it be enough to get a warrant to fully examine the situation at The Center?" Evelyn asked.

"I'm checking with the judge. I expect to hear back from him early next week. It feels to me like a major break in the case," Chief Davis said.

"Isn't that an extreme measure? Going in with a warrant over one misrepresentation?" Court asked.

"No, it speaks to a pattern of behavior," Chief Davis replied.

"Usually someone doesn't stop with one lie. And we know of two other girls who gave birth supposedly to stillborns who may have had the healthy babies on the adoption board for those birthdates," Rance said. "If anything important happens, we'll reconvene, otherwise I'll see everyone at eleven tomorrow morning since I'll be on the call with the Dallas office at ten."

"I'll let you know if I hear anything more on these two girls, Miss Langford. The hotline calls have slowed a lot. Still getting several calls a day about them hitchhiking south and more kook calls than earlier. We have to take them all seriously. You never know which one will lead us to them. Thanks for all your help. Please thank Dr. Merrick for us too." Chief Davis tipped his hat. "Hope to have good news soon."

"So do I, Chief, so do I."

Chief Davis and Courtland Gaines left the conference room. Rance signaled that he wanted the CEO to stay.

"Frank worries me. I know you said he wouldn't hurt you, but…"

She shook her head. "It makes me sad to think about Frank in the middle of this mess. He's not behaving rationally. He told me to call you off somehow. He holds me responsible for the FBI being here. I believe you're going to find something incriminating him or he wouldn't be so desperate."

"Please be cautious around him. I'm sure he is hiding something related to the runaway girls. I hope the Campbells can clear up a lot of this."

****

At the end of the day, Evelyn knocked on the conference room door. Rance had ended the afternoon status call moments before.

"Have you had a good day?" she asked.

"Some frustrating and some positive. The problem is we need to get back into The Center, but your brother is not going to let us waltz through there and talk to whomever we'd like. I've been working on a warrant with Chief Davis, but we have to have stronger evidence before one will be issued. You don't realize how respected the Langford name is in Lansdale. The judge is very reluctant to move forward without more concrete evidence. How do we get back in?" Rance asked.

"Fran Rafferty. She's your passport. I could tell she liked you the first time she met you. Didn't she give you her personal cell phone number? Go see her when Frank won't be there. Take her to lunch. Pump her for information. Turn on the old Thompson charm."

"I appreciate your confidence in my ability to be charming, but…" Rance said.

"On Friday Frank will be going to the Chamber of Commerce luncheon. He never misses it. It's his opportunity to schmooze with all the local bigwigs— people like he wants to be. Call Fran tomorrow and make a lunch date. Offer to pick her up after eleven. Frank will be gone by then. I'm positive she won't say no."

"I only hope Mrs. Rafferty is as taken with me as you seem to think she is." Rance smiled and began packing up for the night. "What about showing me around this charming village in the Wisconsin hills? Maybe dinner and dancing? As I recall, you do a mean samba. And, of course, we could talk about the case."

"Remember, this is a very small town. We only have one place for dinner and dancing, and it is anything but private. Before ten tonight, the whole hospital board would know their CEO was out cavorting with an FBI agent. I'm afraid they would be horrified to know she knows how to samba, much less that she does it well. And if he finds out I've met you before, my brother will be even angrier with me than he already is." She laughed. "What about dinner at my house, instead? I can amaze you with my culinary skills and we won't be interrupted."

"I like the no interruptions part." Rance winked. "I need to file my daily report back at the motel and get more comfortable. Then, I'll prepare to be amazed by Lansdale's own Julia Child."

"Don't set your expectations too high. I'll run by the market to pick up something wonderful to prepare. What about seven thirty for appetizers?"

"Sounds perfect. I'm looking forward to spending the evening with my friend, Evie. I'll see you in the morning, Miss Langford." Rance gathered up his notes, made a small bow, and left.

Chapter Eighteen

As she looked over the available produce at Bob's Market, Evie caught herself humming the song she'd sung on the plane with Rance. This was silly. She was absolutely giddy about having Rance all to herself tonight. Maybe she'd even get an answer to the Mrs. Thompson question. She couldn't remember the last time she cooked a meal for a man. She never had in Lansdale.

****

Rance got to the motel, started his laptop to post his daily report, then called his supervisor to talk to him personally about the progress they were making on the case. As he got out of the shower, he caught himself humming.

What was that song? Oh yes, he remembered singing it on the plane. Evie was quite a woman—two completely different people. So professional as Evelyn Langford, the CEO—he might even say icy or standoffish. But, Evie was so warm, so caring. If he'd never met her at the beach, he was certain he wouldn't be having dinner at her house tonight. He wouldn't want to be. He'd never have known the woman behind the CEO mask. Where was this relationship going? He'd better not put the cart before the horse. First, find the missing children. Then, see what happens next with the lovely Evelyn Langford—a.k.a. his Evie.

****

Evie put the groceries on the counter, freed Gonzo, and grabbed an apron to protect her suit. After thirty minutes, all the prep work for dinner was completed. Evie went upstairs to change clothes. She opted for a multi-colored maxi skirt and a bright yellow peasant top. She slipped into ballerina flats and practically bounced back down to the kitchen. She was excited about having his company. No. She was delighted to have Rance's undivided attention tonight.

Promptly, at seven thirty, the doorbell chimed, and the four-legged alarm announced Rance's arrival. Evie straightened a candle on the table as she passed through the dining room to the front door. She greeted her guest with a lingering hug. "I love a man who can tell time. The brie will be out in two minutes." Gonzo wiggled and snorted in recognition as he wove in and out between their legs.

"I love brie." Rance followed her to the kitchen with the pug close behind him. "With pesto?"

"Absolutely, on hunks of marvelous fresh baked French bread. Make yourself at home." She waved to the stool at the kitchen counter. "Unless you'd rather have appetizers in the living room."

"Won't it be easier for you to monitor things, if we have the brie in here?" Rance settled onto the nearest stool. His curly brown hair was wonderfully out of control and his crystal blue eyes watched her every move. "Besides, don't you need a sous chef? I'm great at making salads."

"Excellent idea. Bottom right-hand drawer in the fridge holds everything we have for salads. It's all washed and ready to go. Call me impressed—on time and willing to help! I'd never pass on assistance in the kitchen, especially from an experienced sous chef." She put the chopping board, knife, and salad bowls in front of him. "We're having the pesto brie, salads, Cornish game hens with a rosemary and thyme sauce, and wild rice. I hope you like it."

"The menu suits me fine. I can do my Henry VIII impression ripping off the hen's legs and gobbling them down." He laughed, got the ingredients out of the fridge, and began chopping veggies for their salads. "Nice kitchen. It's warm and homey. You live in this big house all alone?"

"This is the house I was raised in. I've been living here since I moved back to Lansdale, helping Mama. She was severely injured in the car accident that killed my father twenty years ago. I lost her a month before I met you. The house is all mine now. I bought out Frank's half this week. I know it's silly for one person to live in so much space, but this place holds so many memories. I've lived here for all but ten years of my life. Gonzo and I like it here."

"I'm sorry for your loss. It's good you were here to help your mom. I'm sure she appreciated having her daughter nearby."

Ding. The brie was ready.

"My folks are still alive but residing in an assisted living place. They're moving a little slower these days but are in relatively good health after my dad had a scare twenty years ago. They're together and we're thankful for that blessing."

"Should I ask? Who are the thankful we?" No point in ignoring the elephant in the room.

"Me, Amory, and Kyle—you've met him."

Evie frowned.

"At first, I thought Kyle was your younger brother, until I heard him call you 'Dad' when we deplaned in O'Hare. Is Amory your wife?" Evie asked. Did she sound irritated? She suddenly felt a little angry.

"No, Amory is my older sister. My only sibling." He raised an eyebrow.

"I haven't any right to give you the third degree, but here I go—are you married, divorced, or widowed?" Evie held her breath.

"I've never been married." Her eyebrows flew up. "I guess that raises questions. I'd better explain the whole story, the short version. Kyle is twenty years old. I didn't know he existed until ten years ago. His mother, Mandy, and I dated very seriously our senior year—too seriously for kids in high school. I never saw her after graduation because her family moved to Indiana. I tried to stay in touch. I wrote letters and left messages with her mom, but I never heard back from her. It was pretty traumatic at eighteen to lose my one and only true love. I figured she met someone new in Indiana and was happy to dump me. I poured all my energies into helping my parents, college, and my career. The loss was too new to even think about another relationship."

"I want to hear everything about you since I opened this can of worms, but let's move to the dining room and have our salads while we talk. We're only about fifteen minutes from the rest of dinner."

"We need dressing for the salad. Are you willing to risk the Thompson Secret Salad Dressing?" he asked.

"Sure, what do you need?"

"Dijon mustard, olive oil, little sugar, and

vinegar—apple cider vinegar—if you have it."

"You're in luck." Evie pulled the ingredients out of the refrigerator and cabinet next to the stove. "Here's a bowl and whisk."

In the dining room, she lit the long white candles in crystal holders and dimmed the lights. Rance brought the freshly dressed salads in. Gonzo took a position under the table hopefully waiting for wayward crumbs.

Evie took a bite of salad. "Mmmm. I'll need to remember this recipe."

"Sorry. It only tastes right if I make it. I didn't tell you about the secret ingredient."

"You're an imp. I'll figure it out. Now, back to the story of Rance and Mandy and Kyle."

"I started with the FBI right out of college and time flew by. Ten years ago, I got a call from Mandy's father. Her mom had been gone for five years and Mandy had recently died in an automobile accident. He said, 'I can't take care of your son any longer. It's time you accept your responsibilities.' He sounded more sad than angry. Apparently, since Mandy knew where I was and how to reach me, he assumed I'd been in touch with her on a regular basis. I hadn't seen or talked to her in ten years. Until her father called, I had no idea Mandy was ever pregnant. And certainly not that I was her child's father." Rance stopped and took a deep breath.

"It must have been hard to lose someone you once loved and then find out you'd lost the first ten years of your son's life too." She could see the pain in his eyes. "Rance, you don't have to continue. It was rude of me to ask someone I barely know for their life story. I'm sorry."

"If you're willing to listen, I'd like to tell you everything. You're easy to talk with, Evie. I feel like we've known each other a long time. I hope you want to know everything about me, warts and all." Rance smiled and reached across the table to touch her.

"If you want me to know, I want to know." She squeezed his hand.

"I told Mandy's dad I would gladly step up to my responsibilities and that I would have done so right from the beginning, if I'd known about Kyle. We talked a long time and made arrangements for Mr. Nichols and Kyle to come for a get acquainted visit. I was more nervous than I'd ever been in my entire life."

"I can't imagine."

"Kyle stayed with me after that visit, and we never looked back. Less than a year after our first meeting, he asked his Grandpa Nichols and me if he could legally change his name to Thompson. I've never been so humbled or so proud at the same time. It hasn't all been a bed of roses, but he loved me, and I loved him from the beginning. The bonds of love make everything—even an instant ten-year-old son—easier to deal with. We have a great strong tie to one another. I think it's because we've been trying from the beginning to make up for the lost years and we both loved Mandy." Rance's voice wavered.

The timer buzzed. Rance cleared the salad dishes and Evie plated the hens and rice.

"Do you need anything besides ice water to drink?"

"I see you have some whole milk in the fridge. If you don't mind, I'll have a glass of milk. Helps my stomach."

"No need to explain. Please, pour two glasses.

You'll find the glasses in the cabinet on the left-hand side of the sink." Evie went into the dining room with her hands full, followed by Rance bringing their milk.

"You and Kyle clearly have a great relationship. Like friends, not simply father and son. Why didn't Mandy ever let you know about Kyle?"

"We'll never know. She didn't even tell her parents who Kyle's father was until she was in the hospital after the accident. Then she was worried about who would take care of Kyle, if she couldn't. I'm glad Mr. Nichols was so understanding. He was a fine man. We lost him two years ago."

"I'm sorry for your loss. You're lucky you didn't have a wife to have to explain a sudden son to."

"Yes. I've thought about that more than once."

"Didn't Kyle wonder why he'd never met his dad?"

"Mandy told Kyle his dad had to be away from him and that he loved him very much. She never bad mouthed me or set his heart against me. It meant he had nothing but positive expectations about meeting me."

How many men would take on the responsibility of an unknown ten-year-old son without hesitation? "Your life must have turned upside down when Kyle moved in with you."

Rance laughed. "It was like unleashing a tornado in the middle of an attic. Old habits and things went flying out the window and new ones were sucked in to take their places. Luckily, I was in a two-bedroom condo so Kyle had his own room from the beginning. My sister and parents lived just a few blocks from me, so they were very involved in helping me adjust to instant fatherhood. I never would have made it without my family."

"What did they think about a new nephew and grandson?"

"They showered him with affection from the first minute they met him. It was like they'd known about him his whole life. My mom made a point of including Mr. Nichols in birthday and Christmas celebrations so it was clear he was still part of Kyle's family too."

"No wonder you two get along so well. After Kyle came to live with you, did you ever date? Feel like he needed a mom?"

"No. He'd had ten years of a wonderful loving mom. I focused on being a good dad to atone for missing the beginning of his life." Rance took a bite of his hen. "You're an excellent cook. I'm impressed you whipped this up on short notice. I'm probably not the first man to tell you how much they liked your cooking."

"Not the first, but I never tire of feeding an appreciative audience. I'm really excited about the progress we're making on the case. The Campbells could hold the key to solving it."

"Miss Langford, we'll have plenty of time to talk about our case in the morning. Right now, I want to know all about my Evie. I've spilled my guts. I want to know all about you. How many hearts have you broken? You live here alone, sorry Gonzo, you live here with Mr. Gonzo, so I'll ask you what you asked me, are you married, divorced, or widowed?"

She played with the food on her plate. "My answer is the same as yours. I've never been married."

"I'm surprised." He cocked his head to one side and stared directly into her large sable brown eyes. "Do you have any surprise children I should know about?"

"I certainly do not!"

"That sounded very much like the proper Miss Evelyn Langford."

She laughed. "When I lived in Ohio, I was engaged to a highly successful cardiologist. I broke off the engagement right before I returned home to take care of Mama. Her accident didn't have anything to do with the breakup. We simply weren't a good fit. I was obsessed about being an old maid if I didn't marry by thirty. I accepted Greg's proposal knowing we weren't a lifetime fit, even though I believe marriage should be a once and forever thing. Thankfully, I came to my senses before we tied the knot. Since then I've learned there are far worse things than being an old maid."

"Evie Langford, if you're an old maid, I've been looking for love in all the wrong places! An old maid is unhappy, dried up, ugly, and unlovable. Like Cinderella's step-sisters. You are none of those things."

"Rance Thompson, you're making me blush. It's very kind of you to believe I won't always be alone with only a bug-eyed furball to keep me company. What about having our coffee in the living room?"

"Before or after we do the dishes?

"Be careful. I may lock you in my guest room. How often does a girl find someone who is on time, helps fix dinner, is compassionate, thinks I'm lovable, *and* does dishes? I must be dreaming!" Evie stacked the dirty plates. "It will only take a few minutes to load the dishwasher. Do you know how to make coffee too?"

"You bet. Point me to the coffee maker."

Gonzo retreated to his bed in the corner of the kitchen with a small piece of bread Rance had slipped to him.

They made quick work of the dishes. With mugs of steaming black coffee in hand, they settled onto the chintz covered sofa in the living room.

"Sitting here with someone else makes me realize how outdated the décor is. I don't entertain much. I hardly ever use this room, except when I want a fire. Then I'm concentrating on the book in my hand, not the room's ambience," Evie said looking around the room.

"It's comfy and welcoming. I'm not one to waste a lot of time and money on remodeling and redecorating. I'm sure my years of bachelor living have further reinforced those tendencies. All Kyle and I need is a table to eat at, beds to sleep in, a den with a big TV screen for sporting events, and a pool table in the rec room. Our condo doesn't even have a living room."

"Mama was comfortable with this room, so there wasn't any reason to make changes. I guess I need to start thinking about what I'm comfortable with. I've spent most of my life being strong for other people and doing what I thought they needed me to do. I haven't really thought about what I need or what I want."

"Well, I'm here now. Rance Thompson, super agent to the rescue. My mission is to not only help you discover what you like and want, but to make it happen. At our age, it's acceptable to be a little selfish."

"*Our* age? Stop and do the math, Rance. We are not anywhere close to the same age."

"Are you measuring in years or attitude, my dear Miss Langford? In years, you've probably figured out that I'm thirty-eight; high school fatherhood, twenty-year-old son. I don't think you're a whole lot older than I am."

"Only if double digits, isn't a lot." She shook her head. "I told you my engagement was to avoid being an old maid at thirty and I've been taking care of Mama for twenty years. Rance, our celebration at the beach was for my fiftieth birthday. Don't you think that's a large age gap?"

"As in too large? No. I don't." He set down his mug and clasped her hand in his. "If our ages were reversed, would you think it was an unreasonable difference?"

"No, but who bats an eye when the man is older than the woman. In our case, I'd be called a cougar. An old woman on the prowl for some handsome stud to help her feel young again. I've never thought of myself in those terms, but I know lots of people who would."

"You're not an old woman, but I've always wanted to be some beautiful woman's young stud." Rance laughed. "When you aren't being the prim and proper Garland Regional Medical Center CEO, Miss Langford, no one would ever take you for fifty. You act young. You look younger. I like you and being around you. No, it's stronger than that. Evie Langford, I want to be with you. I need to know everything about you."

She hesitated a moment. Then she squeezed his hand. "We certainly aren't getting any younger. You've coaxed me out of my shell. I enjoy your company."

Rance leaned over and slowly, tenderly, kissed her waiting lips as he wrapped her into an embrace. They stayed entwined. Saying nothing. Breathing in each other's scents. She laid her head on his shoulder.

Evie murmured softly, "The last time I kissed someone on this sofa, I looked up to see my dad with his arms crossed at his chest standing in the living room doorway. He said, 'I think it is time this young man found his way home. It's getting late.' Then he went upstairs, knowing I would obey the directive."

"I hate to say it, but he was probably right then, and he would be now. It is later than I thought. We have a very busy, and I hope, productive day planned for tomorrow. The girls are counting on us." Rance stood to leave. "Evie, you're an amazing woman. Have sweet dreams."

She walked him out the front door. Gonzo trailed behind them. Rance kissed her one more time while they stood on the stoop, scratched Gonzo behind the ears, then he left. She leaned against the front door watching him drive down the street. She picked up the dog and snuggled against him.

How long had it been since she had gotten a good night kiss at the door? Rance thought she was amazing, even knowing her age. She had never connected with anyone so quickly, so deeply. Rance Thompson was…she wasn't sure what. But, she was beginning to believe Divine intervention did bring them together. Constantine said you were never too old for true love. Could she find her soul mate at fifty?

"Hi, Evie." A voice startled her.

"Who's out there?" Evie hugged the dog tighter and peered into the darkness. Gonzo growled softly.

"Just me. Surprised to see you outside at this hour." A figure stepped out of the shadows and into the glow from the porch light.

"Court? What are you doing in my neighborhood?"

"Getting my steps in. Gotta stay healthy. Did you enjoy dinner? Your guest must be from out of state— looked like a rental car. Wait, was he the FBI agent?"

"What? It's none of your business. Why are you walking past my house?"

"I'm waiting for an opportunity to talk to you." Court strode down the walk. "I thought he would never leave."

"Is something wrong at Regional? If you needed to talk to me why not come to the door and ring the bell or, better yet, use the phone?"

"Nothing's wrong at good old Regional. Don't worry, boss." He leered at her. She shivered.

"I don't understand your visit. At this hour. At my home."

"I stopped to tell you good night. Hope you have sweet dreams." He ambled down the walk to his black foreign car parked halfway down the block.

Chills raced down her spine.

"For the record, Gonzo, he's someone you should always growl at!"

How long had this been going on? Why was Courtland Gaines keeping track of her visitors?

Chapter Nineteen

The call from Dallas came in exactly on time. The Campbells were welcomed in the Dallas office by Mark Richards. Special Agent Thompson explained who he was and that he was currently involved in an investigation focused on The Langford Obstetrical Center in Lansdale, Wisconsin.

The Campbells adopted their two children from The Center because they had a national reputation for facilitating private adoptions much more quickly than the usual two to five year wait for healthy, Caucasian children. The fact that the children were redheads, like they both were, was a bonus. Dr. Langford called and told them the birth sibling of their eighteen-month-old daughter, Rebekah, was going to be born in two months, and they jumped at the chance to adopt again through The Center.

"It's sad to see a young girl having two children before she's eighteen, but we liked Rose and she seemed relieved to know her children were going to parents who would love them and could provide a comfortable life for them. She told Dr. Langford she was glad the siblings would be raised together," Millie Campbell said.

"You met Rose? Did she sign the adoption papers for both children?" Rance asked.

"We met her when Rebekah was born. Millie

stayed for two months at The Center and spent a lot of time with her. I only got there two days before the delivery. For Joshua, Dr. Langford said Rose was too embarrassed about being pregnant again to see us face to face. We were told both children have the same father. Rose signed the adoption decrees and so did Frank Raymond, the father. We never met him. Tom Peterman handled both adoptions for us," David Campbell explained. "Is there some problem with the paperwork?"

"I'm afraid it's more than a clerical problem," Rance said. "Rose Rich was not the mother's legal name, it was Rosalie Richardson, and she has been missing for almost three years. There were severe complications when she had Joshua. She was hospitalized and, I'm sorry to have to tell you, she died almost immediately after getting to the emergency room. The hospital was told her baby had been stillborn. But clearly, Joshua was a healthy delivery."

Millie Campbell let out a sob and reached for her husband. "The poor little girl. Now she'll never get to see her babies grow up."

"Why didn't Dr. Langford let us know? We brought Joshua home the day after he was born—just like we did Rebekah. We had an open adoption. We would have tried to find Rose to update her on the kids. The three of us agreed she could see them whenever she wanted." David Campbell's right hand clenched into a fist.

"Where had you been sending the updates on Rebekah?" Agent Richards asked.

"To The Center. To Dr Langford's assistant, Mrs. Rafferty. They agreed to keep tabs on Rose and get our notes to her. Rose had our name, phone number, and address to send cards to the kids or us. We've never heard from her since we brought Rebekah home except for a birthday card on her first birthday. There was no note, it was signed Love, Rose," David said.

"And now we never will even get a card." Millie's shoulders heaved. She was sobbing uncontrollably.

Mark Richards said, "Agent Thompson, she's pretty upset, are you certain we should continue?"

Millie spoke softly, "Please, I'll get myself under control. I want to know what's happened. I need to know."

Agent Richards nodded.

"I'm sorry to have to give you this news this way," Rance began. "Rosalie's death triggered this investigation. It is the first break we've had in her missing person's case. She was not alone when she went missing. Two friends were with her. We're actively trying to find them. We're afraid they are also pregnant and may be in danger."

"Just tell us how we can help. We owe that to our children," David said.

The Campbells agreed to testify, if necessary, about Rose and being told both of the children were hers and Frank Raymond's. They signed a release for The Center to provide Joshua and Rebekah's birth records. Agent Richards said he'd fax it to Rance as soon as the call was over.

David Campbell asked, "How does all of this affect the legality of our adoptions?"

"Honestly, I don't know. You were operating in good faith. I'm meeting with Tom Peterman tomorrow morning. I'll make sure he knows your concerns. We'll be back in touch with you as soon as we have new information. I can't thank you enough for cooperating."

****

Evelyn Langford, Chief Davis, and Rance Thompson were the only ones on the eleven a.m. call. Courtland Gaines was out of the building. Evelyn was relieved he was absent. She had a bad feeling that he was reporting the details of these updates to her brother. Chief Davis believed the judge would be more likely to favor pursuing the warrant now. He planned to bring DA Vanoy up to speed on the case to garner his support as well. They would exercise the Campbells' release for the birth records of their children first.

Evelyn reported Lila Masterson's grandmother would be visiting tomorrow to meet her great grandson. She had alerted the nursery.

Chief Davis had not been able to locate the parents of Sybil Russell and Carley Addams yet. They had been missing six months longer than the Gables and Kelley girls.

****

At the end of the day, Evie checked on the Special Agent in the conference room. As usual, the afternoon conference call with the Chicago office was ending.

Rance hung up.

"A productive day? Mine has been," Evie said.

"Absolutely! First, Mrs. Rafferty jumped at the chance to have lunch with me Friday. She said my timing was 'Perfect' because Frank was leaving at eleven o'clock and wouldn't be back for the rest of the day. He's going to the Chamber of Commerce meeting, as you predicted, and then has a meeting out of town for the remainder of the afternoon. So, I will be doing some serious investigating Friday from eleven forward."

"I knew Fran Rafferty wouldn't pass on the opportunity to spend some time alone with you. Excellent, what else?"

"I'm more convinced than ever that we're on the right trail but, unfortunately, it leads right to your brother and The Langford Obstetrical Center."

"I'm afraid you're correct. There are too many coincidences, even for something Frank is involved in."

"Do you have time for dinner with me?"

"I guess I assumed we had a standing date." Evie smiled.

"Still want to dine in private?"

"I think it's a good idea. Especially so we don't risk running into my brother."

Rance smiled. "Do you have a grill on your patio?"

"Yes, a gas grill. Why? Planning a barbeque?"

"Just dinner for two. I flame a mean steak, if you're interested. Maybe tonight you can be sous chef and handle the salads and baked potatoes."

"Sounds like a wonderful plan. I have potatoes and fixings and salad stuff. You can pick up steaks at Bob's Market. You pass it on the way to my house. See you at our usual time?"

"Seven thirty it is, Miss Langford. I better get going. See you soon."

****

The doorbell chimed at seven thirty. Rance had a bag from Bob's Market in one hand and a sheet of hot pink paper in the other. He handed the flyer to Evie as he came in the door.

"This was under my wiper blade when I got to the car in the hospital parking lot tonight."

You are not needed. Nothing is wrong here. The other girls are gone. The FBI should be chasing terrorists, not harassing the upstanding citizens of Lansdale. It was signed *A Concerned Observer.*

She read it twice. "I think this means you are getting closer to the truth and someone is getting very nervous. I'm a little concerned that this 'Concerned Observer' knows what you're driving. That means you're definitely being watched."

"I thought about the note when I pulled in your driveway. I guess our private dinners aren't going to be secret much longer." He unloaded his market purchases. "I hope you have some garlic for the marinade for the steaks. I forgot to ask."

"Left hand drawer of the fridge. I told you this is a very small town. Honestly, I'm surprised no one has asked about you and me before now. Courtland Gaines knows you've been here and what you drive."

"The CFO? How does he know?"

"It's a little creepy. He's taken to jogging through this neighborhood even though he lives across town. He talked to me after you left last night. I saw his car parked at the curb halfway down the block the night we had pizza together."

"That's stalker behavior. Is he new to the hospital?"

"No, he's been there longer than I have. He has always not too subtly let me know he was interested in a relationship. I told him early on that I don't date co-workers, especially not people who report to me. The warning worked for years, but he seems to have forgotten lately."

"What does the police chief say about his

behavior?"

"I don't want to involve him. Small town. No point ruining Courtland's life over something so minor."

"Think about talking to your HR department."

"I've got it under control. Sorry I said anything. Just wanted you to know we've already been identified as 'being together.' I'm not surprised; it was just a matter of time," Evie stated.

"For the record, I don't like it. At all."

"Duly noted, Mr. Thompson. Back to our case. Have you thought about the best way to charm Fran Rafferty on Friday?" She pulled the salad makings out of the refrigerator and potatoes from the bin and began preparing the sides.

"Can I practice being charming on you tonight? I want to make sure I don't lose my touch at this critical juncture."

Evie laughed. "I guess I can make the sacrifice and take one for the team. Salads are made and potatoes are ready for the microwave. Do you want to eat on the patio so you can keep an eye on the steaks?"

"Excellent idea. How do you like your steak?"

"I'm a medium rare girl. What do you want to drink? What kind of salad dressing do you want or are you making it again tonight?"

"Great, I'm a medium rare guy. I knew there was something I liked about you. A glass of the merlot." He pointed to a bottle on the counter. "I picked it up at the market. Blue cheese dressing on my salad. I saw it in your refrigerator yesterday."

"Okay, I'll bring the salads out and open the wine. Go ahead and light the grill. I'm going to put on dinner music. Is old Blue Eyes okay?"

"Love him. Looks like the patio may even work for dancing later." Rance went out the sliding glass door to the patio with the steaks on a platter. He was closely trailed by a curious little dog. Evie followed with a tray of salads, silverware, plates, the bottle of wine, and two large glasses. She set everything on the picnic table, opened the wine, and poured a glass that she carried to Rance at the grill.

It was a perfect night for dining al fresco. It wasn't too cool, and the stars peeked out of the clear night sky as the sun set. Evie turned on the twinkling white lights ringing the patio once the sun was down. Soon the aroma of sizzling steaks and the soft melody of a classic tune wafted through the air. They sat at the picnic table and ate the salads.

"Why is it food always tastes better outside? It doesn't matter what it is," Rance asked.

"I don't know the scientific explanation. But, you're right, it is absolutely true."

Rance announced the steaks were ready as the timer on the microwave buzzed to alert Evie the potatoes were done. She brought them out with butter, sour cream, shredded cheese, and chives. The steaks were a perfect medium rare—reddish pink and juicy— and the baked potatoes scrumptious with all the goodies melting over them and blending together with the fluffy white interior.

"A toast." Rance raised his glass. "To solving mysteries together."

"Cheers." They clinked glasses.

They ate without talking. The scent of the blooming lilacs mingled with the smell of the steaks in the balmy evening air. She had eaten many meals on this picnic table, but not for years. She needed to remember it would make dinner for one more pleasant too. Evie came out of her reverie when Gonzo barked to remind them he was there not so patiently waiting for a morsel or two. Rance was gazing at her.

"You look beautiful under the stars. I love your hair down, and that blouse is the perfect shade of red for your coloring."

"Has the charm practice begun?"

"No. It was simply a statement of fact. I don't have any plans to see Fran Rafferty by starlight. Not on Friday or at any other time. But you, I could gaze at the rest of my life."

"Good to know. Don't practice too much for Friday or Fran Rafferty might whisk you away from me. Dinner was simply delicious. Sorry, Gonzo, I didn't leave any for you." The pug cocked his head and whimpered until Rance reached under the table and slipped him a tiny sliver of steak. "Rance, you shouldn't feed him from the table. He'll get fat!" Evie carried the dirty plates into the kitchen and quickly loaded the dishwasher.

"We're not finished yet. For dessert we have quadruple chocolate cake, four layers with three kinds of chocolate frosting and filled with chocolate ganache. It should be wonderful with a tall glass of ice-cold milk," Rance announced.

"At this rate Gonzo won't be the only roly-poly one in this house." Evie laughed and poured two glasses of milk while Rance plated the luscious cake. They carried dessert outside and savored the rich chocolate melting in their mouths.

When the CD cycled back to the first song, Rance

stood and bowed. "Madam, may I have the pleasure of this dance?"

"I'd be thrilled." Evie stepped into his strong embrace and danced across the patio laughing and humming along with the song. "I love how a skirt swirls around my legs when I'm dancing with you. I hope I can do this even when I'm old and gray."

"My sweet Evie, you will never be too old for this." He twirled her around ending in a dramatic dip and they both laughed harder.

"My, my, isn't this a cozy picture." Frank stood just inside the back gate scowling with his arms folded across his chest. "What on earth is going on here?"

Evie answered, still laughing, "You can't tell? We're dancing. I know we're not very good, but surely you could tell what we were doing."

"Ha. Ha. Ha. You know very well that isn't what I meant. I have been on your front porch for the last fifteen minutes knocking and ringing the doorbell. No one answered."

"We didn't hear you, sorry." She stopped smiling. "What did you need, Frank?"

"I was worried about you. I could see your car in the garage, but the FBI agent's car was in the driveway. No one answered. I tried to come in to see if you were all right, but my key wouldn't fit in the lock."

"Why should it? This isn't your house anymore. Remember, I paid you off. I changed the locks the same day. Why were you concerned about Mr. Thompson being here?"

"I heard laughter and music coming from the patio, so I came to the back gate and let myself in. And what do I find, but you two plotting against me." Frank pointed at them accusingly.

"We haven't said your name all night. Why ruin a lovely meal? The only thing we've been plotting about is whether to have another piece of the chocolate cake or not. What did you say you needed?" she asked.

"Evelyn Langford, do you think this is appropriate behavior for the CEO of our community's medical center? Entertaining a much younger man in her backyard? What will the neighbors think?"

"I don't believe the neighbors are keeping a close eye on who is in my backyard now or at any other time. To my knowledge they've never checked IDs on any of my visitors. If they are paying rapt attention, they're probably saying to themselves, 'It's about time Evie Langford let her hair down and enjoyed life a little. Heaven knows she's had to put up with her stick-in-the-mud brother long enough.' " Evie's head rolled back as she laughed.

"You are not funny. Not in the least." Frank turned to Rance. "Mr. Thompson, is this ethical behavior for an FBI Special Agent? What would happen if I reported your behavior to your superiors in Chicago?"

"Dr. Langford, my immediate supervisor is William Bartles. You can reach him at the same number as mine. I gave you and your assistant one of my business cards the day we met."

"Frank, what was so urgent it required you see me tonight? Surely, you didn't come over in the hopes of catching an FBI agent behaving badly," his sister asked again.

"Well, forgive me. I was concerned for your safety when I drove by and saw his car in the driveway." Frank turned to leave back through the gate. "Some day, Evie, you'll want my help, and I won't have the time to be bothered. You're making things very hard for me, and they're going to be bad for you if you persist in this behavior. Remember, I warned you in plenty of time for you to back out of this mess."

The back gate slammed shut. "I guess you can tell, Frank got all the dramatic genes in our family."

"His behavior is over the top. Every time I've seen him, he's made some kind of thinly veiled threat directed at you. I'm worried. Has he threatened you in the past? Has he ever been physically violent?" Rance's blue eyes radiated concern.

Evie paced. "He wouldn't hurt me. Frank had trouble with his temper when he was much younger. I found out last year, he took a swing at Dad during an argument the day of the accident. It was only a glancing blow to the shoulder, but somehow Dad ended up on the ground. Frank left without apologizing. He had planned to go on the trip with Dad before their fight. Mom ended up going instead. Frank was inconsolable at Dad's funeral. At the time I didn't know why. Ever since then, he's never been physically threatening, but lately, he is talking a lot more aggressively. I don't think he would intentionally hurt me. I'm more worried about him taking his anger out on you, especially since now he knows you're important to me. Then he could hurt me, without laying a finger on me. The only reason for him to be so upset is if he is involved somehow in the disappearances of those girls. He's my only brother. I don't want it to be true."

Rance's strong arms wrapped around her and pulled her to his chest. She breathed in his scent. She felt so secure, so safe, so...

"Evie, I know the timing sucks and our situation is complicated, but I think I'm falling for you. You don't have to say anything. I'll do everything I can to keep you safe. I hope Frank isn't guilty, but I'm afraid he is. We need to know for sure before we can pursue a relationship, not because it makes any difference to me or how I feel about you, but because I don't want it to cloud my judgment or yours." He kissed her forehead.

"Rance, I know we need to slow down until we get past this mess, but I don't want Frank to be the reason I lose you. I've been praying he will find the heart, the nerve, the whatever it takes to come clean about The Center and the missing girls. It remains my fervent prayer nightly." She laid her head on his chest listening to his heart beat in perfect rhythm with her own. "Tomorrow is going to be a big day for both of us. It's already ten. We should probably call it a night."

"I know. Let me hold you a few more minutes and soak up your affection to steel myself for tomorrow." He hugged her tighter. "I sure am glad I spoke to you that morning on the beach. In kind of an odd way, Frank being a jerk helped us find one another. Funny how things work out."

"Like there's a master plan…I'm glad something or someone made you stop and speak that morning. I never imagined finding you at fifty."

"I'm glad you waited for me." Rance began swaying to the music and pulled Evie along. When the song ended, he spun her around, dipped her almost to the floor, and pulled her into his arms for an ending kiss. A deep soul touching kiss.

"I'll never look at eating on the patio the same way…and I have a whole new appreciation for Dad's

old albums. Thanks for staying a little bit longer."
Reluctantly, she left his arms. He cleaned up the grill
while she cleared away their dessert plates and glasses.

"You'd never know anyone had been here." He
smiled and closed the grill lid.

"Oh, I know…" She winked. "And I'll remember
for a long, long time."

Rance let himself out the front door, making sure it
was locked behind him. He backed out of the driveway
and into the street. A black foreign car pulled away
from the curb as he passed. The driver's face was
partially hidden by a baseball cap pulled low over his
brow.

It didn't take an FBI agent to know he was being
followed. And it was probably Courtland Gaines.

Chapter Twenty

"Good morning, Special Agent Thompson. I'm Tom Peterman." The large, dark-haired man extended his hand across the broad mahogany desk.

Rance Thompson grasped it firmly. "Thanks for making time to see me this morning. I'll get right to the point of this meeting. As a partner in The Langford Obstetrical Center, how much do you know about the investigation we're conducting there?" Rance pulled files out of his briefcase and sat them on the edge of the desk.

"This is a little embarrassing. I'm not aware of any official FBI inquiry related to The Center. I thought your focus was on the runaways who delivered babies there. Am I missing something?"

"Our investigation is more complicated than that. How much time do you have for me this morning?"

"Is two hours enough time to get me up to speed?"

"I'll be as efficient as possible."

The attorney called his secretary and asked her to clear his calendar until noon.

Special Agent Thompson started with the Rosalie Richardson case. He shared the faxed release the Campbells had signed so their attorney could discuss the details of their adoptions. Tom Peterman handled both adoptions of the children of the person he knew as Rose Rich. He confirmed they were both adopted by the

Campbells. He was not aware the mother's real name was Rosalie Richardson or that she died less than a day after giving birth to the second child. The FBI agent relayed the concerns the Campbells had about the legality of the adoptions. Peterman said he would contact them later the same day to allay their fears. He could amend the paperwork to reflect the new knowledge about the mother.

The attorney did not have any records for adoptions with mothers named Sarah Kelley or Sonia Gables. Rance Thompson said he'd send over the aliases they were using at The Center since he did not have those notes with him. He warned the attorney that they were also runaways and had been with Rosalie Richardson at the time of her disappearance.

Agent Thompson told him another runaway under investigation currently was Lila Masterson. Her grandmother, her next of kin, was coming to Garland Regional later today to meet her great grandson. Currently the girl was not tied to The Center. The attorney did not indicate whether he recognized the name or not.

Sybil Russell and Carley Addams were in the attorney's case files. Both young women had a child that was adopted through The Center eighteen months ago. The FBI would need a release from them before Tom Peterman could release further specifics about those adoptions. Agent Thompson explained they were also identified as runaways and law enforcement officials were actively trying to reach their parents.

Peterman had lots of questions and gave the agent a step-by-step outline of how the adoption process through The Center normally worked.

"Thank you for your thorough explanation of things. The moral here is I should have been asking more questions of Dr. Langford all along. The Center has been a business Godsend. My revenue has increased dramatically since we offered the package deal at The Center and tapped into the private adoption market. I've always been a big proponent of adoption. I can't tell you how many waiting lists my wife and I were on before we stumbled on the private adoption option. I can share firsthand with my clients what a joy it is to take a child into your home and provide a life they never would have known with a less financially stable, possibly single mother. Of course, not all of our mothers are unwed. And certainly, not all are runaways. Some are in circumstances where they believe adoption would be the best long-term solution for their child."

"I couldn't put my finger on the problem at The Center until the hospital was told the Richardson baby was stillborn, but the Campbells confirmed they brought the baby boy home. Then we started digging deeper. They were going to contact Dr. Langford for records on both births. We'll want to see what they receive." Rance began packing his files in the briefcase.

"I think The Center's board of directors needs to have a called meeting with you. You should share with them what the FBI is doing in the facility they are responsible for. I'll have my secretary arrange it."

"Good. Please include Miss Langford and Dr. Chase Merrick from the Medical Center. I know they have some questions for your board as well. I'm sure that as a partner in the facility, and as an attorney, you will advise Dr. Langford to be cooperative with any requests. We have a warrant currently in process with the Garland County courts related to all the cases we discussed today."

"Of course. Thank you again."

****

Margie buzzed. "Mrs. Masterson is here."

"Please show her in." Miss Langford got up from her desk and walked across the room to meet her visitor, a short, plump woman with smiling green eyes. Her auburn hair was laced with gray and pulled into a sloppy bun at the nape of her neck.

"Good morning Mrs. Masterson. It is so good to finally meet you. Please forgive me for staring. I was expecting a much more grandmotherly looking woman. You look hardly old enough to be a grandmother, certainly not a great grandmother. I don't believe you're even my age."

The woman laughed. "You're very kind. I'm fifty-three. My son was born when I was less than a year out of high school. My son married and became a father at nineteen. Now his daughter had a baby. That'll get you to great grandma status pretty quickly."

"You're right, it would. And who is this young lady?"

A girl with shoulder length auburn hair who looked to be about seventeen extended her hand. "I'm Lila's cousin, Mikayla. I drove Aunt Zelda here today."

"Welcome." Evelyn clasped her hand. "I'm sure your aunt was happy for the company."

"And the chauffeur service. I had to delay my trip until Mikayla was available to drive me. I'm not comfortable behind the wheel on the highway." Mrs. Masterson chuckled. "Before I forget in all the excitement of meeting my great grandson, thank you,

Miss Langford. The lilac bush you sent me after Lila's service was beautiful and full of fragrant blooms. The nursery men even planted it for me. I'm guessing you paid them for the extra service. I can see it out my kitchen window. Now every time I wash dishes I get a reminder of my sweet Lila. It was extra thoughtful and so very much appreciated." Tears ran down her face. Miss Langford handed her a tissue from the box on the desk.

"I'm glad it worked out so well," the CEO said. "You never know when you're ordering something over the phone."

"I don't want to be rude, ma'am, but could we go right up to see our little guy?" the great grandmother asked.

"Of course, follow me."

Miss Langford led them to the elevator and up to the third-floor nursery. "He was moved out of the high risk nursery yesterday. He's still small, but gaining weight every day. He's a little fighter. The doctors are very pleased with his progress."

The three women pressed against the window gazing at the little blue-blanketed bundle directly in front of them.

"I'd know him anywhere. He looks exactly like Lila's daddy, my son John—cute chin, the dimple in the right cheek, and all that red hair. The doctor was amazed at how much hair John had at birth." Mrs. Masterson beamed. "My great grandson. I wish your mama was here to introduce us." Tears welled up in her eyes.

"Auntie, it's going to be all right. You're here now. We'll make sure he knows who his mama was."

Mikayla hugged her.

"Is it okay for me to hold him?" Mrs. Masterson asked.

"Absolutely. I know just the person who can arrange that." Miss Langford picked up the wall phone and asked Mrs. Bryers to set up the great grandmother and cousin in a visiting room.

"Please stop back in the office before you leave."

"How long can we stay?" Mrs. Masterson asked.

"As long as you want. We do need to talk after your visit about what happens next for Baby Boy Masterson. I'll have some trays sent up for you for lunch. Please let Mrs. Bryers know what you'd like. I'll see you later."

Evelyn smiled as she walked back to the office. It was nice to see some good come out of Lila's tragedy. Baby Boy Masterson was about to get a gigantic dose of love.

Chapter Twenty-One

At one thirty p.m., there was a knock on the door between the conference room and the CEO's office. Evelyn answered it. She opened the door to see lunch for two set up on the conference room table.

"Margie booked the conference room for me today and blocked your calendar for lunch, so I stopped at the market. The woman behind the deli counter told me this was Miss Langford's favorite seafood salad. We have fresh fruit, crackers, and ice-cold lemonade. Your table awaits, my lady." Rance made a little bow.

"How perfectly marvelous. Another surprise from the very special Special Agent Thompson." She sat down in the chair he'd pulled out for her. "How did the meeting with Tom Peterman go?"

"He's very cooperative. He said he wasn't aware that The Center was being investigated as part of the Richardson case. He's been coordinating three to six private adoptions a month from them. He always meets with the adoptive parents. Sometimes he meets with the baby's mother and father. Sometimes just the mother. On at least one adoption each month, he never personally meets either of the birth parents. Their paperwork is coordinated through Mrs. Rafferty. The fee for the legal work is included in the overall fee for the whole event: housing for the birth parent or parents and for the adoptive parents, the delivery, and the adoption paperwork. It makes up a large part of his legal practice revenue."

"I'm sure Frank didn't volunteer any information about the investigation. A joint meeting between the two boards was held before the FBI appeared on the scene. Is Rosalie the only girl who has put more than one baby up for adoption?"

"No. He is going to check his records, but he believes there have been two or three more. Tom didn't realize Rosalie was a runaway. He didn't have information on the Kelley and Gables babies, but those girls are using aliases I need to give him. He did have adoption files for the Addams and Russell adoptions but can't provide any information until we get a release. We can't get that until we reach the parents or find the girls themselves. He didn't seem to recognize the name Masterson.

"I think he hasn't explored the birth mothers' backgrounds much because he couldn't afford to. He prefers to keep making money and stay ignorant of the details. He has great confidence in his partner keeping him out of any shady deals."

"Frank is just as interested as he is in making the maximum amount of money possible. His attitude may lead them both into gray areas of operation. You said he was cooperative."

"He thinks The Center's Board of Directors should get together with the FBI, you, and Dr. Merrick and, of course, Dr. Langford, to further discuss the investigation and what is happening there. He especially wants to know how the birth mothers are vetted by The Center. He said he'd have his secretary pull the meeting together. What have you been doing all morning?"

Evie savored a bite of seafood salad. "I met Lila's grandmother and her cousin who looks like she's a little older than Lila was and could pass for her sister. They've been with the baby for several hours. I have a good feeling about this. I think the boy will be going home with them when he is released."

"What wonderful news. Do I remember correctly that you have a meeting tonight?" Rance asked.

"I do. Quarterly Medical Staff dinner and meeting. It will be a long day."

"Do you have anyone to free Gonzo for a few minutes of romping in the yard?"

"I don't. Poor little guy. These night meetings are hard on him. Last time he growled when I finally got home to let him out. I probably should look for a better situation for him, but I'd miss him," Evie replied.

"Since my girl is tied up tonight, why not let me release Gonzo for a bit around six? I'll grab a sandwich and sit on your patio to eat while he gets some air," Rance suggested.

"What a terrific idea. My little dog will never growl at you again!"

Evie gave Rance a spare key and explained the timing on the alarm system. What a relief to know Gonzo wouldn't suffer tonight because of her schedule.

****

At five o'clock, Evelyn realized she hadn't seen the Mastersons since taking them up to the nursery. Margie hadn't either. She went up to the nursery visiting rooms. They were in Room Two. She tapped lightly on the door. Mikayla answered.

"Miss Langford, please come in."

166

Mrs. Masterson was in the rocking chair with her great grandson cradled securely in her arms. They were both sound asleep.

"Auntie has had a very emotional day. She's exhausted. The baby has been a gem. He only cries if he's hungry or wet. The nurses brought in his formula and diapers. We've had him all to ourselves today. It was just what she needed. It's the happiest I've seen her since we heard about Lila." Tears welled up in Mikayla's eyes.

Evelyn gave the young woman a hug. "I'm so glad things are working out. Do you have a motel for tonight?"

"No. We were in such a hurry to get here she didn't want to stop to find one. We're on a pretty strict budget." The young girl blushed.

"I understand. I'll be back in about fifteen minutes."

Evelyn went down to the Guest Services desk. After she signed some papers, the clerk handed her two keys. She returned to the nursery visitor room.

Baby and great grandmother were both awake now. The infant was vigorously sucking on a bottle and kicking his little legs free from the lacy blue and white crocheted blanket as he ate. His smiling grandmother cooed at him.

"When he gets hungry, he doesn't waste any time. Isn't he a pip? I've decided to call him Michael. It was my John's middle name. Michael John Masterson."

"That's much better than Baby Boy Masterson." Evelyn laughed. "Since you're naming him, should I assume that means you plan to legally adopt him?"

Zelda frowned momentarily. "You mean I can't

just take him home because he's my kin? I'm the closest family he has."

"I don't think it's quite that easy. There will probably be some paperwork to be done. You know how the government is."

"I don't have any lawyer. How would we get all the right things lined up?"

"I'll have Mr. Peterman get in touch with you. He's a local attorney who handles lots of private adoptions. He'll know exactly what needs to be done. Could I have your cell phone number?" She got a pad of paper out of her pocket.

"Auntie doesn't have one, but I do. Here it is." Mikayla showed Evelyn the screen with her phone number on it.

"Is the adoption real expensive?" Mrs. Masterson shook her head. "I really want to take him home, but if it's too much…"

"The hospital has a fund to help in cases like this. I'm sure something can be arranged for little Michael to be with his great grandmother and his sweet cousin. Now, you're welcome to stay as late as you want, but I have a committee meeting to get to. You have a room in our Guest Suites on the third floor, it has two queen-sized beds. That's in the tower located near the entrance where you parked today. Here are vouchers for dinner and for your meals tomorrow in our cafeteria. It's open until nine tonight and opens back up at six in the morning." Evelyn handed the keys and vouchers to Mikayla since Zelda's arms were full of the cheerful little boy.

"Miss Langford, I'm speechless." Tears ran down the woman's face. "You have a special spot in heaven if

I have anything to say about it. Thank you. Thank you."

"My pleasure. I'll check in with you tomorrow. I noticed Michael is wrapped in a handmade blanket. Who gave it to you?"

"A lovely little woman named Mrs. Kapper knocked on the door earlier and introduced herself. She made it especially for Michael. Isn't that sweet?" Zelda said.

"Did Mrs. Kapper tell you that she was the one who found Lila in labor and got her to the hospital by ambulance?"

"No. What a wonderful woman. Michael has received a very special gift."

"Yes, he has. Hope you have a good night."

Mikayla walked her to the door and embraced her. "Thanks for knowing exactly what Auntie needed."

Evelyn had tears in her eyes as she walked onto the elevator. She dabbed her eyes with a handkerchief once she got back to the office. Then she and Margie went to the Medical Staff dinner and quarterly meeting.

****

It was a little past ten p.m. when Evie finally came in the back door. Gonzo was sound asleep in his crate and Rance had properly reset the alarm.

"C'mon, Gonzo. Time to go upstairs and back to sleep. Rance must have played hard with you." The little dog staggered out of the crate and collapsed at her feet whimpering. "What a lazy guy you are!" She picked him up and snuggled him against her cheek. "But I wouldn't have you any other way."

A dozen snow-white roses were in the middle of the round oak kitchen table. The card propped against the crystal vase said "I missed you. See you tomorrow."

She leaned down to smell the sweet scent of the closest velvety bloom. "Rance Thompson, you spoil me. A girl could get used to this. He's a wonderful man, isn't he?" A low snore confirmed, the pug was sound asleep again.

Chapter Twenty-Two

Fran Rafferty was on the phone. She stood by the desk looking stunning in an emerald-green suit with a creamy white silk blouse. The agent took the opportunity to review the baby board again. There had been three new babies, two boys and a girl, added to the board since his first visit. No mothers in the Emergency Room this week so that was a good sign.

"Sorry to keep you waiting, a board member who needed some immediate information." Fran Rafferty touched his arm. "You're always fascinated by our babies. Do you have children of your own?"

"Just one twenty-year-old son. In slightly different circumstances, he could have been an adopted baby. Makes you think," Rance answered distractedly. "Where do you suggest we go for lunch, Mrs. Rafferty?"

"Please, call me Fran. There aren't a lot of local options. Whistler's Diner has great food, but it's the local gossip hub and usually pretty noisy. Shangri-La is more private and has a very good luncheon. You can even get a drink with lunch, if you're so inclined," she said smiling.

"I'm working, so definitely no drinking. I just want an opportunity to talk with you. Wherever you think would be best."

"Oh, I forgot, Fr—Dr. Langford will be at Shangri-

La; the Chamber of Commerce meets in the back room there. I'd rather he not know about our appointment. I'm sure you can understand why. If you're more interested in a private conversation than the food, there's a third option."

"What?"

"My place. I can throw together some salads and crab cakes. It won't take a minute and we won't be interrupted. I promise." She flashed a toothy smile that traveled all the way to her glistening coal-black eyes.

Rance hesitated a moment. "I'm not very gallant; invite someone to lunch and then have them make it. I hate for you to do all the work. I'm a great salad chef. Perhaps I can make the salads while you do the crab cakes."

"Perfect. Why don't I drive?" Fran grabbed her purse and keys from her desk drawer. "My car's right out here, the red one in the administration parking lot."

"The sporty convertible?"

"Yep. A girl's got to have a reliable way to get around." She laughed.

They walked out to the parking lot. Rance opened the driver's door for her, then walked to the other side and crawled down into the passenger seat in the low-slung vehicle.

She put the key in the ignition. "Down or up?"

"It's a beautiful day. Definitely down."

Fran brushed against him as she reached across Rance to unlatch the convertible's top on his side and then flipped open the lever on her side. "Excuse me."

Rance knew the heat in his cheeks meant he was blushing. "I would have been happy to undo the latch."

"It wasn't a problem. It can be a little

temperamental. I know just how to hold my mouth to make it work."

And what a lovely mouth it was. Evie warned him. He needed to keep his mind on the business at hand. Not on Fran Rafferty's shining eyes or kissable mouth. Where did that thought come from? *Pay attention Agent Thompson*!

After a short ride, they pulled into a tree lined driveway and parked in front of a two-story red brick house with white columns in front of it. "My late husband's family was quite wealthy," Fran volunteered, in anticipation of the question on Rance's lips. "I have no children and he was an only, so I am the sole recipient of the Rafferty fortune, such as it is, or was."

"I'm sorry if I was staring. I had the wrong picture in my head. I knew you were a widow. I thought you worked to eat." They both got out of the car. Fran walked over to his side.

"I do in some ways. The Rafferty fortune is primarily invested in real estate, a lot of real estate, and assorted business ventures locally and across the nation. There's not as much steady income as you might think. After Patrick died, I'd have gone stark raving mad if I was idling here all day. And I certainly wasn't ready to move back to Philadelphia. I have too much family there. All of whom are way too interested in running my life. Especially since I'm 'a poor widow all alone in this world.' This job helped get through the grieving process and the regular cash income provides me with some fun money I don't have to account for to the Rafferty family business partners. C'mon in and see the manor." She took his hand and led him up the stairs to the double front doors. "I don't have to be back at The

Center until two."

They walked into the two-story foyer. An elegant staircase wound up to the second floor. The rose-colored marble tile perfectly complemented the large oriental rug in shades of red, burgundy, pink, and black lying on top of it.

Fran pointed to the left. "The library, study, and formal living room are down this way. To the right is the sunroom and the guest suite—a bedroom, sitting area, and bathroom. The perfect hideaway for a long-term guest." She winked at Rance.

Now he was definitely blushing.

"Upstairs we have eight bedrooms and six bathrooms including my master suite. Would you like to see?"

"No, that's not necessary. We probably need to find the kitchen and start lunch so you can get back to work on time," Rance said a little nervously.

Fran laughed. "Of course. The dining room and kitchen are straight ahead. It's such a beautiful day I think we should eat lunch poolside. I have a screened in patio area created especially for lunch or breakfast for two." She walked toward the back of the house and signaled for Rance to follow her.

****

They pulled into the main Center parking lot behind Rance's car a few minutes before two o'clock.

"Lunch was delicious, Fran. It was especially nice to have some private time to get to know each other better and I enjoyed the tour of your home," Rance said unbuckling his seat belt. "Why did you stop here? I planned to walk you back to your office."

"Very sweet idea, but Dr. Langford appears to be

unexpectedly back in the office. I don't want him to see you with me. He'll be angry enough at finding me away from the office when he returned." Fran leaned over and kissed his cheek. "We must do this again sometime soon or maybe something after work one evening, I've been told I make a fantastic martini with blue cheese olives…"

"Thanks again for making lunch and for explaining how The Center's adoptions work. I'm sure I'll see you again before we're through with our investigation." Rance quickly got out of her car and walked around to the driver's window. "Thanks."

"Oh, I forgot to ask. I misplaced your business card; could I get another so I have some way to get in touch with you…if I remember some other detail that could be helpful?" She smiled and licked her bottom lip.

"Sure." He quickly pulled a card out of his jacket pocket. "The contact information is all there." Maybe he was a little too charming. What had he gotten into?

The sporty red car whipped into its space in the Administration parking lot and Fran rushed into the building.

Rance drove behind the main building to take the back road out of the complex. He stopped when he saw a white panel van idling at the back door. A moment later two clearly pregnant young girls were loaded into the back of the windowless van.

Where were they going? What a strange method of transportation for people paying for a deluxe birthing experience.

The van traveled down the exit road until it reached a wide dirt path off to the left. The driver opened the gate remotely, pulled the van through, and closed the gate remotely before driving off down a one-lane rutted path. When the van was out of sight, Rance pulled up to the gate to see if he could get in. A keypad, but no intercom. Only a solidly closed gate. Then he saw a security camera high on a pole and decided he should get out of there before he raised further suspicion. He couldn't see another way into the area, and it appeared to be completely fenced. He couldn't see any buildings, only rolling wooded hills. He waited out of range of the camera to see if any other vehicles came to the gate. After an hour of fruitless monitoring, he drove back into town.

Maybe Evie would know something about it. Could that section of the property be where the runaways stayed before they had identified adoptive parents for their babies?

****

"Miss Langford, it's six o'clock. Special Agent Thompson left a message about an hour ago. It's a little cryptic. 'Usual place, usual time for dinner.' I hope you know what he means," Margie said before she left for the evening.

"Thanks, Margie, I understand the message. I was getting concerned when there hadn't been any afternoon update from him. Have a lovely evening." She smiled thinking of seeing Rance at dinner.

"Have a great weekend, Miss Langford."

"Oh, you too. I'd forgotten it was Friday."

She would stop by the market on the way home and get ingredients for spaghetti. If she started the sauce right away, it would be ready by the time Rance got to the house at seven thirty. Did he like spaghetti? She felt so comfortable with him, she sometimes forgot there was a lot she didn't know about him.

Chapter Twenty-Three

Evie picked up the sock she was knitting but couldn't concentrate enough to actually complete a single stitch. Gonzo snuggled close to her on the sofa. She scratched the pug's ears. "Where's your buddy Rance? He's always so prompt and it's eight fifteen. I hope everything is okay. There's no telling what he found out from Fran Rafferty. I thought he'd call if he was going to be late."

The landline rang. "You're going to lose your promptness merit badge," she said laughing as she answered.

"Obviously, you weren't expecting me. What? Your beau hasn't shown up for dinner yet? Poor little Evelyn. Abandoned almost before her pathetic love affair begins."

"What are you talking about, Frank?"

"Don't you know where your FBI Special Agent is?" Frank snarled.

"He is running late and he's not *my* FBI Special Agent. At any rate, I don't see what concern it is of yours." She couldn't keep the irritation out of her voice.

"I'll tell you what concern it is of mine, Evelyn. The two of you are ruining my life and you're too stupid to realize he's only using you to further his career. He's a young man. Why would he be interested in an old maid, unless he needed information from you

178

to help trap me. Use your brain. You're normally a fairly intelligent woman. He's probably not even going to appear for dinner with you tonight." Frank laughed harshly.

"Stop being so paranoid. No one is plotting against you. Certainly not me, but there will be consequences, if you were involved in any way in Rosalie Richardson's death. Agent Thompson's interest in me is purely personal and only mine to worry about. I don't need any advice from you about my love life."

He let loose an almost demonic laugh, "Oh, that's rich. Evelyn Langford has a love life—since when? Do you know who your lover boy, emphasis on boy, had a lunch date with today?"

"I know he had an appointment over the noon hour."

"No, sister dear, it is an appointment when you go to lunch in a public place. This was no appointment; it was a date. More specifically, it was an assignation."

"What do you mean?"

"He and the young—much closer to his age—attractive widow Rafferty had lunch for over three hours at *her* house. Then when it was over, he kissed her goodbye in the parking lot right outside my office window. Brazenly in public." The malicious glee in his voice poured through the phone.

"You are lying. I don't know what you hope to accomplish with this tale, but I know you're fabricating the whole story. Rance Thompson would not have any reason to kiss Fran Rafferty. Not today or at any other time. It was a business lunch, no matter where they ate."

"You stupid little fool. He's working Fran exactly

like he's manipulating you. Going after you weak-minded women. He thinks he can get away with it because he's good looking, but Fran will never give away any of my secrets. It wouldn't be in her best interest. And she always looks out for herself first."

"Any problems that come out of the FBI investigation are of your own making. I hope they do catch you in something. It would serve you right. You are constantly threatening me, and I haven't done anything to betray you. Your own idiocy will do you in." Evie couldn't control the waver in her voice.

"Shut up. I'm not going down alone for anything. I'm warning you, call Thompson off. I don't care how you do it. Find a way to make all of this end. Soon. Do you hear me?"

The doorbell chimed. Gonzo leapt off the sofa and raced to the front door.

"Goodbye, Frank." She hung up.

She walked to the front of the house and opened the door. "It is you."

"Evie, I'm so sorry I'm late. Are you okay? You look angry with me." He touched her cheek trying to turn her face toward him. She wouldn't look in his direction. He stooped down and petted Gonzo. "Are you upset with me too?" The dog growled lowly and retreated to his mistress's side.

Evie didn't move out of the entryway. She stood defiantly with her hands on her hips. "Is it true? Did you kiss her?" she asked trying to control her anger.

"What? Who?" Rance looked genuinely confused.

"Fran Rafferty. Frank told me you kissed her. He saw you."

"Boy, the small-town telegraph certainly has been

busy. I'm sure it looked that way to Frank. I did not kiss Fran Rafferty. She kissed me and I fled as quickly as possible after she did. Cross my heart." Rance motioned crossing his chest.

"What exactly happened on your three-hour lunch at the widow Rafferty's house that would make her think a kiss was the appropriate way to end your 'business appointment'?" Sarcasm dripped from each word.

Rance laughed. "Miss Langford, I do believe you're jealous of Fran Rafferty. Really? You're the one who recommended I meet with her to charm her. Now you're worried I'm attracted to her?"

"But, Frank said…"

"Since when do you put credence in anything your brother says? I thought you knew how I feel about you. I've tried to make it very clear." He gathered her into an embrace. She didn't resist.

"You're so late. You're never late. Somehow Frank knew you weren't here yet. He couldn't wait to call and give me the news. You said you were going to be charming. Fran was clearly interested in you from the beginning. And she's a lot younger than I am—much, much closer to your age." She sounded pathetic even to herself.

"This is rich." Rance kissed her cheek. Then led her to the sofa. He sat down and patted the spot next to him. She joined him. "We need to have this conversation. Let me be as clear as I know how to be. I don't give a fig about Fran Rafferty's age or yours. I have a job to do, and the widow Rafferty may have information to make solving this case easier. I did not use my 'charms' on her. I did not do anything inappropriate or unethical. I did have lunch at her house. She made crab cakes. I made the salad with the famous Thompson Special Salad dressing. No. I did not give her the recipe or volunteer to make it for her ever again. We had a long conversation—three hours of talking to be precise—about how The Langford Obstetrical Center works, what its financial challenges are, and about the adoption lawyer, Tom Peterman, who is your brother's partner in this venture. All of the discussion helped me develop a much clearer idea of how the whole operation works."

"And the kiss?" She couldn't let it go.

"It is true. Fran did kiss me—on the cheek—in the parking lot at The Center. It was in public. I did not return the kiss. Honestly, she surprised me before I could move out of range. What other questions do you have?"

"I have only one. Are you hungry?"

"Starving! What's that aroma? Smells Italian."

"It's spaghetti sauce. I'll put on the noodles and the garlic bread. Salad is ready. I had some time to kill while I was waiting for my dinner date." She laughed. "So where have you been since Fran dropped you off at The Center earlier this afternoon?"

"There's lots to talk about. I've had a very productive afternoon and I need your help on a couple of issues. Let's talk over dinner. But before that, I do have one more thing to say. Evelyn Langford, I care very much for you. Remember that fact the next time you talk to your brother about where I am or who I am meeting." He kissed the tip of her nose and went to clean up for dinner.

When Rance joined her in the kitchen, she asked,

"Do you want to make the Thompson Special Salad dressing for the second time today?"

"I'd be delighted to." Rance whipped up the salad dressing while Evie put the noodles in to cook and toasted the garlic bread. "Inside or out?" he asked.

"In."

"Kitchen or dining room."

"Dining room. It is a Friday night date."

Evie carried the garlic bread and a bottle of wine to the already set dining room table. She lit the candles and dimmed the lights. Rance brought the freshly dressed salad to the table and poured them each a glass of red wine.

"A toast to the maker of yet another feast," he said as he raised his glass.

"And to wrapping this mystery up soon!" she added.

By the time salads were eaten, the pasta was a perfect al dente. Rance grabbed the parmesan cheese and grater and carried them to the table while Evie brought the steaming bowls of onion, garlic, tomato, mushrooms, and sausage spaghetti.

Rance brought her up to date on what he had observed while leaving The Center.

"You're a terrific cook, but I'm going to have to find somewhere to go running or I'll not fit into my clothes!" Rance said pushing away from the table.

"Thanks. I like to cook when I have time." Evie began clearing the dishes. Once the dishwasher was started, they retired to the living room to enjoy their coffee.

"I do know another way into the property on the backside of The Center. Originally, all that land was a church camp sitting in the middle of twenty acres of woods and streams. Dad bought it when I was about ten. For years, it was a weekend getaway for our family. There were four small cabins and two larger buildings, one with a commercial kitchen and large dining hall and one the church used as an auditorium for large meetings and performances. Each of the cabins was outfitted for five or six people to stay in.

"We used to bring our friends—girls in one cabin, boys in another, and parents in the other two. Frank built The Langford Obstetrical Center on the front half of the property and fenced off the back side. I thought he planned to use it as a retreat. I haven't been out there in the last ten years. When Mama could no longer easily navigate her way between the cabins, we stopped going. I don't know if Frank has continued to hunt and fish out there or not. I have no idea what shape the buildings are in."

"I saw at least two pregnant girls being helped into a van parked behind The Center. I didn't get a good look at their faces. I have a feeling Sonia Gables and Sarah Kelley are out there and they may not be alone. We located the Russell and Addams parents today. They were hopeful. It's been three years since they saw their daughters. I have a gut feeling that if we find Sonia and Sarah, we'll find them. We're getting releases from the parents so we can go back to Peterman, Garland Regional, and The Center to look at their records," Rance reported.

"It sounds like everything is coming to a head. Maybe my prayers for the safe return of all of them are going to be answered. We haven't had any new emergency transfers to our E.R. since you've been on site. I hope it's a sign processes really have been improved at The Center."

"Can you tell me how to get onto the back side of the property?"

"Better than that, I'll take you out there tomorrow."

"It could be dangerous. We know we're being watched. I don't want to put you at more risk than you already are. Just give me directions," he said with a wrinkled brow.

"Nope. I won't. We're going there together. You're at risk as much as I am. I'll feel better if we're together. Then I'll know for sure who you are kissing." She winked.

"Has anyone ever told you how perfectly stubborn you are?"

"Never! Tomorrow, I'll pack a picnic lunch. If someone sees us on the back road, they'll think we're headed to the little lake behind the old camp for a relaxing Saturday afternoon outdoor lunch."

"Great idea. I'll be by to get you at noon. I feel a major breakthrough in this case coming. Thanks for dinner. I promise I will do everything in my power to never be late again." He hugged her close.

"Sorry for being such a ninny. Frank knows how to push all my buttons. He always has. I didn't really believe you dumped me for Fran Rafferty, but I worried you might be in danger. It's hard to believe all this drama and excitement is happening in boring, little Lansdale." She snuggled closer to his chest. "I always feel so safe, so secure, when I'm in your arms. It's like this is where I was always meant to be."

"I like hearing that. When all of this is over, we need to talk about what happens next…with us." Rance tilted Evie's face up and gazed into her sparkling eyes. He bent down and slowly, tenderly kissed her lips. She eagerly returned it pulling him closer. "Now that's kissing someone and being kissed back. Fran Rafferty has nothing on you. Nothing at all." Rance chuckled.

Chapter Twenty-Four

At eleven a.m. the doorbell chimed. Evie was in the middle of making chicken salad for the picnic. She wiped her hands on the apron tied around her middle and hurried to the front door. Gonzo was only a step behind her.

She opened the front door saying, "Do you think coming early today makes up for being late yesterday?"

Her smile dissolved. She gasped and tried to close the door.

Courtland Gaines shoved his way past her. His eyes were coal black. His jaw was set as if he were grinding his teeth.

"I'm not going to tolerate any more. Not one minute longer," he shouted.

Gonzo stood between his mistress and the unwelcome guest emitting a low growl.

Evie left the door standing open. She walked into the living room. He followed. She sat down on the sofa. "Sit down, Court. Tell me what's bothering you." Gonzo stayed between her and the visitor continuing to growl.

"Don't act the innocent. You know damn well what's wrong," he continued shouting. The vein on his neck throbbed. His face was flushed. Sweat beaded across his brow.

"Please don't shout. I'm right here. I'm sorry but I

don't know what the problem is," Evie spoke softly, she hoped calmly. "Please, sit down." She patted the sofa cushion next to her.

"No. You're not sweet talking your way out of this. Almost every night this week you've had dinner with him. You've worked side by side—all day—every day for two weeks. I haven't had fifteen minutes of your time alone all week. It's clear in the morning updates that you already know the information he reports there. Pillow talk or something like it?" He paced back and forth gesturing wildly with his arms. He stopped and ran his fingers through his hair leaving it spiked wildly in all directions so he looked totally maniacal.

"Pillow talk? What are you saying? Is something wrong at work? I didn't know you were trying to get in to see me. It's not like Margie to ignore a meeting request for something urgent."

"This isn't about Margie. This is about you! You and me!" He plopped down next to her. Gonzo parked himself at her feet.

"I don't understand. Court, there is no you and me. There never has been. There never will be. You know I do not date people I work with, especially not people who report directly to me. It's been my rule since the beginning." She stood and walked to the opposite side of the room trailed by the pug.

"You seem to have changed the rules. I should get a chance now. New rules, new game."

"What are you talking about? What game?"

"You're dating someone you work with. You know I've been waiting twenty years for you. If you're going to date people you work with, I'm supposed to be the first one. I'm at the front of the queue. I've been in line all of these years. No one gets you before me. It's only fair." Court rose. He crossed the room in three steps and loomed over her.

Evie moved to the right. He shadowed her. She stepped backward. He went forward. He towered over her by at least six inches. Gonzo barked and bared his teeth.

She spoke to the dog, "Hush." To Court she said, "Please sit back down. We need to discuss this. Calmly."

"That's what I said." He moved closer to her. "It's my turn, Evie. Not his. He wasn't even here until last week."

"Court, I haven't changed my rules about dating co-workers or subordinates," Evie almost whispered.

"But you're working with that blasted Special Agent all day every day at Garland and seeing him every single night. Here. In your home. If that's not dating, what is it?" he roared.

"Please, Court. Stop shouting. Special Agent Thompson is here on an assignment. He is not a Garland Regional employee. He is not my subordinate. When this case is over, he'll go back to Chicago where he is based. The 'no dating rule' still applies to you and me. You're my co-worker and I'm your boss. Nothing about our relationship has changed. Absolutely nothing," she said firmly with her hands clenched into fists at her side. She stared directly into his darkening eyes trying not to flinch at the madness she saw there.

"One very important thing has changed. *Me*! I can't wait any more!"

He moved toward her. She ducked under his outreached arm. He grabbed her right arm and tried to pull her to him. The pug got in between them, bit at his ankles, and growled loudly. He loosened his grip on her and kicked at the animal, who raced for shelter behind his mistress. She took the opportunity for freedom and quickly backed up, tripped over the dog, and fell to the floor. She hit hard on her right shoulder. There was a popping sound, then nauseating pain.

Courtland knelt next to her. "Evie, I didn't want to hurt you. I've always loved you. What have I done?" He stroked her cheek as tears wetted her face. He tried to move her off the floor.

A scream rang out.

Hers.

"Don't touch me. I can't stand it. My shoulder," she cried. "Court, I need help. Please call an ambulance."

"Don't worry. I will take care of you. This wasn't supposed to happen. You weren't supposed to get hurt. Let me help you stand up and I'll drive you to the emergency room. Then you'll know how much I care for you," he insisted.

"It hurts when you pull on me. Please call an ambulance," she begged. Gonzo was at her side whimpering.

"Don't cry, Evie. I can't stand to see you cry. I never meant to hurt you. This was all an accident. If I call the ambulance, will you tell them it wasn't my fault?" He sounded like a child negotiating his punishment.

"Yes. Yes. Of course." She gulped for air.

"I promise I'll call. First, I just want one kiss. That's not too much to ask, is it? Please, Evie."

A shadow covered Evie's face. Courtland Gaines

flew to his feet. Rance Thompson held his arm.

"Why don't you try manhandling someone your own size?" Rance demanded.

Court raised his free arm to shield his face. "I didn't mean to hurt her. She tripped over that ugly dog. It's not my fault. Tell him, Evie. Tell him it was an accident."

"Rance, it happened like Court said. I tripped over Gonzo. Please help me."

Rance released his grip on Court and bent down to look closer at her injury. Court scrambled quickly out the door. He never looked at Evie. The door slammed shut.

Rance knelt down next to her on the floor. "Are you going to be all right?" Gonzo licked the tears streaming down her cheek.

More tears blurred her vision. "I'm glad you came in when you did." She petted the dog with her left hand. "I hope he didn't hurt you when he kicked, or I didn't when I tripped over you." The pug whimpered and tried to snuggle closer to her.

"Can you move?"

"Maybe if you'll help from my left side. My right shoulder is throbbing. I think it may be dislocated."

"Grab a hold of my arm with your left arm. I won't let you fall." Rance helped her struggle to a sitting position and then to her feet and walk over to the sofa. He gently lowered her to the cushion.

"I can't raise my right arm at all." Tears poured down her cheeks. "I need some ibuprofen."

"You need to go to the Emergency Room."

"Please get me some water and the ibuprofen first."

"Of course, Miss Langford. Whatever you say,

Your Stubbornness," he said with a smile, but concern showed in his eyes.

He retrieved the medication and poured a glass of water which he brought into the living room. She popped a couple of pain tablets in her mouth and washed them down.

"We need to go to the Emergency Room," he reiterated.

"Just give me a few minutes for the ibuprofen to kick in."

"If you don't like the idea of the Emergency Room, you're going to like this one even less. You need to call Chief Davis. He should arrest Gaines after you file charges. I'm not sure Courtland Gaines is in his right mind. He left, but I'm not certain he won't return. He's obsessed with you. I'm worried about your safety."

"No. No police. No charges. Yes, Courtland did come here to convince me he loved me, and he wanted me to be with him instead of you. He didn't attack me. He didn't intentionally hurt me. When I tried to move out of his reach, I backed up and tripped over Gonzo. He'd run behind me after Court kicked him. I don't think Court would intentionally hurt me. He was pretty distressed that I was crying. I think your timely appearance will make certain he doesn't come back."

"Okay. I won't argue with you. Please can we go to the Emergency Room? I can't stand to see you in pain."

"Yes." The ibuprofen hadn't touched the pain radiating across her shoulder, up her neck, and down her arm. Her head pounded without relief. Tears streamed down her cheeks and pooled in her lap.

"I'm witnessing a minor miracle. Let's go before you change your mind," Rance said.

"If the FBI doesn't work out for you, try stand up comedy. You're a laugh a minute." Evie tried to force her lips into a smile. "I'm ready to go."

"Your wish is my command, my lady."

Evie accepted Rance's assistance from her left side to get to her feet and into the car. Gonzo was whimpering at the door when it closed. Evie couldn't stand to have the seat belt touching her shoulder. He fastened it behind her so the alert would stop beeping and off they went.

Chapter Twenty-Five

Rance dropped Evie in the Emergency Room and took her office key to go retrieve a different blouse from her closet. She wanted one that would be easier to get on, one that buttoned up the front instead of having to be pulled over her head. It was right where she'd said it would be. He was locking the office door when someone tapped him on the shoulder. He turned around.

Courtland Gaines.

"What are you doing here?" Rance asked. He backed up prepared to defend himself.

"It's okay. He's with me." Chief Davis stepped out of Mr. Gaines's office across the administration lobby from the CEO's. "He called to tell me he'd hurt Miss Langford and asked me to meet him here."

"I needed to pick up some of my personal things and leave this." Courtland held a long white envelope marked *To Evelyn Langford. Personal and Confidential*. "Would you please see that she gets this?" He passed the envelope to Rance. "And tell her how sorry I am. I know the word doesn't begin to cover what happened earlier. I never intended to hurt her. It was an accident. I hope she can find it in her heart to forgive me."

"She's in the Emergency Room now. I'll make sure she gets your letter when they're finished treating her."

"The E.R.? Because of me. How could I hurt her? I

love her." Court covered his face with his hands.

"Come with me, Mr. Gaines." Chief Davis steered him toward the door.

"Chief, Miss Langford doesn't want to press charges. It was a misunderstanding and it resulted in an accidental injury," Rance said knowing Evie wasn't going to reconsider charges.

Chief Davis said, "Then you are free to go, Mr. Gaines. You may want to consider leaving town before the lady changes her mind."

"Thank you, Chief. Mr. Thompson, please thank Miss Langford and tell her I intend to take the chief's advice." Courtland Gaines left administration with a small box of personal items in his hands.

Rance returned to the E.R. and handed the blouse to the nurse at the desk. He paced the small, crowded waiting room with its scarred end tables and uncomfortable Naugahyde-covered metal frame chairs. He wanted to be in the examination room with Evie, if for nothing but moral support; except he had no standing suitable for being in the room with her. Especially not in *her* facility. Good friends didn't count in a case like this. Not even special friends who wanted to be more. Someday. Now was not the time to make public romantic overtures.

About an hour later, a nurse came to escort him to Miss Langford's exam room. Evie was sitting on the padded table in the new blouse, her old one in a plastic bag at her side. She was milk-white and her eyes showed no twinkle, only pain-dulled flatness induced by medication. Someone had brushed her hair and pulled it into a ponytail. She smiled weakly when he came into the room. The doctor was still there.

"Good as new?" Rance asked.

"Not quite," Dr. Merrick replied. "But her shoulder is back in place. I had to sedate her to get the reduction done. She can't drive and she shouldn't try to do much of anything for the next couple of days."

"Shouldn't or can't? There's a big difference with this patient," Rance clarified.

"I understand. Let's say it would be best for someone to wait on her hand and foot at least until Monday." Dr. Merrick turned to his patient. "You heard me. Right, Miss Langford?"

No response.

The doctor stepped in front of her. "Did you understand my instructions, Evelyn?"

"Yes. Yes. How long do I have to keep this arm in a sling?"

"Three to four weeks. You'll need to ice down your shoulder for twenty minutes every four hours for the first twenty-four hours. A prescription for a muscle relaxer for today and tomorrow has been called into your pharmacy. It's the same medication as the injection I just gave you. Take it every four hours until you go to bed, whether you think the pain is 'bad enough' or not. I know you don't like being groggy, but you need to rest after the trauma you've experienced, and we need to stay ahead of the pain, or we won't be able to control it. By Monday, the pain should subside enough to have the extra strength ibuprofen alone do the job. You have a large bump on the back of your head, but it doesn't appear to have caused a concussion."

"I didn't realize I'd hit my head too. Thanks, Chase. I'm glad you were the doctor on duty. Special

Agent Thompson, I guess it's time for your babysitting duties to begin." Evie held on to Rance's shoulder as she slid off the table into a standing position.

"My pleasure." He stabilized her with an arm around her waist and they walked to the car.

Evie gave him directions to the pharmacy. He whipped into the drive-thru lane. She gave him the necessary birth date and other information to pick up the medication.

Rance glanced at his passenger. Her head lolled back against the headrest and little snuffling sounds emanated from her. She had fallen asleep almost as soon as he pulled out of the pharmacy drive-thru lane. She was pretty loaded with sleep-inducing medications.

She was beautiful. Thank God he got to her before something worse happened. He wasn't totally convinced that Courtland Gaines was harmless or that her injury was an accident.

Evie stirred as Rance pulled in the garage. "We're home?"

"We are. Stay where you are. Give me your purse. I'll go unlock the house and come back for you.

Using her good arm, she heaved her purse up from the car floor. He rummaged through the bottom of it until he heard metal on metal. House keys. He opened the kitchen door. No need to disable the alarm because he hadn't set it on the way out. Gonzo ran into the garage barking. Rance went around to the passenger side. Gently, he picked up her legs at the knee and pivoted her around. "Okay. Grab my shoulder with your good arm and on three we'll get you standing. One…Two…Three."

She grimaced as she pulled herself into a full

standing position. Then she was toe-to-toe with Rance. He laughed and kissed her cheek. "Some girls will do anything just to be near me."

"Don't quit your day job yet, Special Agent Thompson." She cuffed him playfully.

"I'd say the pain meds are kicking in." He smiled broadly.

Side by side, they waddled into the kitchen. Rance deposited Evie in a chair in the kitchen while he went outside to close the car doors and run the garage door down. Gonzo sat at her side whimpering. He rubbed against her leg.

"Okay. Where do you want to hold court? The living room or your bedroom?"

"Poor choice of words. It's going to have to be the living room. I'm too exhausted to get to the bedroom and I'm afraid we'd both get hurt if you tried to haul me upstairs. But, before we go anywhere, let's talk about Court. I'm still having trouble believing what happened. I keep walking through it in my head. Do I need to reconsider pressing charges?"

Rance pulled the envelope from his shirt pocket. "Chief Davis already knows you were hurt. Courtland Gaines was in Administration when I went to get your blouse. With the chief. He asked me to give you this."

She opened the envelope. It was a handwritten resignation letter. At the bottom he apologized for causing the accident and said he'd loved her since the first minute he saw her. He said she'd never see him again because he was leaving Lansdale immediately. Probably going out of the country.

Tears streamed down Evie's face.

"I thought you'd be happy he did the right thing."

"These are happy tears and relieved ones. Did you tell the chief and Court that I didn't plan to press charges? I feel so bad about our misunderstanding."

"I did tell them there were no charges. Since he's leaving town, it's all over. You have absolutely nothing to feel bad about. You are in no way responsible for Courtland Gaines's misplaced obsession with you. Neither am I. It's all on him and only him." Rance knelt down next to her. "I'm just glad I was here to intervene."

"I'm exhausted. Could we move into the living room now?"

Rance helped Evie to her feet. They picked their way through the house and into the living room. She sat down with a sigh. She slipped her shoes off. The sigh became a sob. Soon she was shaking. Non-stop tears flowed down her cheeks. The little dog jumped into her lap and licked the falling teardrops.

"I'm sorry. I can't seem to stop."

"You're in shock. I think you're having a natural response. You've been injured. You're heavily medicated, and I'm willing to bet you didn't eat much breakfast."

"You'd win that bet. Oh no, the chicken salad will be ruined."

"No, it won't. I stuck it in the fridge before we left for the E.R. Is that what you want to eat for lunch?"

"It wasn't finished. Help me to the kitchen and I'll finish making it. I'll need help chopping celery." She slipped her shoes back on.

"I am a bachelor dad. Don't you think I can whip up some chicken salad sandwiches? You can ice down the shoulder while I cook. You stay here. Doctor's orders. Remember?" Rance scurried into the kitchen. He returned with the ice wrap out of the freezer and put it on the hurt shoulder. Gonzo settled next to her on the sofa and worked his way under her hand to be petted.

Evie heard chopping, mixing, and muttering coming from the kitchen. A couple of "where is…oh never minds," cabinets opening and closing, and finally, "that's pretty good if I do say so myself."

Rance came into the living room and set two TV trays side by side in front of the sofa. "Luncheon is served, madam." He made a formal bow from the waist, then returned to the kitchen. He brought sandwiches and chips on plates and two tall frosty glasses of lemonade into the living room and deposited them on the trays.

His patient nibbled a corner off her sandwich. "You weren't kidding when you said you could cook. Does this chicken salad have paprika in it?"

"You have excellent taste buds. And a teensy, tiny splash of hot sauce. Do you approve?" He remained standing.

"One hundred percent. Please sit down and join me." She patted the sofa next to Gonzo.

They ate in silence. It was as if talking would take too much energy. Eat or talk. They couldn't do both. Being so hungry meant the food won.

After lunch Rance gave her the first of her every four hour medications. He retrieved the pillow off her bed and sheets and blankets to cover her. Evie took off her shoes and lay on her "good" side.

Rance checked on his patient after he loaded the dishwasher. Sound asleep. Good. Dr. Merrick said she needed to sleep. This was an opportunity for him to get online and do some more research on the missing girls.

Chapter Twenty-Six

Two hours later, Evie woke up. She stretched and then struggled into a sitting position. She looked around, then stood teetering on wobbly legs. Hadn't Rance been here when she went to sleep?

She cautiously wandered into the kitchen. There he was at the kitchen table. His laptop was open in front of him and there was a pile of notes next to him.

"Having any luck?"

"Hello, sleepyhead. I didn't hear you stirring." Rance flashed one of his "glad to see you" smiles at her. "Tons of luck. I've been running files through facial recognition. Rosalie's friend, Sarah Kelley is definitely using the name of Sally Kaiser. That's the same name her blood tests had been under earlier. She was seen recently. The nurse practitioner treated her strep throat and noted she was eight months pregnant."

"That's great." She sat down at the end of the table.

"And Sonia Gables was seen last year at this time in the urgent care clinic requiring stitches in her arm. The report said she cut it while hiking. She was treated under the name Sofia Gates. That's the same name from her earlier blood test too. At least they're only using one alias. No mention of pregnancy in the medical records."

"Great detective work. The pieces seem to be falling into place."

"They are. There is one thing that's bugging me. If the runaway girls have been seen at Garland Regional, how is it they never asked for help while they were there? Especially the Addams and Russell girls who came into the Emergency Room and were inpatients?"

"I can answer that. They are never alone as outpatients. A staff member from The Center stays with them the entire time. They are never able to talk privately with anyone at Garland."

"What about the girls who came into the E.R.?"

"Shortly after they arrived unconscious by ambulance, The Center sent sitters to be with them around the clock. I thought at the time The Center staff was showing genuine concern about them. Now I realize it was to make certain that once they regained consciousness they wouldn't have an opportunity to ask for help. They covered their bases very well."

Rance shuffled through his notes. "Oh, and the Campbells contacted the Dallas office again. They asked The Center for their babies' birth records. The Center will have to be more forthcoming to the two-time parents."

"We're so lucky you have a good memory for faces to link them to both the Richardson children. Lila's grandmother, Mrs. Masterson, is totally in love with her great grandson. I'm so glad we found her."

"Another piece of the puzzle. But we haven't tied Lila to the Center yet, have we?" He referred to his notes.

"No. But I have a gut feeling we will. Frank tried to see Lila the day before she died. Since he wasn't listed as her physician, he didn't get in to her, but I thought it was strange after he had vehemently denied she'd had anything to do with The Center." She rubbed her neck and grimaced.

"It's not time for more meds yet. Are you hurting?" Rance turned off his laptop and closed the cover.

"Just a little stiff. Could be sleeping on the sofa or my earlier adventure—probably a combination of both."

A cell phone chimed.

"Yours or mine?" Rance asked.

"Yours."

"Special Agent Thompson…Kyle, is everything okay?…I'll call and tell them to give you a key to mine…in the morning we can all do brunch…call me in the morning…love you…see you tomorrow."

"Where is your son?"

"On the way here. Just a minute." Rance called the motel. "Okay, he's all set. I'll see him in the morning."

"Why won't you be there to let him in tonight?" Evie raised her eyebrows.

"Because I'll be here. Sleeping on the other sofa nearby. I can't have you getting up in the night alone and falling. I have nursing responsibilities. Besides, there are meds to give and ice packs to apply. You can't do all those things on your own. And Gonzo is in no position to help." He grinned at her.

"Thanks for taking your responsibilities so seriously. Now what happens? Do you still have work to do?"

"I always have work to do when I'm out in the field, but it will keep until the next time my patient falls asleep. Are you hungry? Thirsty?"

"A little thirsty and, hard to believe since I just woke up, but a little tired." He poured her a glass of cold water and carried it while he helped her back into the living room.

"What about an old movie? Or two?" she asked.

"Sounds great. What do you want to see?"

"You pick." She pointed to the closet next to the television. "I'm still old school. Physical stuff, no streaming services.

The closet was filled with floor to ceiling shelves lined with video tapes and DVDs. Old TV shows. Movies. All alphabetically arranged. He spent a few minutes perusing the selection.

He pulled a DVD off the shelf. "What about this? I haven't had an Ingrid fix in a while. Love her sultry voice. And those 'kiss me' eyes. And especially that hat."

"Perfect. Do we need some popcorn too?"

"Absolutely. Do you have some microwave kind?"

"Third shelf from the bottom. Left hand side in the pantry."

In a few minutes, the smell of popcorn wafted into the living room. Rance came in with a large bowl of buttery kernels. Then disappeared momentarily and returned with two glasses of ice and two soda pops.

"Keep this up and I won't ever let you go home." She smiled broadly.

He set their movie-watching feast on the coffee table and popped the DVD in. Soon, they were sitting in a café listening to Sam play the piano.

During a musical number in the café, Rance leaned over and kissed her cheek. "What could be better than a Saturday night movie date with my best girl?"

"And Bogie."

"And Ilsa."

At the end of the movie, Evie's tears returned.

"Hey, from the way you said the lines along with Ilsa, I was certain this wasn't the first time you'd seen the movie. You must have known how it was going to end."

She smiled and brushed the tears from her cheeks. "I have seen it dozens of times. I cry every time. Even when I'm alone. What can I say? I'm a sucker for lost causes and love stories."

"Nurse Thompson says it's time for some meds and the ice wrap. Then we can decide what to watch next." He popped off the sofa and went to the kitchen. He was back minutes later with the ice wrap fresh from the freezer, pain medications, and a small water to wash them down.

The landline rang. After he got his patient situated, Rance answered the phone.

"Who is this? Where's my sister?" Frank snarled.

"Rance Thompson. She's right here." He put his hand over the mouthpiece. "Do you want to talk to Frank?" She shook her head.

"Put her on."

"She can't come to the phone right now. Would you like to leave a message?"

"No. I want to talk to her," Frank insisted.

"I told you she isn't available. Is there anything else?"

Dial tone.

"Guess he didn't want to leave a message. How is my patient feeling?" He sat down on the sofa and adjusted the ice wrap on her shoulder.

"Better. But, I'm so tired. I hate to fizzle out on you. It's been a long time since I've had a Saturday night date. I need a little nap. Can I take a rain check for the second movie?"

Evie's cell phone rang.

"That's Frank's ring tone. I might as well take it or we'll get no peace the rest of the evening." She answered, "Hi Frank...yes, I'm recovering...no, Rance Thompson is helping me...I know you're a doctor. I don't need another doctor...I don't think it's any of your business...I don't know...I'm too tired to talk about that right now...check with me when I'm back in the office on Monday...I'm hanging up now..." She pressed End Call.

"Sounds like he's worried about you," Rance said.

"Not really. More like he thinks my strength is down so he can bully me about your investigation. He wants to know when you'll be finished. I can't deal with him tonight." She handed her phone to Rance. "Would you mind keeping this? I can't turn it off completely in case the hospital calls."

He put the phone in his shirt pocket. "You bet. Lie down. I'll unplug the extension in here. If you need anything, ring this bell. I found it on the coffee table."

She laughed. "It's the one I had for Mama to use. You can hear it all over the house. There are more pillows and sheets in the linen closet at the top of the stairs. For your bed."

"I'll be in the kitchen for awhile. When you're ready for the second feature just ring. I'm game."

He turned off the living room lights and went back to the kitchen. Gonzo followed close behind Rance and lay under the table at his feet.

Chapter Twenty-Seven

Rance checked on his patient every thirty minutes. She was sleeping soundly. About eleven thirty he helped her into the bathroom to brush her teeth and prepare for bed. He'd gotten her nightgown off the bed upstairs. He helped her remove the sling, got her out of her blouse, and unfastened her bra, then draped the gown around her neck. The blouse and bra were removed under the gown, and she carefully worked her arms into the sleeves. Then it was time for more medication.

Gonzo went and sat at the bottom of the stairs waiting to go upstairs to bed. When his mistress lay down on the sofa instead, he went to her side and whimpered.

"Rance, he's used to sleeping with me but there isn't really room for both of us here. Would you mind bringing in his bed from the kitchen and put it beside the sofa? Then I can reach out and pet him if he gets anxious."

"He sleeps with you? Good to know. Talk about a spoiled little critter," Rance teased, but did as she requested. He put the dog's bed close to Evie. Gonzo jumped into it, circled three times, cocked his head, and barked twice at Rance as if to dismiss him. "Definitely spoiled rotten," he muttered.

He covered Evie with a sheet and blanket, and she

quickly fell asleep again with her good arm hanging over the edge of the sofa so the little dog could snuggle against it. He returned to the kitchen, grabbed a tall glass of ice water, and turned on the laptop. He sat down at the kitchen table and started back into his searches where he'd left off earlier.

At two in the morning, his bleary eyes couldn't look at one more screen of information. He grabbed a flashlight and turned out the kitchen light. He heard something in the back yard. When he shined the light out the kitchen window, he spied a man letting himself out the backyard gate.

Rance hurried to the front door and cracked it enough to see Frank Langford getting in a car at the curb. What was he doing skulking around in Evie's backyard? He knew his sister wasn't alone. They hadn't taken any pains to hide the rental car. It was parked in front of the house. Was he planning to break in to look for the FBI files on him? Just to be safe, Rance went back in the kitchen and packed up his notes and laptop and brought the briefcase into the living room. He'd sleep with it under the sofa he lay down on.

****

"Good morning, sleepyhead. It's already eight o'clock. I thought you'd never wake up."

Rance slowly opened one eye. Sitting on the coffee table in front of his "bed" was his patient—all smiles. "Good morning. Guess yesterday took a lot out of me too. It took me a while longer than usual to fall asleep because someone—the only fur covered creature in the room—snored all night long."

Evie laughed. "I'm so used to Gonzo's night sounds that I can hardly fall asleep without them."

"Good to know. You look much improved this morning. Do I smell coffee?"

She tousled his hair. "You do indeed. I could reach everything I needed to brew a pot, so I decided to surprise my nurse."

"Your nurse is surprised and very pleased." He pulled himself into a sitting position. "Hope you don't mind—I took one of your spare toothbrushes last night. And I found a comb still in plastic wrap."

"That's what they're there for. Come on into the kitchen." Barefoot and still in her nightgown, Evie led the way. "Black, right?" She took two mugs off the hooks under the cabinet, filled them both, and handed Rance one.

The sun streamed in the windows and onto the kitchen table. "This is a very cheery kitchen. First time I've seen it in the morning." Rance sipped his coffee and looked out at the yard. "Is that an apple tree?"

"Yes. Yellow delicious. If I can beat the squirrels to them, they're usually juicy and tasty. Mama always liked to have her morning coffee in here. She said it gave her a happy start to the day. I was a little surprised it was all cleared off this morning. When I went to bed it was completely covered with your work."

"It was necessary." He hesitated. "Your brother was in the backyard at two o'clock this morning. I believe he was planning to try to get in, possibly to take some of my files. So I packed them in my briefcase and slept with them under my sofa."

"I wish I could say I was shocked. I'm not. There is a reason Frank's so edgy about the investigation. I wouldn't put anything past him." She shook her head. "He hasn't always been this way. He was a great big brother when we were children. He defended me more than once. There wasn't any pair of siblings tied together more closely than we were. Then we lost Dad. I think opening The Center really taxed Frank— financially and mentally. It was a lot of added stress, and he began to show it."

Rance's cell phone played a guitar riff. He smiled.

"Good morning, son of mine. Did you sleep well...I need to come to the motel to get cleaned up...We have ten thirty reservations...I need to check with Miss Langford...I'll call you right back."

He ended the call. "Do you need my help to get dressed for brunch? Obviously, I can't go like this, so I'll take a quick shower and get dressed at the motel."

"I'm not going. This is a father-son outing. Not father-son-stranger outing."

"You're not a stranger. Kyle has danced with you."

"Okay. He's met me. This is a family bonding moment. Probably to let you know how the proposal went. And I don't think I have the energy to shower, change, dine out, and be decent company. I'd like to stay in my nightgown and robe and relax today. I want to be well enough to go to work tomorrow. If you would get the novel off my bedside table, I'll have everything I need until you return."

"But..."

"Please. Humor me. Let me have a free day to recuperate. I so rarely have a 'do nothing' day."

"You are a very stubborn patient, but I'll grant your wish with one big if. You lock the door and don't let anyone in. I'll use the spare key to let myself out and back in."

"Courtland Gaines is out of town. What are you

worried about?"

"Your brother. Especially after he was skulking around in your yard last night."

"I think I'm safe, but I agree to the terms of my parole." She batted her eyes.

"You are one spoiled rotten, but absolutely beautiful woman." He leaned down and kissed her forehead. "I'll be back in a minute with your book, your medicine, the ice wrap, and another cup of coffee for you."

When he got Evie situated, he kissed her again. At the front door, he turned and said, "Remember. No one comes in. No one. Not for any reason."

Chapter Twenty-Eight

Rance drove straight to the motel. Kyle embraced him in a bear hug when he walked in the room. He hadn't realized how much he'd missed the kid even though it had only been a week. He quickly showered and changed clothes. They walked into Shangri-La at ten thirty on the dot. They made the first pass of the buffet table and sat to talk over their full plates.

"I assume she said yes. Did you and Jamie pick a date yet?" Rance asked.

"She did. We are very close to deciding the when. Since we're planning a relatively small affair, we'd like to get it done this summer before Jamie goes back to teaching. Then we can have a more leisurely honeymoon. Talking about the ceremony is what brought me back to see you so soon."

"I wondered why I got to have Sunday brunch with you on back-to-back weeks. Not that I am not always happy to see you."

"Jamie would like to get married in her family's church by the pastor who has known her all of her life. When we met with him, he asked about my family. Questions like whether my parents had used a special verse of scripture at their wedding, my mom's favorite Bible passages, things like that."

"Sorry, if it made you uncomfortable."

"My discomfort didn't last too long. Pastor Kessel

is a sensitive, kind man. But the questions prodded my memory. I remembered I have the Nichols family Bible, the one Mom kept on her bedside. Grandpa Nichols gave it to me along with a stack of photo albums when I came to live with you. I'm a little embarrassed to say I haven't opened it since I got it. I had to dig around in my closet a while before I unearthed it. I thought if Mom had a favorite verse or chapters, she might have made some notes in the Bible or on papers stuck in it."

"Good thinking. We were both active in the church youth group in our area when we were in high school. I never asked, did you go to Sunday School before you came to my house?"

"I did. But once we got together, it seemed there were so many other things to do on Sunday morning. We had so much time to make up for that I never really missed going to church and Sunday School. Don't feel bad that we didn't. I think we were doing the right thing investing so much time in each other to strengthen our new family ties," Kyle said.

"Thanks for the pass. Sounds like Jamie will get you into a new Sunday habit."

"I didn't come just to tell you about the ceremony. I could have done that over the phone. Dad, this is what I found in Mom's Bible tucked into the section of 1 Corinthian's Chapter 13, where it defines what love is." Kyle reached into his jacket pocket and passed a large, yellowed envelope to his father. It was not sealed. The flap was tucked into the back, as if it had been opened and closed frequently. The front said, "To be given to the love of my life, Rance Thompson, upon my death".

Rance's hands trembled when he took the letter from his son. "It's her writing. I'd know it anywhere.

Have you already read it?"

"Of course not. It's addressed to you. That's why I had to see you in person. Dad, I'm sorry I hadn't looked in the Bible sooner. You've had to wait ten years longer than you should have to get her letter."

"Thank you for making the extra effort to get it to me now." He tucked the thick envelope into his jacket pocket. "I think we should eat before our hot food gets cold and the chilled food gets warm. I'm going to have to think about this before I open it and I'm sure I'm not able to read it without having a bawling fit, so I'd rather not be in a public place when I look at it."

"Good idea. I totally understand."

Throughout the meal Kyle shared the details of the planned wedding ceremony. The reception would be in the Colbys' backyard. They had a pool and beautiful flagstone patio around it. Mrs. Colby looked forward to pulling out all the stops for the party celebrating the marriage of her only child. Rance was having trouble concentrating on all the details. His mind was on the envelope burning hot against his chest.

"Dad…what do you think?"

"I'm sorry, Kyle. I didn't hear what you asked me. I'm having a little trouble keeping my mind on our conversation."

Kyle laughed. "Guess I should have started with the other reason I needed to see you and left the envelope until the end of the meal."

"What was the other reason?"

"Dad, I'd like you to be my best man."

Tears welled up in Rance's eyes. "Oh, my son. I would be positively honored. Are you sure you don't want one of your good friends to be at your side for this once in a lifetime event?"

"I'm certain, Dad. You are the best friend I have. I can't take this major step without you next to me."

"I will be there! How did I get so lucky to have such a fine man as my son?" Rance brushed away the tear escaping down his cheek. "Today, the check is mine. You've got a honeymoon to save for."

"No arguments here!"

****

What was that sound? Evie rubbed her eyes and slowly sat up. The book was on the floor. How long had she been asleep? There was that noise again. She slowly turned and looked at the window behind the sofa. Frank's face was plastered against the windowpane. He pounded on the glass and waved wildly. She couldn't understand what he was screaming. She pointed to the front door. She would have to talk with him before the neighbors called the cops. Frank left the window.

She carefully made her way to the front door, put the chain lock on, and opened it a crack. "What do you want?"

"Open the damn door." He pounded his fist on the door. Gonzo ran into the front hall barking all the way. Evie shushed him.

"Tell me why you're here."

"We need to talk, and I don't feel like airing my personal business in front of all your nosy neighbors."

"Apparently, that wasn't a concern when you were standing at the living room window raving like a lunatic moments ago," she muttered. "I'm not sure you're calm enough for me to feel safe letting you in."

Frank jammed his foot in the narrow opening. "Open the damn door, Evie. This is not funny. Let me in." Gonzo grabbed his pant leg and pulled on it growling loudly. Frank kicked at him. The dog didn't let go.

She didn't move. His hand shot through the door and grabbed her sling. New pain rocketed through her shoulder. He jerked her again. Tears ran down her cheek. She wouldn't give him the satisfaction of crying out.

"If you want me to stop hurting you, then let me in. Now!" Frank insisted.

"I don't believe she will." A hand gripped Frank's shoulder and jerked him away from the door. "What do you want?"

Frank stepped toward Rance until they were toe-to-toe, his index finger poking the agent's chest. "This is none of your business, Mr. FBI Special Agent. This is a family matter, and you are not family. Evie, open the door."

"No. Tell me what you want from there," Evie said.

"This doesn't concern him. Let me in." Frank glared at Rance.

The flashing lights of an approaching silent patrol car distracted Frank. It pulled up in front of the house. The officers got out of the car and walked onto the porch. The lights continued to flash.

"You stupid b—" Frank snarled.

"Gentlemen, we got a call from one of the neighbors about a disturbance at Miss Langford's. Can one of you tell me what the problem is?" the officer asked.

"There's no problem. I believe this *gentleman* was just leaving." Rance pointed to Frank.

"No, I was not. The problem is my sister refuses to let me in my house to speak with her. This man has no reason to be here. This is a discussion between siblings," Frank explained.

Evie pulled Gonzo away from the door, closed it long enough to release the chain lock, then reopened it. "Officers, thank you for coming. This is not my brother's house. It is mine. The last time I checked, that means I have the right to turn away anyone I don't want to see, and I definitely do not want to see or talk with him." She pointed at her brother.

"Don't be ridiculous. We're family. You have to talk with me," Frank demanded loudly.

"No, I don't. Make an appointment to see me in the office if there is something important we need to discuss."

"Well, if I have to leave, so does he." Frank pulled Rance's arm.

"Rance, please come in." Evie opened the door wider and stood to one side.

Frank charged at the door. "You can't do that." One of the officers grabbed him before he cleared the doorway.

"Look, buddy. Do we need to go to the station? Or will you leave peaceably?"

"If he'll leave and promise not to come back, I won't press any charges," Evie tried to diffuse the situation.

"I'm leaving, but we're not through by a long stretch, darling sister of mine. You won't have FBI protection forever." Frank wheeled around, pushed between the two officers, and got in his car.

"Ma'am, you might want to talk to your attorney

about a restraining order. Sometimes that is enough to make a bully change his mind," the taller officer recommended.

The policemen nodded and left.

Rance stepped into the house and closed the door. Evie fell into his arms.

"I was actually scared of him. What am I going to do?" she sobbed.

"Frank needs to be locked away."

"You're probably right."

"Are you okay? It looked like he was pulling hard on your sling."

"I could use some ibuprofen and the ice pack. It is hurting."

Rance went into the kitchen and returned with the medicine, the ice wrap, and a small glass of water. Evie took the ibuprofen and helped Rance get the wrap in place.

"How was brunch with Kyle? Where is he?"

"On the way home. She said yes so there is going to be a wedding. I'll fill you in," Rance replied.

"How exciting to be doing wedding planning. You're going to be a father-in-law. How does it feel?" Evie hugged Rance.

"I don't know. I'm barely used to being a dad. Jamie's a sweet girl. Kyle has been a one-woman man since their first date. It's been kind of fun to watch. He's a lot like his mom. Jumps into things with both feet and knows what he wants," Rance said.

"You don't think he got some of that from you?" Evie asked.

"I don't think I was ever as confident as he is at twenty. I've always envied him the easy way he tackles the things he wants."

"Maybe that's because he believes he will be successful. It's the mark of knowing you're loved. You've done a wonderful job with him."

"He had a good head start before he ever met me. I'm just glad I didn't screw it up."

"How could you mess up being a father when you both love each other so much?"

"I didn't appreciate how much he loved me until today. Evie, Kyle asked me to be his best man." Tears welled up in Rance's eyes again.

She threw her good arm around him. "You said yes, didn't you?"

"I did. I never expected that in a million years. And there's more. Look what he found in Mandy's Bible." He pulled the yellowed envelope from his jacket pocket and handed it to her.

"From Mandy?"

"Yes."

"It looks like you opened it? What did it say?"

"No. I didn't open it. She had never sealed it. I'm working up the nerve to read it. It's so fat. It looks like she wrote a novella to me."

"I'm sure there was a lot she wanted you to know. Maybe now you'll find out why she didn't tell you about Kyle earlier."

"Maybe. I'm not quite ready to open it. Are you getting hungry? I ate so much at lunch, I shouldn't be, but I am."

"I am too. I think there is some left over beef stew in the freezer, and I have biscuits we can bake to go with it. You know where the salad stuff is," Evie replied.

"You stay right where you are. Is the ibuprofen kicking in?"

"Surprisingly, after Frank's manhandling, it seems to be enough. I think I can wait until bedtime for the final dose of the good stuff."

"I'll go to explore the frozen tundra of the freezer. Make yourself comfortable. It may be a few minutes to get everything thawed and ready."

Rance called Evie into the kitchen when supper was on the table. "Are you okay with sitting in here or should I move it to the TV trays?"

"This is fine. I need to move around a little or I will be too exhausted to make it all day at work tomorrow."

"Whether you're exhausted or not, I'm not sure you should plan on a full day tomorrow. You've been through a lot of trauma the past two days. Your job is no picnic. Why don't you see how you're feeling in the morning before you commit to a full day in the office?"

"I hate to say it, but you're probably right. Thanks for making supper. You're pretty handy to have around. I won't know how to act when you're gone."

"We'll cross that bridge after we solve this case. Or I should say cases? I'm planning to stay here tonight to monitor you and to make sure your crazy brother doesn't put in a repeat appearance this evening. I'm not sure the officers' warning was sufficiently frightening to keep him at bay."

"I don't think it's necessary for you to continue babysitting, but I'm a little relieved you want to. I've never seen Frank like he was this afternoon and after Court's unexpected appearance yesterday, I'm a little jumpy."

"Let's talk about more pleasant things. Are you up

for the other movie tonight?"

"Great idea. Tonight, what about a western?"

Rance tipped his imaginary cowboy hat. "It'd be my pleasure, ma'am."

He selected a classic Duke movie. They snuggled together on the sofa and enjoyed the Western. By the end of the movie Evie was fading.

"I thought I might be able to do two, but I think I better get some sleep if I have any hope of going into work tomorrow. I'm glad I didn't bother to get dressed today. I don't have the energy to be wrestling into my nightgown before bed."

"I want to wrap up some things before I call it a night."

When Rance finished his work, two sets of snores were echoing through the living room. He was tired enough, they didn't bother him at all.

Chapter Twenty-Nine

Rance poured them both another cup of coffee. "Are you certain you should try to work today?"

Evie grinned with all her teeth showing. "You know the answer to your silly question. I'm going to hurt whether I am sitting in my living room or in my office. I wouldn't be able to rest here knowing issues were needing my attention at work."

"Okay, your stubbornness. Shower upstairs or down?"

"I think it needs to be upstairs because my clothes are upstairs. You're welcome to use the first-floor shower. I saw you brought a bag back from the motel with you yesterday."

Rance helped Evie slowly navigate the stairs to her bedroom. "Do you need any help to get in the shower?"

"No. I'm just glad we got an early start on all of this."

"Okay. I'm going down to get my shower and get ready for the day."

Evie wiggled loose of the sling, then peeled out of her nightgown, and left it in a heap on the cedar chest at the foot of her bed. Into the shower. Thank goodness it was a low entry walk-in so she didn't have to use her bad arm for balance. She acrobatically washed her waist length hair one-handed, then stood with the hot pulsating spray beating down on her sore shoulder until it changed to tepid. Hopefully, Rance had enough hot water for his shower.

Drying her hair required nearly as much Houdini-like dexterity as washing it had. Finally, her hair and body were dry enough to get dressed. She selected a pantsuit so there would be no need to wrestle herself into a pair of pantyhose. She was certain that would be an impossible task one-handed. A hook-in-the-front bra and a button-up-the-front blouse. Those were hard enough to get on. Flat shoes.

What could she do with her hair? She was going to need help. She carefully made her way down the stairs and into the kitchen where Rance was dressed and ready to go.

"I need help." She held out a hairbrush, elastic, and ribbon that matched the green of her pantsuit. "Could you brush my hair into a ponytail at the base of my neck and put this ribbon on it? I never wear my hair down at the Medical Center but today it will have to be that way."

"Sure. I don't have much practice with long hair, but I think I can make you presentable."

After ten minutes of Rance corralling her tresses, she looked in the mirror and pronounced it, "Good enough for today."

"I'll take you into the office and get you situated before I start my work."

"Have you heard back yet about a warrant?"

"No. I'm expecting to hear today and confirming Sonia and Sarah's aliases will definitely help incline the judge toward granting my request."

****

Rance helped Miss Langford into her office.

Margie had been watching for her. News had spread through the hospital staff that the CEO had been injured Saturday. And that they were looking for a new CFO.

"The Chairman of the Board called first thing this morning. He told me to look at your calendar and schedule a special meeting to talk about Mr. Gaines's replacement. The soonest everyone could do it was next Tuesday at noon—same day as the regular meeting—so it will be the primary agenda item," Margie reported. "He'd like you to call him this morning."

"Thank you. Efficient as usual." Miss Langford looked at the files laid out on her desk, preparation documents for her day's meetings. "Looks like now is the best time to call the chairman." She turned to her temporary chauffeur. "Thanks for the lift. Can we plan a late lunch to catch each other up on events? I have an hour at one thirty."

"Yes, ma'am." Rance waved and left the room.

"Chairman Jungers is on line two."

"Thank you, Margie…hello, Mr. Jungers…"

****

At one thirty, there was a knock on the door between the conference room and the CEO's office. Evelyn opened the door and saw lunch for two set up on the conference room table.

"Wonderful. Mac's cheeseburgers are one of my favorite guilty pleasures," she said with a smile.

"People have been talking about them since I arrived, but I hadn't had one yet. Mac knew exactly how to dress Miss Langford's, so it seemed like the ideal lunch," Rance said.

A cell phone chimed.

"Mine." Rance reached into his pocket. "Hello,

Fran. What a nice surprise…Yes…I know the place…six o'clock…back booth in the bar…I'll see you there."

Evie's eyebrows shot up. "Another date with the beguiling Mrs. Rafferty?"

"Well, when you've got such animal magnetism…" He winked. "She said she has important information for me. About Rosalie's children. Too good an opportunity to pass up."

"I agree. Maybe Frank's insanity is bothering her conscience. I have a Personnel committee dinner meeting tonight, so you and Mrs. Rafferty can take your time."

"Okay…how are you going to get home?"

"Margie can drop me. She stays to take minutes in the meeting."

"Are you recovered sufficiently to stay alone tonight?"

"Yes. I believe I am. Just how late are you planning on being with Mrs. Rafferty?" Evie waggled her eyebrows at him and laughed.

"On the important news front, we are getting the warrant today for The Center related to records for all the missing girls except Lila Masterson because we haven't succeeded in tying her to The Center yet," Rance reported.

"That's terrific news. I'm sure it will create another wave of angst for my brother. Let's hope we can link the Masterson baby to them soon. Did Tom Peterman have adoptions for Sonia and Sarah's babies once he knew their aliases?"

"He did indeed. And the father of record was Frank Raymond again. Same as the Richardson babies."

"Maybe the records review at The Center will tell us more about this Mr. Raymond."

"We can only hope."

****

Rance Thompson pulled up to the front of The Garland Bar and Grill at five minutes before six. He spotted the red convertible on the far side of the parking lot. So much for being a little early. He walked through the front door of the neighborhood bistro. The bar was on the left and the dining room to the right. He walked through the beads hanging across the entrance to the bar. It took a second for him to see through the smoky haze and dim lighting to find the back booth.

No doubt she was there. Those legs couldn't belong to anyone else. Crossed at the knees. Bright red stiletto heels. No skirt in sight from that angle. The floor to ceiling booth dividers hid the rest of its occupant. He walked over and slid into the seat across from her.

"Special Agent Thompson. Do you always show up precisely on time?" she purred.

"I try to. Working on my promptness merit badge." Why was he flirting with her?

A bottle of merlot and two glasses were sitting on the table. "I decided you looked like a merlot kind of guy. Hope I wasn't too presumptive."

Did she just bat her eyes? "Guess you thought I was a more than one glass guy too."

"I wasn't sure, but I know I'm the kind of girl who can't stop after just one…of anything. Not ever."

Yep, she was definitely flirting with him.

She poured a full glass of wine for each of them and raised her glass. "A toast."

Rance picked up his glass. "To what?"

"To a developing friendship." She smiled, winked, and took a long slow drink of the wine.

Better rein this in.

"I was surprised by your call. You said you had details I needed to know about Rosalie Richardson's babies?"

"First, I need your solemn oath that you will never let Dr. Langford know who gave you this information." She wrapped his hand in hers. "Please. You don't know how he can be when he believes he's been betrayed." Her voice wavered.

Oh yes I do. "I will make every effort to keep your name out of all of this. But, I can't promise you'll never have to testify, if things come to trial." He laid his free hand on top of hers.

"I understand. I can't ask for more." She took a deep breath. Then looked directly into his eyes. She had tears in her own. "Rosalie's second baby wasn't stillborn. The baby lived. And was adopted by the Campbells—the same couple who adopted her first baby. I didn't know for sure until I got a request this week for birth records on both children." She stopped and looked around the bar. "Frank would kill me if he knew I was telling you any of this."

Rance patted her hand. "He won't know. Did you send the records out?" Either this woman was giving a best actress award winning performance or Langford had terrorized her like he had his sister.

"Yes, I did since they were requested by the parents. I wasn't revealing anything that they didn't already know. They can always have access to their children's records."

"Telling me was the right thing to do. There are two other babies I need to track down." He pulled out his notes. "A baby boy born August 10th last year and a girl born August 22nd. They're both on the adoption board. I need the names and contact information for the adoptive parents."

"I don't know. I'm taking a gigantic risk talking to you here now." She shook her head.

"Please, Fran. This is a major break in these cases. There are parents wondering where their daughters are. They've been praying the girls are still alive. They've been missing a long time. Please. You've been brave. I need you to do a little more."

She took a big gulp of wine, then quickly looked around the bar once more. "I guess I'm in for a penny, might as well be in for a pound. Give me the dates again."

He pushed a small piece of paper with the dates written on it across the table. "Thank you. Please call or text me as soon as you get the information on the other two. You have no idea how much I appreciate this."

"I'm sure I will think of some way for you to show your appreciation when this is all over." But there was no smile on her face. She shoved the slip of paper into the side pocket of her purse. "Please wait at least ten minutes after I'm gone before you leave. No sense giving people any more to talk about."

"Are you certain I can't buy you dinner? I mean, Frank has already seen you kissing me." He tried to keep his tone light and teasing, but it fell flat—even to him.

She didn't respond. She picked up the red purse on the seat, poured another glass of wine, and downed it in one gulp, then strolled to the door. Her swinging hips got appreciative leers from a couple of beer drinkers on stools at the bar. A woman who wasn't interested in attracting attention should never leave a room like she just did.

Ten minutes later, Rance paid for the wine without ever finishing a glass of it, then left.

****

Margie dropped Evelyn at the front door and idled at the curb until she was safely inside the house and had turned off the porch light. Evie kicked her shoes off as soon as she got inside. Even being barefoot didn't relieve the throbbing in her legs. It was spooky quiet. She walked through the house turning on lights in every room.

Surely Frank wasn't insane enough to try and see her again so soon after the police warning. She hoped…

Her cell phone rang. She jumped. What a nervous Nellie.

"Hi…just got home…long meeting…Glad it was productive…Sorry, I ate at the meeting… I'm wiped out…Thanks for understanding…I'll see you in the morning…Oh, okay…seven? I'll have coffee ready for my chauffeur…Have sweet dreams."

She walked into the kitchen long enough to release Gonzo from his crate. She gave him some water and he made a quick trip outside. Evie checked all the locks. Twice. Tonight she was going to sleep in her own bed. No matter what it took.

This old house didn't have the broad, gentler sloping staircases of today's construction. She carefully pulled herself up the steep stairs. One step at an exhausting time. Gonzo sat at the bottom of the stairs whimpering.

"Sorry, fella. I have a hard enough time getting myself up these stairs with my arm in this sling. If you're sleeping with me tonight, you'll need to get to the bedroom on your own." The little dog barked sharply twice in disapproval, then slowly climbed the stairs after his mistress.

She sat on the edge of the bed in sheer exhaustion after working her nightgown over her head and through one arm. She missed Rance's assistance. She awkwardly reached down, scooped up the pug in one hand, and put him on his pillow. Remembering how long this morning's shower took, she set the alarm for an hour earlier than normal. A little pain medication to help her sleep and she slid under the covers. To sleep. Out as soon as her head hit the pillow.

****

Was that the doorbell? Or was she dreaming.

Evie struggled to a sitting position on the edge of the bed.

No. It was the landline. She reached over to the phone. The clock flashed 2:33 a.m. Another ring tone as she took the phone receiver off the cradle. The doorbell?

"Hello."

"Why don't you answer the door?" the voice slurred.

"Frank. Are you at my front door? It's the middle of the night."

"Come down and let me in. I've been out here forever."

"You've been drinking and I'm in bed. It took too long for me to get up the stairs for me to come down now. I'm not letting you in. If you keep ringing the doorbell, I'll call the police. This time I will have them take you to the station after I press charges."

"But, Evie, I need your help. You don't understand. I'm in bad trouble. None of this is my fault," the soft voice insisted.

"Go home and sleep it off. Your emergencies are never real. We can talk at the office tomorrow."

"We can't. Someone might tell her. What I have to tell you is confi…confi…secret. It's a really big one. This time I'm telling the truth. I swear I am."

"I'm hanging up. Please go home and go to bed." Evie put the phone back on the cradle.

Someone knocked at the door. The phone rang again.

She answered on the first ring. "Frank. Go home."

"Miss Langford, this is Officer MacPherson. I'm out on patrol and saw a male on your dark front porch. After the recent problems, I wanted to make certain you were okay."

"Thank you for checking. I'm fine."

"When I parked in front of your house a man jumped over the hedges and ran down the street to a car idling at the curb. I didn't pursue him."

"I know who it was. No pursuit is necessary. Thanks."

"Good night, Miss Langford."

Chapter Thirty

"It would almost be funny, if it weren't so creepy." Evie laughed as she poured Rance another cup of coffee. "I can't imagine what the big secret is. He'd definitely been drinking."

Rance told her Fran's news and the mission she was on at his request to find the other adoptive parents. "She seemed genuinely terrified of your brother's temper. Having seen it myself, I'm thinking she has had firsthand experience with Frank in high dudgeon."

"Then why does she keep working with him? She has money of her own. Something about this whole scenario seems a little off to me." Evie shook her head.

"Is it because you're jealous of Fran?" He winked over the coffee cup.

"No. Not in the least. Maybe you don't sense anything amiss because you're so taken with saving a damsel in distress that you're blind to how dangerous the lady is. I think you've misidentified who needs a knight to rescue her. I can't believe Fran Rafferty has ever felt helpless and in the need of saving in her entire life. She knows more about this than she's told even her favorite FBI very special agent."

"We'll see if she comes through with my request. Now, Miss Langford, it's time I delivered you to The Garland Regional Medical Center for another day of toil."

He cleared the table, rinsed the dishes, and loaded the dishwasher while Evie got her work things together.
****

Margie buzzed. "Dr. Langford is here to see you."

"Send him in please." She stood at the table where she and Rance were reviewing files. "Good morning, Frank. It's a nice to see your manners have improved and now you to wait to be announced before bursting into my office."

He hobbled to the middle of the room leaning on a cane with one foot in a boot. "Lot of good it does."

"What happened to you?"

"I sprained my ankle last night. Didn't the cops tell you?"

"They did say a man leapt over the hedges around my front porch. I assumed it was you. Looks like your track and field days are behind you. Now what did you need from me?" Evie had a hard time suppressing a laugh.

"I want to see you in private." He glared at Rance.

"I can wait in the conference room." Rance began to gather his files.

"I want you to stay here. What is so confidential that the FBI can't know? Secrets are their business."

"You are a ninny who's being played for a fool. Do you know where your Special Agent was last night? And who he was with?"

"The Garland Bar and Grill. Drinking merlot with Fran Rafferty in the back booth of the bar, if my memory serves me right."

Frank's jaw dropped. "How? Who? Did you follow him?"

"No. He told me this morning over coffee. Was

there another earth-shattering secret I needed to know?" Evie asked with a smile.

"No. It would just get back to the enemy."

Frank hobbled out of the office and slammed the door.

"Who do you think is the enemy?" Rance asked.

Rance's phone chimed. A text from Fran Rafferty. "That was fast. She just sent the names of the adoptive parents for the babies from last August. I'm sure they're from the girls who came to the Emergency Room with supposedly stillborn babies, Carley Addams and Sybil Russell."

"I have a good feeling about all this," Evie said enthusiastically crossing her fingers.

"I'll call Tom Peterman. We need to contact the parents for releases. I'll be back in touch by the end of the day."

"Would you please tell him I'll need his help on the in-family adoption of the Masterson baby?"

"Sure. Oh, if you're up to it, I'd like to go exploring this evening. Where we intended to go on Saturday before Courtland Gaines foiled our plans."

Evie shook her head. "Hard to believe that was only Saturday. Today's Tuesday. I'll never complain about Lansdale being too quiet again."

****

"Good morning, Miss Langford. Michael weighed four pounds and twelve ounces this morning. Dr. Wetzel said if he continues to make such good progress, we may be able to take him home in the next two weeks. He's breathing well on his own and eating like a full-term baby." Mrs. Masterson's smile spread across her face.

"And the doctor said all the hugging and rocking is helping him want to thrive," Mikayla added.

"That is good news. I'll get you in to see Mr. Peterman soon so all the paperwork will be ready when Michael is released."

"And our room is lovely. You are a wonderful hostess. Mikayla and I both really enjoyed supper last night after Michael went down for the night. You've made this whole situation so much less stressful."

"My pleasure. You know where my office is. Let me know if you need anything else. If I'm not in, my assistant, Mrs. Wright, will be happy to help you. I'll check in later today."

****

Rance picked Evie up in front of the Medical Center at five thirty. They drove over to the Purple Cow for burgers, fries, and milkshakes before going exploring. Eating in the car was a lot more private than any restaurant. Almost as good as eating at Evie's house.

"Tom said he'd be happy to prepare Michael's adoption papers. Do we know who the father was? That could be a sticking point," Rance reported.

"Lila never told anyone. She got pregnant several months after she ran away so her grandmother can't be any help identifying the dad. He won't be the first baby ever with a certificate that says Father Unknown."

"Tom's reaching out to the August adoptive parents to explain the situation and ask if they are willing to talk to the FBI. One family is in Colorado and the other in Alabama."

Evie slurped the last of her milkshake through the straw. Then she laughed. "My mother hated when we did that. She thought it wasn't the least bit polite."

"She was right!" He slurped loudly. "One other interesting fact. The father of both the August babies was listed as Frank Raymond, the same father as the Campbell children. Tom hadn't noticed the father earlier. He'd never met him. Fran Rafferty handled the paperwork and got Mr. Raymond's signature. He's going to check how many adoptions have gone through with the same father."

"One busy guy."

"Or a completely fictional person. We'll see. Are you ready to go exploring?"

"Full speed ahead."

****

The white van turned left in front of them. It drove to the gate, entered a code, and drove down the rutted path. Rance continued on the road that ran parallel to the one the van took. Evie watched for landmarks. There it was. Church Camp Road. She instructed him to turn left.

They drove a quarter of a mile and a sagging metal gate with a string of barbed wire across the top loomed in front of them. With a rusting padlock on it. She dug around in her purse for a few seconds, then got out of the car. In a couple of minutes, the padlock was off and the gate swung open. Rance drove through. Evie closed the gate and hung the open padlock on the barbed wire strand running across the top.

The road couldn't have been used routinely. It was severely rutted and in low lying places it had been washed out more than once. Thick vegetation hid part of the original path. They drove straight ahead until the ruts reappeared. The rooftops of the church camp cabins were visible at the top of the hill, but they couldn't continue any farther. A giant oak tree lay across the road. The tree had been down a long time. The leaves were all gone, and the mud had completely washed off exposing the bare roots. No wonder the road hadn't been used.

Rance put the car in Park close to the downed tree. "We wouldn't want to drive any closer and risk being seen even if the road was open. This should provide cover to anyone looking down the hill. Let's turn off our phones so no ill-timed call or text gives our location away. Ready for a hike?"

"Yep. Got my walking boots on."

The terrain was steep. It alternated between a muddy mire and tangled vines. It hadn't seen a mower or a trimmer in years. At the top of the hill, they ducked behind a lean-to shed within thirty feet of a cabin. Weeds had grown all around the cabin's entrance. Glass was broken out of the windows. A massive branch stuck out of the roof. No one was staying in this building.

Rance took Evie's hand and led her to the edge of the next cabin in the line. It was in similar shape. No signs of activity or life anywhere near. They crept up the hill farther. A white van was parked in front of the cabin directly across from the Fellowship Hall. Lights were on in both the Hall and the cabin. The aroma of hamburgers on a grill wafted across the compound. It was coming from behind the Hall.

They sidled close to the end of the brightly lit cabin. The frosted windows were open several inches so the interior was partially visible. Cross hatched bars covered the exterior of each window. The bunk beds were all neatly made. It looked like only the bottom bunks were being used. No occupants were in sight. They waited.

Ten minutes later, the double doors of the Fellowship Hall swung open and four young girls in various stages of pregnancy marched out—herded along by two middle aged women in jeans and tee shirts—and followed by a large man carrying a rifle across his protruding midsection. The women accompanied the girls inside, then came out and bolted the cabin door behind them. The man with the rifle was posted outside the locked door. Rance crept a little closer to hear.

One of the women patted the man on the back. "Well, Jack, this is our last night. The boss paid us off earlier."

The other woman said, "Nice little nest egg. How much longer are you here?"

"I think only a day or two. You know they don't tell you what's going down too far in advance. It's been good working with you both. Good luck." The man sat down in the chair outside the door.

The women walked to a dark blue SUV parked next to the Fellowship Hall and drove away.

Rance moved back to join Evie who was plastered against the end of the building. They could hear voices from inside. They tried to identify the girls in the room.

"I wonder if Lila made it home?" the strawberry blonde said.

"I still don't know how she managed to get out. They sure have beefed up the security since she left. Do you think that old fart could actually shoot us if we all stormed him at one time?" the ebony-haired girl with wild curls all over her head asked.

"I think he could and would. Count me out," the long-haired blonde said.

"Why does it matter how you die? I'm sure Rosalie is gone, and she wasn't shot. We have not heard a word about her since she had the baby. If she was still alive, she'd be back here with us waiting her next turn," the brunette said quietly.

Their backs were to the window. Rance wanted to see the faces that went with those voices and hair. Maybe a noise would make them turn around. Of course, it might make the guard curious too.

Rance made a sound like a cricket. A little louder. A little louder.

One of the girls stood up and waddled toward the window. "If that bug is inside, we need to find him or I'll never get to sleep tonight." Chirp chirp. "Help me, Sarah. He sounds too close to be outside."

All of the girls stood and slowly walked toward the "cricket." Each one was responsible for a specific section of the room. The chirping continued periodically. They slid chairs and tables away from the wall, looking for the noisy culprit.

"Give it a rest, Sybil. He must be outside. Let's just close the window."

The window slid shut and Rance grabbed Evie's hand. They picked their way back down the trail to the fallen tree. They got inside the car before they spoke.

"Rance, those are all our missing girls. They knew Lila and Rosalie."

"Yes. And all alive...so far. But all appear to be pregnant. Sybil and Carley have already had one baby that we know of. Someone is afraid they'll escape and expose what's going on. Otherwise, they'd be at the main Center facility. I don't think they are here by choice, or they wouldn't have an armed guard outside their cabin. And those women were paid off tonight. I don't think we have too much time before they'll be gone. We need to get back to my files while their faces are fresh in our minds."

Rance turned the car on and cautiously turned it around. The falling dusk made headlights necessary, but at least they were pointed away from the cabins. Evie opened the gate, then closed it and reinstalled the padlock once the car was through. Then the jarring ride back to the county road.

"My computer and files are in the trunk. Where do you want to review them?"

"Let's go back to my kitchen table. We have plenty of room to spread out there."

****

Gonzo finally settled down at Evie's feet after a quick trip outside and licking Rance's hands.

"Do you want something to drink? Coffee? Wine? Lemonade?" Evie cleared the salt and pepper shakers and napkin holder off the kitchen table.

"Maybe a glass of wine if you have some open. After all, this may turn into a celebration." Rance winked.

Two glasses and a bottle of merlot. He opened the four files with the pictures of the missing girls on the inside on the left.

"The girls are older now and weren't smiling, but it was definitely them. They are all alive. No doubt Rosalie was with them at one time. Lila had been there too and found a way to escape."

"What happens next?" Evie poured the wine.

"We know where they are. Now we need to link them to the stillborns and to The Center and, I think, the mastermind behind all of this is your brother."

"I don't believe Frank could orchestrate all this alone. Organization was never his strong suit, and this would require lots of planning and structure to pull it off."

"Then we need to capture him and his partner or partners. Oh, I forgot to turn my phone back on."

"So did I."

Both phones began chiming with messages as soon as they were turned on.

"Tom Peterman found the adoptive parents for Sybil and Carley's children. Neither family met their baby's birth mother. Or Frank Raymond, the listed father. Both said they'd be happy to help in any way possible. I'll send a quick text back and follow up with Tom in the morning." Rance began typing in the text.

Evie frowned as she listened to her voice mail. "I need to return this call."

"Bad news?"

"I'm not sure. I can't make sense of the message. Listen to this: *Miss Langford, this is Mikayla. Auntie is very upset. He told us we can't have Michael. He's sold him to someone else. What are we going to do?*"

"Sold Lila's baby? You better call her back."

"Hello, Mikayla. This is Miss Langford. I got your message, but I don't understand it…When did that happen?…No. He can't take Michael…I have a meeting for you with the attorney tomorrow morning at eight thirty…He's coming to my office…Get some sleep…Assure your aunt we'll get to the bottom of

242

this…I'll see you in the morning."

She immediately made a second call. This time to the nursery. "Under no circumstances is anyone allowed to have contact with the Masterson baby except Zelda and Mikayla Masterson and Dr. Wetzel or myself…Thank you."

"If Tom Peterman is coming to your office, we can cover Lila's baby and the adoptive parent information both. Who upset Mrs. Masterson?"

"Three guesses."

"Dr. Frank Langford?"

"My brother told Mrs. Masterson she can't adopt her great grandson because he'd already paid Lila and the baby's father—Frank Raymond—five thousand dollars for the baby and the child has been promised for adoption to a couple from Massachusetts."

"Frank Raymond again. We need to find out if this person exists or not."

"How do we do that?"

"DNA testing on the babies would be confirmation of genes in common. We have his name on their birth certificates: Rosalie's, Sybil's, Carley's, and now, Lila's. It should tell us whether they really all have the same father. If they don't, it's part of the fraud going on at The Center. If they do, we need to find the guy. We have to get the testing in the works first thing in the morning. Oh, I need to check with Tom. He has the aliases for the Kelley and Gables mothers, but I haven't heard back if they've had babies earlier. Clearly, they are pregnant now." Rance sent the text and made some notes.

"If there's an adoption contract for Lila's baby, wouldn't Tom Peterman know? You said he acted like he'd never heard of Lila Masterson. And shouldn't there be a canceled check?"

"Yes, and yes. We need to nail down the process with Tom when we see him in the morning."

"And I think it may be time for a certain charming Special Agent to contact his mole and find out how much she knows about all of this. I'm sure she's been holding back critical information."

"Tomorrow's Wednesday. A good day for lunch with the lovely Mrs. Rafferty. I'll text her an invitation right now. Miss Langford, you may have a future as an FBI agent."

"Not sure I could stand all this drama on a regular basis." She laughed.

Rance's phone chimed. "The lady said yes. She'll pick me up at the Medical Center at noon. Speaking of pick ups, I'll be back to have coffee with you at seven tomorrow morning before we go to work together."

"Better make it six thirty. I want to go into the office a little early to see Mrs. Masterson before our meeting. Have sweet dreams."

Rance leaned down and kissed her cheek on his way out.

"C'mon, Gonzo. Time for bed. Sorry you didn't get much playtime today. I hope tomorrow I'll be home on time. You still need to climb the stairs though."

Chapter Thirty-One

The CEO found Mrs. Masterson and Mikayla in the cafeteria having breakfast. Their red eyes and sad faces told her they were worried about little Michael. She reassured them Tom Peterman was a good attorney who agreed to represent them in the adoption proceedings. She explained about the FBI investigation underway and asked for permission to do a DNA test on Michael related to identifying his father. Mrs. Masterson agreed without hesitation.

"Isn't Dr. Frank Langford your brother?" Mrs. Masterson asked. "That's part of the reason I believed what he said."

"I apologize that he upset you. He is my brother, and he does help match adoptive parents with available babies, but he denied that your granddaughter was one of his patients at The Langford Obstetrical Center. If she wasn't at The Center, he has no say over who adopts her baby. Mr. Peterman would normally be the one who draws up those contracts and issues the checks to the mother. We'll straighten all this out when we meet with him in a little bit. Finish your breakfast, then come over to my office. Mr. Peterman will be here at eight thirty."

****

Tom Peterman was in the Administrative Conference Room talking with Rance when Evelyn returned to her office. She told them Michael could be DNA tested. Tom texted the adoptive parents in Alabama and Colorado about the testing and Rance contacted the Campbells. The Chicago, Denver, Birmingham, and Dallas FBI labs had all been notified there was priority one DNA testing to be done. They should have results in twenty-four to forty-eight hours.

Tom said eight adoptions in the past two years showed Frank Raymond as the birth father: Rosalie Richardson as Rose Rich; Sarah Kelley as Sally Kaiser; Sonia Gables as Sofia Gates; Sybil Russell; Carley Addams; and two names the FBI had not found yet. Michael Masterson would be the ninth one. Fran Rafferty had coordinated The Center's end of the paperwork for all of those adoptions and gotten Frank Raymond's signature. The birth father signatures on all eight certificates matched.

Mrs. Masterson and her niece arrived at eight thirty and joined the trio at the conference room table.

Tom Peterman extended his hand to Zelda Masterson. "Ma'am, I am Tom Peterman, your attorney for the adoption proceedings for your great grandson, Michael John Masterson."

Mrs. Masterson shook his hand. "I'm glad to meet you and especially happy to hear you to say we can adopt Michael."

"I have not drawn up a contract or made any payment related to the baby now known as Michael John Masterson. I believe Dr. Langford confused the Masterson child with another in process adoption. I will personally talk with him to resolve his confusion. Since we have identified who the father was Special Agent Thompson will talk with Mrs. Rafferty about getting

Frank Raymond's signature on the adoption papers since she has obtained them in the past."

The CEO said, "It sounds like all the loose ends related to Lila's baby going home with his great grandmother and cousin are about to be neatly tied up."

Zelda Masterson burst into tears. "You don't know how worried I've been all night. I know Miss Langford told me not to worry but I couldn't lose Michael. Not after losing John and then Lila and wondering what had happened to her for so long. I'm sorry. I promised myself I wouldn't cry."

The CEO walked to the woman's side, bent over, and hugged her. "You cry all you want, as long as they are happy tears. Michael will legally be yours soon."

After thanking everyone, Mrs. Masterson and Mikayla returned to the nursery for Michael's next feeding.

****

Fran Rafferty pulled up in front of the Garland Regional Medical Center promptly at noon to pick up Rance Thompson. Once again, they lunched at her home.

The FBI Special Agent filled her in about finding the four runaway girls out at the old church camp on the back of The Langford Obstetrical Center property. Fran didn't respond with surprise or volunteer that she knew anything about it. He didn't press her. She seemed to be mulling over this new information and her options.

When he told her about the DNA testing to determine if all the children who had Frank Raymond as their birth father were actually from a single person, her right eyebrow shot up.

"I could have saved you a lot of time and expense.

They are all half-siblings as I am certain the testing will prove. I personally got Frank Raymond's signature on all the adoption papers," she said with a smug look on her face.

"Good, because I need his signature one more time."

"For what?"

"Lila Masterson's son who is in the Nursery at Regional right now."

"Masterson?"

"The girl who was 'found' in Mrs. Kapper's orchard and died after having the baby at Regional. Her son survived."

"I didn't think she was a mother from The Center."

"Dr. Langford told Lila's grandmother yesterday that Frank Raymond was the baby's father."

"Well, he should know." She pursed her lips. "Do you believe Dr. Langford is behind the mysterious deaths and stillborn babies at The Center?"

"Honestly, yes I do."

"Will the evidence you've found so far and the DNA testing be able to link him to your case? Allow you to finish the investigation?"

"Not definitively. I'm struggling with how to accomplish that. Ideally, I'd want those runaways to confront him. They know what happened to them and, I believe, to Rosalie and Lila. If they can testify about how Dr. Langford is involved, then we are finished."

"You've come to the right girl. What if I could help you set a trap to accomplish all your objectives and more?" There was the cat lapping cream look again.

"Why would you want to help me? Ruin your boss's career? Maybe send him to prison?"

"I've invested a great deal of time and money into The Center. I have reason to believe Dr. Langford is siphoning off money from the practice and is planning to flee the country once he has *enough*. I don't appreciate being conned. Maybe if he is out of the picture, I can recruit a medical director who will make The Center a profitable enterprise again and I can recoup my investment," Fran Rafferty explained.

"Okay. What's the plan?" Rance began to take notes.

Chapter Thirty-Two

"Frank, what is this nonsense about there being a contract and payment already in place on the Masterson boy?" Tom Peterman asked.

Frank Langford paced in front of the attorney's desk chain smoking particularly foul-smelling cigarettes. "I have a line on someone who'll pay double for a little red-headed boy. Since the mother is out of the picture, I thought we could enjoy a little extra profit. I desperately need the money."

"I was told Frank Raymond is the father…again. What is the deal with this guy? Is he really the dad to all nine of these kids or do you just pay him to sign the adoption papers?" Tom held up his hand. "Stop. Don't tell me. I can't deny it in court if you tell me straight out. Client privilege or not."

"So will you back me on this?" Frank questioned his partner.

"It's too late. Wish you'd clued me in on your plans. This Masterson baby is a pet project of your sister's. She asked me to draw up the paperwork for the great grandmother to adopt the boy. You'll have to find your client a different red-headed baby."

"Damn my sister." Frank slammed the coffee cup on the desk. "She ruins everything for me. If it's not her, it's that blasted FBI special agent. Fine. If you won't help me, make the paperwork out as Father

Unknown. I can't afford for Raymond to get involved with this one if I'm not getting paid. My client will have to wait a month longer for their baby. Hope it comes out male and red-headed." He snuffed his cigarette out in the ashtray and immediately lit another.

"As you wish. I know you won't listen to me Frank, but you're skating on dangerously thin ice. If you continue being careless, the entire enterprise may come down around our ears. I, for one, like having a profitable practice and those private adoptions are critical to my income being able to maintain the lifestyle I've become accustomed to. Don't screw it up—for any of us," the attorney warned.

The doctor glared at him. Then wheeled around in a cloud of cigarette smoke and slammed the door on the way out.

Tom Peterman picked up the phone. "Please get Miss Langford at Garland Regional for me. If she's not available, ask her to call back at her earliest convenience."

Then he texted a message to Rance Thompson.

—*Pkg w my asst. Ready 4 pick up.*—

That would be the last of the paperwork he owed the FBI agent. Those last two girls were a surprise. He wondered if the other Frank Raymond babies had runaway moms too.

He leaned back in his overstuffed burgundy leather chair and put his feet on the polished desk. "Frank, Frank. You aren't going to know what hit you. If only you hadn't persisted in being so pig-headed. You have definitely tangled with the wrong people. I tried to warn you. We both did. But you refused to listen. It's time to pay the piper."

Chapter Thirty-Three

"Do you trust her?" Evie set their dessert on the dining room table.

"Not entirely, but her reasons for cooperating seem sound. You said Frank found the money he needed overnight when you didn't give it to him. Fran Rafferty must have been the funding source and now she's watching him jeopardize her investment. I'm supposed to call her back tomorrow afternoon about whether we're in or not."

"We?" Her brow furrowed.

"She thought your presence at the sting might soften the blow for Frank."

"Right. Better to be certain your own flesh and blood betrayed you rather than only think they did." Evie shook her head. "I'm extremely uncomfortable with this plan. Can we wait to implement it until the DNA tests come back? Including the one from this afternoon?"

"I think so. They should all be in by Friday morning. We're planning this operation for Saturday morning."

Evie's phone chimed. A text message from Tom Peterman. She read the message and made a call. "Mikayla, please tell your aunt that the attorney will bring Michael's adoption papers for her signature tomorrow morning…Can you both be in my office at nine?…Terrific…see you then."

She hung up. "At least one good thing will come out of all of this. The Mastersons are over the moon excited. Thanks for your help with Michael's adoption."

"I didn't do anything except bring Tom Peterman up to speed. It's him you need to thank." Rance pushed back from the table. "Another delicious meal. You continue to amaze me."

"Am I a better cook than Fran Rafferty?" She tried hard to suppress a grin.

"Hmmm…I may have to have another sample or two of Fran's to have a fair comparison."

She cuffed him. "You are incorrigible."

"And pretty exhausted. Pick you up at seven in the morning?"

"Please. Someday soon I'll need to try driving one-handed, but right now I'm enjoying being spoiled by the chauffeur service, especially the good-looking guy they keep sending over as my driver." She winked.

"Good night."

"Sweet dreams."

Could Frank have gotten into this mess totally on his own? Masterminded the entire operation? She couldn't believe it.

"It's bedtime, Gonzo. I saw Rance slip you a treat." She opened the back door. The dog made two laps around the yard, then stopped for the reason he was outside, and returned to the kitchen. "You're getting pretty good on the stairs and I think it's great exercise for you. I may have you continue to walk up on your own even after this sling comes off."

The pug cocked his head and barked twice. Evie

laughed.

****

Rance was exhausted. But too tired to sleep. Could they solve all these cases with Fran's help? It was an exciting prospect and one he was dreading. When the cases were finished, did it signal the end to Rance and Evie's growing relationship? What did he want it to mean? That was the billion-dollar question. He couldn't sleep. Now was as good a time as any to read Mandy's letter. Maybe reading about the true love who escaped would steel his resolve about what should happen with this one.

He pulled the yellowed envelope out of the file folder he'd stuck it in earlier. There were at least thirty pages. He put on his reading glasses, sat with his back against the bed's headboard, and stretched his legs out in front of him. Not terribly comfortable, but better than the chair at the desk where he'd already spent far too many hours.

My Dearest Rance. Her handwriting was neat and easy to read. Seeing it again set his heart racing remembering their last night together.

You are holding my woefully inadequate attempt to introduce you to our son. If you are reading this, he is with you, but I have gone on ahead to join Mom. I don't intend to be overly dramatic. Sorry if it sounds that way. She wrote exactly like she spoke. This vibrant, fresh, stream of consciousness flow, as if she'd invited you deep into her mind to see the words as she thought them.

He's the most amazing child—even more so because he was born from nothing but our pure love. But I'm getting ahead of myself. I decided to make a diary for you of all of our son's most important moments. Then one day, you and he can sit together and read about the beginning you missed. I can see you wrinkling your brow and that pouty but kinda sexy frown painting your face. You've always wanted to be in on everything at the beginning. You're ready to ask me why you weren't with me for Kyle's beginning. Right? I know you so well. Of course, he would have preferred to be there from the beginning, if he'd known there was a beginning.

You had plans, Rance. Gigantic, well-thought out, marvelous plans for your future, for our future. They all sounded perfect for us. You earned your appointment to West Point. You'd attend and, without a doubt, graduate with honors. Then you'd serve your country in return for your education. You always said that we'd serve our country, recognizing the sacrifices an army wife makes. You wanted me at your side as soon as it was possible, and, more than anything, I wanted to be there. I was, I am, so proud of you. Of the amazing man you are. A great role model for our son.

I couldn't tell you our last night together resulted in my pregnancy. You were always the first one to get in line to do the right thing and you would have married me immediately. We both knew West Point cadets could not marry until after graduation. I couldn't let our night of passion destroy our dreams for tomorrow.

"Mandy, why didn't you read any of my letters? You just cruelly marked each one *Return To Sender* in black marker. You would have known. We could have been a family right from the beginning."

You know I'm right about marriage and West Point. There's that wrinkle knitting your eyebrows together again. Now you want to know why I didn't contact you after you graduated. We could have married then and had a head start on beginning our family. I intended to become your bride then. It was in my master plan. Then life intervened. What is the saying, something about man planning and God laughing? Something like that.

My mom was diagnosed with early onset Alzheimer's the year Kyle was born. Dad desperately wanted to keep her at home. He could only do that if Kyle and I stayed to help them both. Dad was floored by her illness. He'd always joked that he'd robbed the cradle when he married a woman fifteen years younger than he was so he'd have someone to look after him in his old age. Now he was her caregiver. I couldn't leave him to deal with the devastating news alone. I know I disappointed you, but I couldn't have lived with myself if I'd walked away from them.

I added another step to my master plan. I kept house for everyone. I cooked, did laundry, shopped—all the things Mom insisted I learn to do if I was ever going to marry. The bright side of my new "job" was I got to be with Kyle while I was caring for Mom. I'm sure you'll remember how wonderful I thought it would be to be a stay-at-home mom, if we could ever afford it. In a bizarre twist of fate, I got to be that mom to take care of my parents and your sweet son.

He pictured Mandy, the super organized, incredibly compassionate woman he had loved, in the middle of it all. He could forgive her not coming to him after four years. She always wanted to do the right thing too. It was one of the things that made them so good together. And, apparently, so good apart.

Mom forgot lots of things, but never how to care for a baby. She loved feeding him and rocked him for hours until they both fell asleep. Kyle was her rock star. He made her face shine with love just by crawling on her lap and saying "Memaw, Kyle wuvs you." Dad said Kyle was the best medicine Mom could have. I think he was right.

We lost Mom shortly after Kyle turned five. He was as devastated as Dad and I were, maybe more so. He didn't lose a grandmother as much as a playmate, a friend, and the person he never doubted loved him totally without reservations. I have to confess, there were times when I was jealous of their relationship. But I wouldn't have had it any other way. Our lives were all richer for those last years with her.

Shirley Nichols had never treated Rance with anything but kindness. How wonderful that she got to share her unique personality with his son, her grandson.

According to my plan, now I would take the step to join you wherever you were stationed and share your life as an army wife. But I couldn't. Dad and Mom never knew who Kyle's father was. They didn't press me. I believed they were thankful to be so involved in their grandson's life, whoever his father was. Dad never directly asked me to stay with him after Mom was gone. He was accustomed to living with us and we were comfortable with him. I simply couldn't kick him again when life had been hammering him so relentlessly. You didn't know about Kyle. You had no idea you were missing anything. Dad would have known we were gone every single day. He would have been totally alone. It would have been a painful loss for him. And I was worried about Kyle losing Dad so soon after losing

Mom. He clearly loved them both. I'm sorry, Rance. I modified my master plan once more. I hope you can forgive me. Again.

How could he do anything else?

I've kept in touch with Amory over the years so I would be able to find you when I got to the step in my master plan where we three became the family we were always meant to be. She knew nothing about Kyle. We made a pact not to discuss you, at least not the specifics of where you were and what you were doing. I'm not so brave that I would have been able to have that information and not be torn between the two men I love, you and Dad.

I've missed you every day of Kyle's life. I couldn't figure out another way to handle this situation. I hope you two will love one another as much as I have always loved you both. Now that you are together without me, I pray you'll always remember that everything I did, every decision I made, was done with a heart filled with love. All my love forever, Mandy.

Dozens of pages of diary-like entries followed the main letter. From the first pregnancy test taken in the bathroom at Mandy's work to the week before Mandy died. The last entry was penned immediately after a birthday extravaganza for Kyle's tenth birthday. It was getting late and harder every minute to read with tear-filled eyes. She was an amazing woman. A terrific mother. A steadfast daughter. And his wife of ten years without a wedding ring or a ceremony. He'd never looked at anyone else in all those years even though he'd thought she'd dumped him. Without knowing why, he'd stayed available for the step in the master plan of life when he became an instant father to a ten year old boy who loved him without question. Somehow Mandy knew what would happen. She'd prepared Kyle for their life together and, through this letter, was preparing Rance for the next steps and answering the questions he'd had for the past ten years.

He leafed through the diary pages planning to sit down and binge read them one day when he didn't have to be up first thing in the morning. He noticed his name on an entry when Kyle was four.

Mom's Alzheimer's is worsening but she doesn't miss a thing. Kyle told her a knock-knock joke but couldn't remember the punchline. Mom said it for him. They both roared laughing. When he left the room, she said, "His laugh sounds like Rance's and the way he crinkles his eyes when he's tickled looks just like him." I gasped out loud. She winked at me and said, "Don't worry. I won't tell anyone." So much for keeping Kyle's paternity a secret. She was right. I see you in him all the time. I thought it was only a mother's hope for her son to look like his father.

Rance folded the packet of papers and stuffed them back into the envelope before they got wetter from his tears. *Oh, Mandy. How I loved you. Thank you. Thank you. Thank you.*

Chapter Thirty-Four

Rance walked into Evie's kitchen at five after seven. She had just coaxed Gonzo into his crate so they were ready to leave for the day.

"Running a little late this morning, Mr. Special FBI Agent," she teased.

"Yep. Sorry. Got wrapped up reading a letter last night and lost track of time."

"Mandy's letter?"

"That's the one."

"Did it give you any answers?"

"Yes. Some more questions too. I haven't finished reading everything. Maybe we can talk about it later. I need to deliver you to Garland Regional so a sweet baby boy can be adopted today."

****

Tears ran down Zelda Masterson's cheeks as she signed the adoption papers. "Mr. Peterman, Miss Langford, thank you. This is wonderful. Dr. Wetzel said Michael is doing very well. We hope to take him home by the end of next week."

"I'm going home later today to get the nursery ready. Auntie is going to stay here so Michael gets all his hugs and keeps growing," Mikayla said. "I should be back to pick them both up in about a week."

"He's one lucky little boy." Miss Langford hugged Mrs. Masterson and Mikayla. "I'm so glad I got to meet you."

"We're the blessed ones. We thought our darling Lila was lost forever, but Michael will make sure a part of her is always with us. Thanks again," Zelda Masterson's voice wavered.

****

Rance tapped on the CEO's door, then entered, and closed the door. "We're beginning to get the DNA results back. So far the Campbell babies and Michael Masterson have paternal DNA in common. Exactly as Fran predicted they would. Still waiting on three others."

"Thanks for the update. Heard anything else?" Evelyn shuffled papers on her desk but didn't look at him.

"I have to call Fran and confirm for Saturday morning. I need a definite yes or no from you about whether you're willing to participate in this operation." He walked around the desk and stood at her side.

"Until we get the situation with Frank resolved, we can't move forward with this." She gestured between them. "I'm not comfortable with the plan but I haven't been able to devise a better one. It's a yes. I'm in. You knew I would be."

"I'm hoping we might begin to cement this relationship in a public way. What about dinner at Shangri-La this evening? We can go right after work so not a late night. What do you say?"

"You mean we might as well confirm the gossip swirling around everywhere that the prim and proper medical center CEO has a fella? A good-looking, younger one?" Evie laughed.

"And that the FBI Special Agent has a beautiful

older woman prowling around him?"

"It's a date." She kissed his cheek and shooed him out of her office.

****

On the way to Shangri-La, Rance began talking about Mandy's letter.

"Did it answer the biggest question you had, the why she didn't tell you about Kyle earlier?" Evie asked.

"Yes. She didn't want me to have to give up my dream of a West Point appointment. They don't allow married cadets."

"I thought you went to college in the Chicago area, not West Point."

"I did, but when did I tell you that?"

"On the plane coming back from the beach."

"I'll have to be careful what I say to you if your recall is that complete." Rance laughed.

"So it was a sacrifice for nothing?"

"Not exactly."

"Okay. Sounds like there's more to the story. Why didn't you go to West Point as you planned and Mandy believed you would?"

"I was supposed to leave for the academy in August. In July my dad had a massive stroke. He was hospitalized and it was pretty touch and go about whether he'd live, much less be able to ever come home. I couldn't go hundreds of miles away and leave Mom and Amory with so much up in the air, so I went to a small liberal arts college nearby instead."

"So you wouldn't have been comfortable getting married at that time either?"

"It would have been a difficult situation. Mandy was dealing with medical issues with her mom too. In some ways, her decision to raise Kyle without me made the other things we had to deal with easier. She kept referencing her 'master plan' in the letter. I don't know if it was hers or someone's higher up the food chain, but I truly believe the situation worked out for the best for all of us," Rance hesitated before going on. "And I think it made it possible for you and me to become us. There's more but I'd rather not discuss it in public."

"I understand." Evie leaned over and kissed his cheek after he parked in the Shangri-La lot.

The restaurant wasn't very busy when they sat down, but more people came in during the course of the meal. They were out of the main traffic flow seated in a corner booth. But not so far away as to be totally unnoticed. A tall, older man walked over to their table as their entrees arrived. He extended his hand to Rance.

"Don't worry. I'm not staying so long that your food will get cold. I'm Charles Jungers, might say I'm Miss Langford's boss. I'm chairman of Garland Regional Medical Center's Board of Directors. I'm guessing you are the FBI Special Agent working at our facility."

Rance stood and took the extended hand. "Yes, sir. FBI Special Agent Rance Thompson. You should be very proud of Miss Langford and the employees at Regional. They have all been very cooperative and are top notch to work with."

"I've always thought so, but it's good to hear the praise from someone official. Please sit back down and enjoy your meal." The chairman walked over to the group in the far corner who appeared to be his wife and other family members.

Evie said, "Now the cat is officially out of the

bag."

"I think it must have been mostly out already or he wouldn't have made the assumption about who I was. Are you concerned?"

"No. Mr. Jungers has always been reasonable to work with and listens to all the facts before he forms an opinion."

Rance and Evie lingered over a shared crème brulee. Dr. Frank Langford and Fran Rafferty were seated at the table across from them. Her brother's face turned beet red when he saw who was in the booth. Evie thought his reaction was anger, not embarrassment. Fran merely nodded and smiled. Not at Evie, at Rance. Luckily, they were able to finish the last couple of bites and escape Frank's glare.

On the way to the car, Evie said, "I'm glad they didn't come in sooner. It was uncomfortable being there with them. I'm glad they didn't ruin a lovely dinner."

"Why were you uncomfortable? Aren't we entitled to eat out in public?"

"Yes, we are allowed to go out, but I felt like Frank was looking daggers at us the whole time. And she couldn't stop ogling you."

"Ogling? Do women do that?" Rance laughed.

"Fran Rafferty does when she sees you. Each and every time that I've witnessed your encounter."

He put his arm around Evie's waist. "I think you're a little silly, but I love that you're jealous of her attention to me. Fran doesn't mean a romantic thing in the world to me. She's a necessary contact to solve this case. That's all. Besides, she's much too young for me." Rance laughed.

Evie kissed his cheek. "And don't you forget it!"

Chapter Thirty-Five

Margie Wright tapped lightly on her boss's office door. "Got a minute?"

"Sure, come on in." Evelyn got up and moved to the table in the corner of the office and motioned for Margie to sit down.

"Miss Langford, you know I don't spread gossip," Margie began, "But when it's about my boss, I think she should know the lies that people are saying about her."

"My heavens, you sound so ominous. What's the rumor that has you so upset?"

"While I was eating breakfast in the cafeteria, three different people came to me asking about your relationship with Special Agent Thompson," Margie said.

"What business is my relationship to anyone?" Evelyn asked with an edge to her voice.

"I told them they should stick to their own knitting, not get in the middle of yours. But they said not only were you seeing him every night, but his car had been parked all night outside your house. More than once."

"Goodness. I guess people must be looking for some kind of scandal to entertain themselves. It is true, we have been spending a lot of time together. It's no secret. Special Agent Thompson did stay overnight in my home on the weekend after I was injured. He slept on the couch to make sure I was all right and to give me my medications on time. Nothing went on that was improper," Evelyn said through clenched teeth. "I guess people who are looking for dirt can always dig up some true fact to expand and misconstrue into a lurid lie. I had no idea so many people had so much interest in the cars parked outside of my house. What must their lives be like if they have to look to mine for something exciting?"

"I told them you're an honorable woman and they should be ashamed of themselves. One of them said you were having a love affair with the FBI agent and that's why Mr. Gaines left in a hurry. They said he had a fight with Mr. Thompson, and it was over you. Then they told me Mr. Thompson forbade your brother to see you in your own house and set the police on him to make sure he stayed away."

Evelyn took a deep breath. "Mr. Gaines left Garland Regional because he resigned his position for personal reasons. They are no one's business except our Board of Directors'. The issues between my brother and me are a lingering family issue that has absolutely nothing to do with the FBI special agent or my job. Mr. Thompson and I have enjoyed meals together in my home on several occasions and we had dinner together at Shangri-La last night. My goodness, I have no spouse whom I'm cheating on. I'm a single fifty-year-old woman. Agent Thompson is a single man. I'm not some love-struck teenager who's going to elope in the middle of the night abandoning her responsibilities. Thanks for letting me know what people are saying and for standing up for me. Margie, I'm sorry you were put in a position to feel you had to protect my reputation and defend my personal morals. I hope you can laugh off those overly interested people. There is no need to worry. I'm touched that you would come to me so I know what is being said."

"Thanks for listening, Miss Langford. I can't stand to hear people disparaging you. It's simply not right."

Margie returned to her desk in the outer office.

****

Just before noon, Rance walked into Evelyn's office from the adjoining conference room and put the latest lab results on the CEO's desk. "All the children do indeed have the same father, exactly as Fran Rafferty believed."

"Now to find him."

"We already have." He slid another result across her desk. "If that's not a direct tie-in to The Center, I don't know what is. This is indisputable, clear, and positive proof."

She read the lab report, then paled. She closed her eyes and took a deep breath. Then she read the report again. "I think I'm going to be sick." She raced into her personal bathroom adjoining her office.

When Evelyn returned to her desk, she could see through the crack in the ajar door that Rance was in the conference room on the phone.

****

The FBI agent had errands to run in mid-afternoon. He pulled to the curb in front of Garland Regional at five thirty. Evelyn came out immediately and got in the car.

"Special Agent Thompson reporting for chauffeur duty." Rance tipped his imaginary hat. "How about dinner out again tonight? Can't let my best girl sit at home on a Friday night?"

"Tongues will really be wagging now." Evelyn wasn't smiling. "I should never have agreed to dinner in public last night. What on earth were you thinking when you sent flowers to me at work today?"

"Madam, I have absolutely no idea what you're talking about."

"Pull into the parking lot and come to my office."

She led the way back into administration. There in the middle of her small conference table were two dozen snow-white roses in a crystal vase with a card that said, "All my love, Rance."

"Believe me. I did not send these flowers. What a waste to send them to the office on Friday afternoon. Someone is spending a boatload of money trying to get me in trouble. What florist are they from?"

"Shaw's on Main. Why would someone do this? It piles more fuel on the rumor fires ablaze all over town about us," Evie said sharply.

"What are Lansdale's gossipy tongues wagging about now?"

"Us! Having dinner last night. You staying in my house all night after I was hurt. You having a fight with Courtland Gaines. You warning Frank to stay away from me or else. The police coming to the house to remove Frank from my front porch. Margie said people make it sound like we're so insanely in love that we're likely to chuck everything and run away together. Any day now."

"Oh, let 'em talk." Rance chuckled. He tried to embrace her.

She pushed him away and stepped farther from him. "This isn't funny, Rance. I have a professional reputation to maintain. I can't deny how I feel about you. I hate people twisting our very proper and innocent relationship into fodder for their nasty overactive imaginations. And like all gossip, part of it is true. So denying it does little or no good." Tears welled up in her eyes.

"This will all be over by tomorrow afternoon, and I'll make an honest woman of you. Cross my heart. You'll believe I didn't send these flowers when we get to your house."

"What?"

"Come with me." He took her hand in his. "I knew you'd say no to going out tonight. I have dinner in the oven at the house. Your key has come in handy."

Evie allowed him to lead her back to the car.

The rich, onion-filled aroma of Beef Bourguignon greeted her when she opened the kitchen door. In the middle of the dining room table was a bouquet of delicate lavender orchids.

She burst out laughing. "They must pay FBI agents a lot better than I thought. What, no card? The people at the florist's must think you're nuts."

"Or just a fool in love. Unfortunately, the roses did come from the same florist where I bought the orchids. Someone had to have seen me there and called later to order the roses. A very malicious someone. Appetizers will be ready in twenty minutes. Get comfortable."

Rance freed Gonzo from the crate while Evie slowly made her way upstairs. It had been a day of surprises, most of them bad. Rance must have recognized the dinner in public last night was a major mistake. She should have known better. Rumors. DNA tests. Flowers.

A whirlwind of uncertainty swept through her mind. What had Frank done? What had she done? Was there a future with Rance after the dust settled from the drama surrounding The Langford Obstetrical Center? Right now, she couldn't imagine hers in Lansdale. Not after this debacle. No matter how things turned out tomorrow.

Evie pulled on a comfortable pair of navy-blue knit pants and a patterned cotton knit sweater in Kelly-green and navy, slipped into the navy ballet flats, brushed her hair out, and prepared to rejoin Rance in the kitchen. She had become quite proficient at one-handed dressing. She would hardly know how to act once the constricting sling was gone for good.

Soft candlelight glowed in the dining room. The salads were on the table with a crusty baguette of French bread and a bottle of red wine. Rance stood behind her chair and pulled it out as she approached. Evie sat down.

"Your dinner awaits, madam. Tonight, we're having tossed salads with the soon-to-be-famous Thompson Secret Salad dressing followed by a hearty serving of Beef Bourguignon over rice. All accompanied by a delightful cabernet sauvignon the sommelier just got in today. For dessert we have delectable chocolate covered cream puffs with freshly brewed decaf coffee."

"It all sounds perfectly marvelous. I'm beginning to understand why you're a special agent. There is nothing ordinary about your many and varied talents." Evie smiled.

"I'm glad to see you smile at me." Rance poured the wine and raised his glass. "A toast to an end to this intrigue and the beginning of the next chapter of the Evie and Rance story."

"Amen. To us," Evie responded.

Chapter Thirty-Six

Saturday morning, they lingered over breakfast enjoying their second cups of coffee when Rance's phone chimed.

"The text from Fran. Frank is at the church camp. He's doing the weekly prenatal checks on the girls. They're all in the Fellowship Hall. Time to roll." He sent two texts, then took Evie's hand. "It's all going to be okay. I promise."

He coaxed Gonzo into his crate with an extra treat. Evie locked the door and activated the alarm. They got in the car.

"Please don't promise things you can't guarantee. I want this to be over, but I can't imagine what Frank has done. When did he go off the deep end? How did I miss it?" Evie stared out the window without seeing the passing scenery.

"Don't be so hard on yourself. It's hard to catch irregularities in behavior when someone is being so secretive."

"But there were signs I ignored. Over the past three years he has made at least one trip every quarter to Chicago. Said he had speaking engagements to promote the birthing and adoption experience at The Center. He'd get antsy before he left and then be quite full of himself once he returned. Thinking about it now, I realize he behaved as if he was a junkie needing his next fix. I thought maybe he had a new girlfriend or some other sexual liaison there.

"He spends more time at The Center than at his home. He'd been snappish about Mama, about medical staff rules at Garland, about money. He'd been morphing into someone I didn't know and I'm just now recognizing the accumulated change in his personality."

"Please don't fret. I don't see what you could have done to stop this from happening."

"I'm his sister. We have deep family ties. I should have sensed something was wrong. I should have been able to do something to head off this disaster."

"Evie, you're only his sister, not his keeper."

They drove to the church camp in silence the rest of the way. They stopped at the gate across the rutted path. Rance punched the number that Fran had given him into the lock keypad. The arm flew up. He slowly followed the road to the Fellowship Hall trying to avoid most of the major potholes and parked on the back side of the building.

The armed guard outside the Hall nodded as they approached the front door. "They're expecting you."

Three girls were sitting on chairs in a semi circle on one side of the nearly empty cavernous room. Frank, in a white lab coat with his stethoscope draped on both sides of his neck, led a fourth girl out from behind the curtained examination area behind where the girls were sitting.

"What in blue blazes are you two doing here?" Frank snarled.

"Personally checking on some of your patients." Evie glared at her brother. "I wanted to meet them before they ended up in my emergency room or worse, the morgue. Will you make the introductions?"

"You're insane. I don't have time for this nonsense." Frank turned his back to her and stomped to the other side of the room.

Rance approached the girls where they huddled together holding hands watching his every move with wide eyes. "I believe I can make the introductions. Let me see if I get it right. You must be Rosalie Richardson's friends."

Rance pointed to the freckle-faced strawberry blonde. "You're Sarah Kelley, right?" The girl nodded. Then he pointed to the girl with a swath of out-of-control ebony curls ringing her head. "And you're Sonia Gables. Am I right?"

She nodded her head.

"And this lovely blonde must be Sybil Russell, and the brunette with pink tips on her hair is Carley Addams, right?"

"Yes, sir," they said in unison.

Evelyn Langford stepped toward the quartet of young women. "This gentleman is FBI Special Agent Rance Thompson, and my name is Evelyn Langford. I'm the CEO at Garland Regional Medical Center where some of you have already visited as patients."

"The FBI? Does this mean we finally get to go home?" Sarah asked wide-eyed.

Frank rushed across the room. "No way in hell. They aren't going anywhere, and neither are you. Who let you in here?"

"I did." Fran Rafferty strode across the room—her black stiletto heels made a staccato click with each step on the tile floor.

Rance nodded to their accomplice. "Thank you,

Fran." He turned to Sarah. "Yes. You're all going home."

The girls hugged one another as tears streamed down their cheeks.

"When?" Sybil asked.

"As soon as we can get you safely out of here and contact your parents," Rance replied.

"You mean they're still looking for us?" Sonia asked.

"They are. And they're very excited that you've been found alive," Rance explained.

The tears were soon replaced with smiles of disbelief.

"What a made for TV moment. The brave FBI agent frees the trapped runaways aided by the love of his life, the spinster CEO." Fran laughed harshly. Rance stared at her, mouth agape. She pulled a revolver out of the large black purse on the table. Chills raced down Evelyn's spine. "Sorry, my very dear Special Agent. I'm afraid no one is going home, not these young ladies or you or your lady love. Not today. Not ever."

"That's more like it," Frank crowed as he came to Fran's side. "I knew you wouldn't betray me."

"The only way I'm not going home is if I'm dead," Rance declared.

"Correct. That, my dear sir, is exactly what I have arranged," Fran replied.

"You'll never get away with it. I'm a Federal agent. They'll be looking for me—for all of us."

"No. They won't. Everyone of any importance believes you and the spinster, Miss Langford, have fallen madly and passionately in love. It's being discussed all over town. It is a small leap for the rumor mongers to be convinced you two lovers have eloped and fled overseas with money the CEO embezzled from Garland Regional Medical Center.

"Dear besotted Courtland completed that half of his job. The money was efficiently paid out to multiple bogus vendors over the past two and half years and deposited into an offshore bank account in Evelyn Langford's name. People will think the CEO was just waiting for her mother to be gone to take the opportunity to flee this hick town. And magically, she found someone other than Courtland Gaines to accompany her.

"Thank you, Miss Langford, for not pressing charges after Courtland's crazy-in-love-with-you performance in your living room accidentally injured you. He was certain you would have compassion for him after you'd played coy and led him on all these years. It would have thrown a major kink in our plans if he had been incarcerated. Dear Court was undoubtedly our weakest link and probably would have crumbled under Chief Davis's questioning and most assuredly would have under the FBI's. He took the chief's advice and, last I heard, was a half a world away from here." She cackled maliciously. "I need your cell phones and wallets, and your shield and gun, Special Agent Thompson. Frank, collect them."

"No one will believe I stole from my employer or that I ran away with Rance Thompson," Evelyn insisted.

"Then why did you leave your loyal assistant, Mrs. Wright, a tear-stained note confessing to everything? And take your passport out of the safe?" Fran waved the small blue book in the CEO's face. "All the gossips in town know you two are quite an item. They have been devouring all the information I've let slip about your assignations over a private dinner in your home, sleepovers more than once, lavish floral surprises, and front porch kisses. I've even heard new rumors that I never planted. Lots of wildly creative and wicked imaginations around here. Everyone believes that your uncontrollable lust for one another drove poor Mr. Gaines insane and your FBI Special Agent lover drove your beloved brother away from your family home at the point of a policeman's gun."

Frank took the personal items and piled them on the table next to Evelyn's passport. "What are we going to do with them?"

"We have a permit from the county to conduct a controlled burn today. These old camp buildings are being burned so the area can be bulldozed to be ready for new construction. The Langford Obstetrical Center has so much demand for its beautiful babies that it needs to expand to this part of the property. We have plans on file with a local architect for more cottages to be built here.

"The Lansdale Fire Department will be here in a couple of hours to conduct a practice using the burning buildings. They greatly appreciated our civic mindedness in offering them this opportunity. Only we're going to start the fires a little sooner than they thought. Someone must have written down the wrong time. On your feet, everyone, we're taking a little walk," Fran announced waving the revolver in the direction of the door.

Frank led the way to the cabin the girls had been living in. Halfway to the building, Rance spun around and began running toward the car. The armed guard stepped in front of him. Then shoved the butt of the rifle into his stomach. Doubled over and gasping for breath, Rance returned to the line of people marching down the hill.

Inside the cabin, Fran instructed everyone to lie down on a bottom bunk. While she stood watch, Frank and the guard duct taped each captive spread eagled to the bunk bed frame by their hands and feet.

"Are you sure these girls have to die? My babies are worth a pretty good bump in our coffers. We could move them to a new location until they give birth," Frank suggested.

"It's not worth the risk, Frank. You've been getting greedy. You put the whole operation in jeopardy with your delusions of manhood. The runaways you brought here are what attracted the FBI. If you hadn't been so out of control, things could have continued as they were for a long and profitable period with no runaways drawing unwanted attention. If you'd had the guts to pull the trigger when the FBI Special Agent first arrived, the problem would have been immediately resolved." Fran spewed out the words hatefully.

"She is my sister, and she cares for him. I couldn't," Frank said sheepishly.

"Too bad that infamous red-headed temper of yours couldn't ignite when we most needed it. No matter. I'm a patient woman. It's all going to work out swimmingly well," Fran almost purred.

"It is working out. They fell into your trap. Now what?" Frank asked gleefully as he finished taping his sister to a bed.

Frank and the guard pulled the mattresses off the

top bunks and piled them in the middle of the room. The guard retrieved two five-gallon cans from outside the cabin door. The smell of gasoline permeated the room. He gave one can to Frank, and they poured it all over the room concentrating most of the liquid on the mattress pile. The guard opened all the windows. Lots of oxygen. More fuel for the fire.

"Anything else, Mrs. Rafferty?" the guard asked putting down the empty gas can.

"Thanks, Jack. Just one more thing. Then you can take their car to the shop and trade it for a different vehicle. Dr. Langford's car was moved offsite earlier."

"Where's my car? Are we leaving together?" Frank asked.

"No. We aren't doing anything together. Ever again. Sit down on the floor there." Fran pointed to the end of the bunk bed his sister was bound on. Frank stared at her unmoving. "I'm not kidding. Now!" She waved the revolver in his face.

Frank sagged to the floor. "Why? How can you do this? You need me. I'm the juice that keeps the whole operation running."

"Hah! I'm tired of trying to keep your libido and those idiotic notions under control. You've been living on borrowed time for twenty years. You had a much longer run than you were ever meant to. You have nothing to complain about," Fran snarled.

She instructed Jack to secure the still mewling Frank to the bed his sister was on. The guard pulled his arms behind him and duct taped them to the leg of the bunk bed. Then taped his legs together and swung them the length of the bed before taping them to the opposite bed leg.

"Thanks for your help. You may leave now." She handed him a fat envelope that appeared to be full of cash. "Forget you ever met me, and you've never been in Lansdale, Wisconsin. Have a nice relaxing life on a beach somewhere far from here," Fran instructed.

Jack thumbed through the cash in the envelope. "This will buy a whole lot of amnesia. It's been a pleasure doing business with you, Mrs. Rafferty." He strode out of the room, slamming the door on the way out of the cabin.

"I don't understand, Fran. How can you do this to me?" Frank moaned.

"You should've been in the car. Your mother was never supposed to go on that trip," Fran hissed as she stood back admiring her handiwork. "Both the Drs. Langford were supposed to meet their Maker together in that wreck."

Evelyn gasped. "My father didn't die in an accident? He was murdered?"

"Give the lady a prize. Maybe a dozen white roses. No. Make it two," Fran snorted. "And throw in some orchids for good measure."

"But why?" Frank was pale and sweating.

"A little family business my brother, Ricco, was conducting. You screwed up the plan when you had a fight with your father and stayed home. We were certain you knew the same information your father did, but I think you're really as clueless as you seem to be. You'd have to be more clever than you are in order to hide that kind of knowledge all these years. Now what you do or do not know will not be an issue. The problem will be corrected, and the plan neatly wrapped with a bow on it. Just a couple of decades later than originally expected. The family appreciates this loose end being tied up. It's been a real pleasure."

Fran lit a rolled-up newspaper and touched it to the mattresses. Flames leapt to the ceiling. Smoke billowed out of the pyre.

Then she walked out of the cabin, laughing demonically all the way. She slammed the door shut and the lock on the outside of the door bolted loudly into place.

The girls sobbed hysterically, "We're going to die. All of us."

"Quiet. Don't panic," Rance hushed them. He listened. The sports car sped away from the compound in a hail of gravel.

"Don't cry. It's only going to pull the smoke over to you faster. Try and work down into your shirts so they cover your mouth and nose. If you can move at all, turn your heads toward the wall." Rance tried to follow his own advice.

"Rance, I love you. I'm sorry we won't have a chance..." Evelyn couldn't hold back the tears overflowing and streaming down her cheeks.

"We will be together. I promise. This is not over. Have faith."

The stuffing of the mattresses seemed to be smoldering more than burning to ash. Maybe someone would see the smoke and report it. But would the fire department realize the controlled burn started earlier than planned? And there were people still in the cabins?

A finger of fire spread from the mattresses along the gasoline trail toward the edge of the room. "My pants are on fire," Frank screamed.

"You have to roll over," his sister yelled. "Or raise

up and tamp it down with my mattress."

Frank continued screaming but was able to get his legs free from the bed frame. They were still taped together but were mobile. He extinguished the pant leg fire. At least, temporarily.

Listen.

What was that sound?

Sirens.

Lots of sirens.

Fire trucks?

The roar of an engine, crunching gravel, and yelling voices sounded a short distance from the cabin. Nothing happened. No one raced to their rescue.

More sirens.

"They think it is supposed to be burning," Rance said. "All together. We need to scream the same thing. The word *help* twice then count to three and do it again. All together now!"

Help! Help!

One. Two. Three.

Help! Help!

An axe broke through the front door. Water began showering down from the roof and through the open windows. They were getting soaked but the mattress pile flames died down. Firefighters rushed in and quickly freed the captives.

Coughing and bleary-eyed, everyone stumbled out of the cabin under their own power. Two ambulances arrived and Chief Davis with two patrol cars joined the three fire trucks. The EMTs hustled the young mothers-to-be into the ambulances two to a vehicle and tore out of the compound sirens blazing to get them to the Emergency Room for smoke inhalation treatment.

While Frank drew oxygen through a mask covering his face, the burn on his leg was cleaned and bandaged by a deputy. He was medically stabilized.

Chief Davis quickly walked over to where Frank sat on the ground, the officer bent over and clapped handcuffs on the doctor. "Frank Raymond Langford, you are under arrest for the attempted murder of a Federal agent and other parties. You have the right to remain silent..." Once he was read his rights, Dr. Langford was transported to jail in the back of a police cruiser.

Rance and Evie had moved away from the traffic and collapsed on the ground. She leaned against him too stunned to speak. Her shoulder throbbed and her lungs ached. She kept taking deep breaths and saying prayers of thanksgiving with each one.

Rance reached up from his sitting position on the ground and shook hands with Chief Davis. "I was beginning to wonder if I'd told you the right time. Thanks."

"The permits for the burn said it was to start at noon. Not ten. We had a ranger in the fire watch tower on alert. He signaled us at the first sign of smoke. Good thing you didn't follow Fran Rafferty's instructions to keep the police out of this."

"Amen to that." Rance hugged Evie.

"You were so calm because you knew the chief would come. Why didn't you tell us?"

"I knew he *should* come. He was the second text I sent before we headed into the camp. When you're waiting for something you believe is going to happen, you can get panicky when you think it's not working. We all needed to stay calm. And I didn't want Fran and

Frank to become suspicious if we didn't seem to believe there was no way to escape our situation."

"We have an A.P.B. out for the red sports car convertible and have alerted authorities at all airports, all bus terminals, and all train stations within three hundred miles. Your FBI counterparts have confirmed their net is in place," Chief Davis reported.

"I want to go home. Rance, please come with me." Evie kissed his soot-streaked cheek.

"If Chief Davis will give us a lift, I think that's a great idea. Do we need to stop at the Emergency Room first?"

"No. I just want to go home."

"Your personal belongings are gone. They were probably removed to make it believable that you had fled. Your official chauffeur would be more than happy to take you home. We can get your statements later this evening. Everyone is worn out now. The fire chief told me they'd be out here several more hours to make sure everything is extinguished. The burn won't be continued until we can confirm we aren't destroying evidence in this case." Chief Davis led them to his car.

Chapter Thirty-Seven

Gonzo began barking as soon as the front door closed. Evie went into the kitchen and freed him from the crate. He made a beeline for the back door barking all the way.

"You're being a spoiled baby. We haven't been gone as long as a normal workday," Evie scolded the little dog. She dished him out some food and put fresh water in his bowl. When he came back into the kitchen, he barked his approval.

"We stink. First order of business is showers and clean clothes," Evie announced as soon as the pug was happily munching kibble.

"A shower sounds great. What am I going to wear?"

"Sweatpants and a tee shirt? I'm sure I can scrounge up something that will work. Follow me." Evie slowly led the way upstairs. "You can use the guest room and connecting bathroom. There are sweats in the dresser in there and tons of tee shirts. Help yourself." She ducked into the master suite.

An hour later, two floral smelling people in blood donation tee shirts and navy sweatpants met in the living room.

"Funny that we picked matching outfits," Evie laughed. "Or maybe not."

Rance pulled out a cell phone. "I need to check to

see what happened with the girls."

"I thought Frank took your phone."

"He took a phone. Not the only one I had. Thankfully, he didn't check very well after he found one. This is a backup. Messages go to both of them."

The phone chimed for an incoming phone call.

"It's Kyle. Hey son…yes…tomorrow? I think we can…just a minute…" He put the phone on mute. "Jamie and Kyle want to come and have brunch with us in the morning."

"Both of us?"

"Yep."

Evie nodded.

"Sounds great. Ten thirty?…Where are you?…Really?…I'll call them…see you in the morning…" Rance hung up. "The motel has all my belongings in the office. They got a message that I was checking out immediately due to a family emergency and would pick my things up later. Fran Rafferty certainly was efficient setting the stage for our sudden departure." He called the motel office and straightened things out.

"While you were getting our social life and your stuff in order, I called in a pizza for delivery. It will be here in about twenty minutes. Hope that's okay."

"Perfect."

"Would you stay here in the guest room tonight? I have no desire to be alone in the house after this day, this whole week. I know it's not rational. Courtland is out of the country and Frank is in police custody, but I have the willies about being alone here with only Gonzo for protection." The dog raised his head from his spot on the sofa next to Evie and she scratched his ears.

"Sure, but we'll need to run over and pick up my things. I can't go to Shangri-La in sweats tomorrow morning. And we have some things to discuss before we meet my son and his fiancée for brunch."

The pizza was delivered on time and hit the spot. They were both hungrier than they expected to be. For a long time after eating, they sat side by side on the sofa in the living room holding hands in perfect silence.

The doorbell rang.

Evie answered it with Gonzo close behind her.

Chief Davis.

"Stopped at the motel to talk to you, but they said you checked out and were here. I took the liberty of bringing your things." The officer handed two suitcases to the FBI Special Agent.

"Thanks. You saved us a trip later." Rance could feel heat flooding his face. He was certain his blush mirrored Evie's. "Miss Langford wasn't comfortable staying here alone after all that's happened these past two weeks. What did you want to talk about?"

"Don't worry. Your sleeping arrangements aren't any of my business and have nothing to do with this case. I thought you might like to know Fran Rafferty was arrested at the airport in Chicago where she was trying to board a plane for Belize using Evelyn Langford's passport. She wasn't traveling alone. She was with Rance Thompson, an FBI Special Agent who looked remarkably like our local attorney, Tom Peterman. The FBI took them both into custody," Chief Davis explained.

"She had everything finely orchestrated." Evie shook her head. "And it almost worked."

"What about Dr. Langford?" Rance asked.

"Dr. Langford is being held on multiple counts of human trafficking and kidnapping, in addition to multiple counts of attempted murder including that of a Federal agent. I'm certain the FBI will have additional charges to bring when all the facts of the case are known. Miss Langford, I thought you'd want to know that he did not rape the girls, at least not in a traditional way. According to their statements, they were sedated so they were aware of what was happening but unable to move. He artificially inseminated them with his own sperm. I'm certain that still constitutes a sexual assault.

"A warrant has been issued for Courtland Gaines for embezzlement of the funds they deposited in Miss Langford's name. If they can find him, there will probably also be fraud and conspiracy charges related to the rest of this case."

"I'm sure the FBI will have a whole slate of charges for them all," Rance confirmed. "Chief, we need to check on Fran Rafferty's brother, Ricco, who apparently had something to do with the accident that killed the elder Dr. Langford and maimed his wife."

"Will do. Francesca Scacchi Rafferty was originally from back east. There were rumors that she and her late husband were from an old Philadelphia crime family that was spreading across the country. They came here from Chicago. All the investigations into their local activity have shown legitimate business transactions, so far," Chief Davis said. "Around the time of Dr. Langford's death, we'd had a spate of drug overdoses and there were concerns that a drug syndicate had found its way to our small town. Shortly after his death, the problem seemed to evaporate. Maybe that's what they thought Dr. Frank Langford knew about and they rethought setting up in Lansdale. It definitely bears further investigation."

"Where are the girls?" Evelyn asked.

"They're getting settled in at your facility. They didn't want to be apart tonight. I dispatched a policewoman over to the Budget Boutique to get them clothes and toiletries. We checked them into your family guest rooms that have four beds in them."

"That was a great idea," Evelyn said.

"It was Dr. Merrick's suggestion after he and Dr. Wetzel examined them and double-checked on their babies. None of them suffered anything but some minor smoke inhalation. We have a policewoman staying next door. I'm sure by now it's an all-out slumber party. They were looking forward to hot showers and softer beds. One of the girls wanted to know if we had a fast-food place called Taco Insanity. When I told her no, she said the first thing she was getting when she got home was a Taco Insanity Porkarito Taco—whatever that is."

Evelyn laughed. "That must have been Carley Addams. Remember, the manager at the one location said she ate them daily before her disappearance and she wasn't even having pregnancy cravings then."

"You're right. I'd forgotten. The families have all been notified and are on their way. They should be here tomorrow. I interviewed the young women when they were medically released. They were remarkably calm considering what they've been through. Sonia Gables said it was easier to stay hopeful because they had one another. They confirmed Rosalie Richardson and Lila Masterson had once stayed at the cabin too. All four of the girls you found today are pregnant for the second time since going missing. There is a great deal to untangle in all of this."

"And we need to get a look at Peterman's adoption records. He showed nine adoptions had been done with Frank Raymond as the father. I'm afraid there are still some girls unaccounted for. It's going to take some time to resolve all the lingering issues here," Rance said. "Did anyone go out to The Center?"

"Yes. The head of the Garland County Health Department. There are only two mothers-to-be and two sets of prospective adoptive parents in residence. He interviewed all of them. Young women in their twenties, no runaways. Those births are expected in the next two weeks. The Director of Nursing at The Center has staffing under control, so nothing needs to be done there today. Of course, we're going to need to find out if other mothers are expected in the near future," Chief Davis reported.

"I'm certain the FBI will pull together a team to help determine the future status of The Langford Obstetrical Center," Rance said.

"This has been a lot more excitement than I was expecting in the last months prior to my retirement. I've asked for them to find a new police chief when reappointment time comes up in November. It's time I got to enjoy my family while I'm still healthy," Chief Davis said.

"Thank you for everything." Evelyn kissed the chief's cheek. "We're so lucky to have you here."

"If you don't have any other questions, I'll leave you folks until Monday. I can stop by Regional to get your statements Monday morning, if that will work for you," Chief Davis said with a hint of red in his cheeks.

"Perfect. Thanks, Chief. Good night." Rance

walked him to the door.

As soon as the chief was gone, Rance asked, "Miss Langford, could I interest you in a nightcap to enjoy while we discuss the future of us?" He held out his hand to lead her to the kitchen.

"That sounds wonderful." Evie clung to him smiling.

Gonzo trailed behind them barking his approval.

Chapter Thirty-Eight

Rance and Evelyn walked into Shangri-La at ten thirty a.m. trailed by Kyle and Jamie. The hostess greeted them, "Good morning. You gentlemen are becoming our most loyal customers. Three weeks in a row for brunch! Nice to see you have some lovely company today. Right this way."

Evelyn adored Jamie. She was bubbly and beautiful. She clearly loved Kyle. Her eyes rarely left him. She and Kyle made a striking couple.

"Dad, does all this mean you've wrapped up your case and will be coming home soon?"

"Soon is a relative word. I'll probably need to get back to the Chicago office this week to finish some paperwork, but I'll have to be back here for some of the loose ends. Why? Tired of Sunday brunch at Shangri-La?"

Kyle laughed. "No. We've chosen a date and I wanted to make certain my best man will be in town at the end of July."

"I think that can be arranged. Which day?"

"Saturday the 28th at two p.m. in the Colby backyard. We're doing the ceremony and the reception both there. My parents are so excited," Jamie said.

"Where are you honeymooning?" Evelyn asked.

"We're catching a ten-day cruise out of Mobile on Monday the 30th," Kyle responded. "Why?"

"Perfect. Can you extend your stay on the Gulf through the second Saturday in August?" Rance asked.

"We already planned to take a couple of days on the Alabama coast. Kyle wanted to show me where you went fishing this year," Jamie said. "He said the area was beautiful."

"It is quite lovely. I think you'll like it," Evelyn said.

"So, Kyle, are you up for being my best man while you're there?" Rance asked.

Jamie squealed. "Are you two getting married soon?"

"We are. We decided life is too unpredictable for long engagements. You two didn't let any grass grow either," Rance said.

"I would be totally honored to stand up with you." Kyle beamed at his dad.

"Congratulations!" Jamie said.

"Oh, Kyle, I have an important question before this engagement is finalized," Evelyn said.

"What's that?"

"I know you've traveled a lot with your dad. Did you share a room?"

"Yes, why?"

"I need to know if he snores."

"I hope it's not a deal breaker, but he sounds like a little motorboat all night long," Kyle said laughing.

"No, that's absolutely perfect," Evelyn said watching their confused expressions.

Rance laughed. "It's a long story. Now, I think the prime rib is calling my name again," he said as he pushed back from the table.

****

Evelyn Langford stopped at her assistant's desk on the way into her office Monday morning. "Margie, would you please grab us both a cup of coffee and come in my office. Please ask one of the other secretaries to cover your calls for the next thirty minutes. Thanks."

Ten minutes later, Margie came in carrying the coffees. Evelyn motioned toward the table. "Let's sit over here."

"Am I in trouble?" Tears threatened to fall.

"Goodness, no. Sorry if I sounded ominous. I had no intention of frightening you. I have a lot to get done today, but I wanted you to be the first to hear my news. First, thank you for being my reliable assistant and my dear friend all these years. I know part of my success here has been due to you always having my back and always having the best interest of Garland Regional Medical Center at the heart of everything you do. No one could ask for a more loyal and capable assistant. You are truly a gem."

"Miss Langford, are you dying?"

"Goodness no. I thought I had complimented you before so you would be used to it."

"You have. You just seem so serious."

"Quite the contrary. I'm delighted. I'm starting a new chapter of actually living. FBI Special Agent Rance Thompson has asked me to marry him, and I accepted his proposal. I'm sure that won't be a surprise to some of the rumor mongers here. I don't believe it will be possible to command the same support and respect from the community after my brother's crimes are widely known. It's time for someone else to take over the reins here at Garland Regional Medical

Center."

"Congratulations. I'm very happy for you. I hate that Dr. Langford's behavior is driving you away, but I'm so glad you've found someone to love. Agent Thompson looks at you like my John looks at me. You're a very lucky woman."

"Thanks, Margie. Would you please call Chairman Jungers and see if he can join me for lunch today in my office? Until I meet with him and determine the next steps, I'd like this news kept confidential."

"Absolutely, Miss Langford. I'll go take care of that now."

She expected to be sad about resigning, but the joy of living with Rance for the rest of her life pushed all the unhappy thoughts away. Maybe life did begin at fifty. At least for her.

****

Chairman Jungers was shocked by Miss Langford's resignation. She explained she was getting married in six weeks but would work out a six-month notice if it was necessary to assure a smooth transition of responsibilities to a new CEO.

"What are you planning to do in Chicago?" the chairman asked.

"I am looking at the national health care accreditation company there. They are always looking for experienced administrators to conduct training and to do accreditation surveys. It would be a change of pace to be the one making all the notes instead of figuring out how to resolve the facility issues to meet their standards."

"Best of luck. If I can provide any personal and professional references, I would be delighted to do so.

I'll get in touch with a headhunter immediately and this will be the first agenda item on next week's board meeting. I'll see you then, if not before."

Courtland Gaines shouldn't have been impatient. He could finally have gotten to sit in the CEO's chair. Instead, he'd be looking at the world from inside a jail cell, once they found him. If Frank had never gone off the rails, would she have found Rance again? Maybe Rance's Mandy was right about Master Plans—not mortal ones, but Divine ones.

****

Rance and Evie had lots of decisions to make. Condos to sell? The Langford house to sell? A lifetime of treasures to move? A new place for them to start out in? The details of the rapidly approaching wedding?

One decision was made easy. Katrina Merrick called three weeks before the wedding and asked if Gonzo was making the move to Chicago with Evelyn. The Merrick children held a family meeting and voted to ask if Gonzo could live with them. Mama's little furball would be spoiled rotten in the midst of five little children who loved him.

A husband-and-wife team of obstetricians expressed an interest in The Langford Obstetrical Center property. Her sister was an adoption attorney who decided to move to Lansdale and set up practice. The Center continued to run under the supervision of the Director of Nursing there until new management was in place. Once the legal entanglements were resolved, it would reopen as The Lansdale Family Creation Center.

A new physician moved to town in early August. He made an offer on Evelyn Langford's home. He planned to move his family to Lansdale in September; his nurse wife, a ten-year-old boy, and a seven-year-old girl. Evelyn thought it was fitting that the home would still shelter a physician's family.

Epilogue

The sun barely peeked over the undulating horizon. Pinks, yellows, reds, and oranges streamed in all directions above the azure ocean. Waves gently lapped onto the shore darkening the sugar-white sand. A violinist stood on the right-hand side of the white rose-covered arbor. Rance Thompson, wearing an elegant satin trimmed black tuxedo, stood with the pastor in front of the arbor. Muted strains of violin music wafted softly through the air.

Everyone turned and looked down the sandy path between the small group of white fabric-skirted chairs.

The Merrick twins, Tracy and Mallory, dressed in matching bright purple dresses and broad-brimmed lace hats, led Gonzo between them down the aisle. When they got to the row their parents and brothers were in, they made a brief detour to kiss the top of their baby brother, Jimmy's, head as he snuggled peacefully on their mother's lap.

The pug strutted as if he knew all eyes were on him. His tongue lolled out of his mouth and a low snore came from his mashed-in nose. He was clad in a purple vest with two bows tied on the back where simple gold bands were secured. When he reached Rance, Gonzo sat at his feet and barked twice. The twins moved to the opposite side of the arbor.

Pam strolled down the aisle in a flowing green

dress the same color as her twinkling eyes and a matching lace hat. She was accompanied by a tuxedo-clad Kyle.

Beverly looked radiant in a bright-blue off the shoulder dress and matching lace hat as she made her way down the aisle on John's arm.

Liz slinked down the aisle in a flame-red strapless sheath and a matching lace hat holding Peter's arm.

The music stopped briefly, then restarted the bridal march with great exuberance. The audience stood and turned.

Evelyn Louise Langford stood at the end of the path in a flowing white satin gown covered in Chantilly lace and seed pearls with a three-foot train. She wore a broad-brimmed lace hat with her long silver-streaked brown hair draped loosely on her shoulders and down her back to below her waist. She walked slowly down the path smiling broadly and looking from side to side taking in all the details, etching every moment of this once-in-a-lifetime event on her heart.

When she reached the arbor, Evie handed her bouquet of white roses, gardenias, and ivy to Pam and took Rance's hand. She closed her eyes and took a deep breath. When she opened them, she peered directly into her soon-to-be-husband's eyes. He winked. She laughed out loud.

The pastor began, "Dearly Beloved..." Then it seemed like only a moment later he said, "I now pronounce you husband and wife. You may kiss the bride."

And kiss Rance did. So long that the audience tittered happily. Rance announced everyone was invited to a special wedding brunch at Constantine's.

****

After everyone had filled their plates from the brunch buffet and gotten a starter glass of champagne, the toasts began.

Rance stood first and toasted his bride. "Please stand up, Evie. We make great partners when we're solving crimes. I'm sure we'll be even better at figuring out marriage. To my lovely bride, I love you, Evelyn Louise Langford Thompson."

The happy couple clinked their glasses and locked arms to sip the bubbly. After refills all around, Evie raised her glass. "Thank you, Rance, for being brave enough to help a lady in distress, and to approach me again after I was so rude the first time. You were worth waiting for. I love you, Rance Russell Thompson."

As best man, Kyle said, "Dad, I only hope that you and Evie will be as happy as Jamie and I are. Cheers!"

Pam raised her glass saying, "It took a once-in-a-lifetime event, but we finally got all the Fantastic Four spouses and families to Constantine's. Wishing you both as much happiness as Jerry and I have shared together."

A table of teenagers stood and cheered, "Yea, Mom! We love you."

Pam laughed and said, "And displays like that are the reason it's taken so long for you to be invited down here. I love you." She blew kisses to the table of rowdy young people and her husband, and to the bride and groom.

Beverly toasted saying, "I too am glad my sweet husband got to come to this place that has been so special to me to witness the marriage of my extraordinary friend. To your love, Evie and Rance!"

Liz laughed and raised her glass. "I'm only doing this for you once. After waiting fifty years to get married, would it have killed you to stay in bed for a few more hours this morning? I love you, kiddo. Wishing you tons of joy!"

Beverly became the wedding photographer taking lots of formal and informal pictures of the assembled crew. The cake was cut, and hours of laughter spent reminiscing about the past thirty years of Fantastic Four adventures on the Gulf of Mexico. After many glasses of champagne, Rance and Evie said their farewells. They had a plane to catch in Mobile.

Amid a shower of rice, tears, and good wishes, Liz shouted, "Where are you going on your honeymoon?"

Rance laughed and said, "Would you believe Belize?"

A word about the author...

I grew up in a small town in Wisconsin. I had a career in Healthcare Information Technology, most recently as CIO for a small hospital group in Alabama. Now, I am focused on creative endeavors - writing, spinning, weaving, knitting and crocheting. I have been married to my own Romance hero for almost forever. Follow my adventures at www.spinningromance.com.

E-mail me at kimjanine@spinningromance.com. I'd love to hear from my readers!

Thank you for purchasing
this publication of The Wild Rose Press, Inc.

For questions or more information
contact us at
info@thewildrosepress.com.

The Wild Rose Press, Inc.
www.thewildrosepress.com